Twice Cursed

DEMON CAT CHRONICLES 2

MARIE FLYNN

Small Fish
Fish
publishing

Small Fish Publishing
USA

First edition

Cover design by Stephanie Flynn

ISBN ebook: 978-1-952372-34-6

ISBN paperback: 978-1-952372-35-3

ISBN hardcover: 978-1-952372-81-0

ISBN large print paperback: 978-1-952372-80-3

Also By Marie Flynn

Demon Cat Chronicles series
Demon Experiment special report
Demon Curse
Twice Cursed

If you like steamy romance mixed in with your paranormal tales,
check out Marie Flynn's other name, Stephanie Flynn!

I

Cake

iKat

MOST HUMANS DREADED SHOWING up each morning to their cubicle farms, but here in the belly of Hell, I loved it. Maybe because I wasn't human. Maybe, having spent the majority of my adult life scrubbing human toilets, my bar was really low. Regardless of the reason, the expanse of endless orderly rows of bright lights, clean gray modular cubes, and humming computers put my mind at ease. My best friend, Andras, used to visit me at work, and we'd chat about things humans did that drove us nuts. I'd been raised with the primitive but numerous cretins, and only Andras was kind to me.

A *demon*. A real one.

My mother had been a Field Agent, and she'd been trapped at the surface when she went into labor. As a newborn demon, I'd been whisked away by human hands and shuffled through their foster system until I'd aged out. Growing up, I didn't know what

I was. Demon puberty was awkward as hell, and I spent time in churches against my will. At the time, I thought they were joking when they'd claimed I was a demon.

Turned out they were right.

I learned to hide my emotionally charged red glowies, my desire to flame-on, and my convenient teleporting for the sake of survival, until Andras introduced himself one lonely night at NBB pharmaceuticals. I had earbuds in and almost didn't hear him over the hum of the floor washer. How I could've missed him was beyond me. The dude was enormous by human standards, but only slightly more than average by demon standards. I preferred all demons without the glamour, but after seeing many of the natural demon shapes, sizes, and colors, I still held back reactions of shock. Hey, I was used to humans of a same size and shape. The coloring on them wasn't much different from one to another—unlike that of demons. Unfortunately, I was technically half-demon, so I was stuck looking like a human all the time. Lame.

Anyhoo, after bonding over basketball, Andras admitted he'd been looking for me, explained what I was, and he wanted to bring me home, where I'd get to watch a better version—demon basketball. He'd also explained my mother died in childbirth, but he said nothing about my father. I'd tried tracking them down a couple times but working every waking minute to keep the lights on left little time for hobbies.

Or investigating one's birth parents.

I'd needed serious time to swallow all Andras told me, but for some reason, I felt drawn to him, comfortable, as if I had known him a long time. It sounded baffling to me now, but I considered him a friend right away, and I trusted him. So when he told me about this Desk Agent job, I jumped at it. Buh bye, toilets.

After two exciting weeks, I was still working on learning the ropes, so after work, I study the manual at home, alone in my single bedroom apartment. Having recently moved into the towering complex in Hell City, I hadn't made friends with the neighbors yet. They almost seemed afraid of me, but from my experience living among humans, demons weren't unique in being wary of strangers.

I'd terrified a few sets of foster parents along the way, but I hoped demons would be more understanding. They just needed time.

When I'd settled in, I set up my home gym. Always wanted one but never could have one in my sparse and dank apartments on the surface. Newsflash: janitorial work didn't pay well. Sometimes Andras joined me on the rower or pounding the treadmill. When he couldn't, I watched demon basketball alone while pumping my heart rate. All the different breeds of demons had different strengths, and their size differences were quite pronounced. How that made the game fair was beyond me. But watching purple iridescent lizards on two legs running down the court with a thick swishing tail, bouncing a larger-than-human-regulation basketball, and blocking a minuscule smooth-skinned yellow demon was entertainment unmatched. Those yellow demons used their slime. I never wanted to touch one, but my eyes were glued to the screen with horror and fascination.

When I didn't have television to entertain me, I researched how to build a saltwater reef aquarium. I didn't know why the idea struck me in the first place, since down here in Hell, we didn't have any aquatic stores or fish farms or any oceans to collection them myself. And I'd never get permission to visit the surface just for pets. And I'd never be able to afford one, so I'd relegated the unusual desire to a daydream.

Which I doodled in my notebook between customers. It helped me think and plan. While Andras and this job were life changing, I suddenly felt the need for more. I wanted to become a Field Agent like my mother. I wanted to track down my human father and ask him about her. Large pieces of my memory were garbled, and when I asked Andras questions about my past—since he'd been looking for me—he carefully explained that I'd suffered some brain damage during an accident with electricity and water, of which I didn't remember, naturally. But most of all, I wanted to do the job well—getting my own tiny piece of vengeance on humans for scrubbing their toilets all those years.

And shuffling me from home to home, hating me but loving the checks.

And all those exorcisms, which were quite traumatic if I was being honest with myself.

To do all that, I had to impress The King of Hell for a promotion. I'd already found a way to organize the demons to demand a new coffee pot, which the manager wasn't thrilled about, but we won. And results were what mattered. And it was my idea to display a progress chart for everyone, initiating a friendly competition. And I wanted to win. See, Hell's customer service department was responsible for assisting humans with their moral quandaries in a manner beneficial to Hell. For each successful sway, the agent responsible earned a star. Having hard data to prove my worth was my best chance of negotiating a promotion to Field Agent.

The north end of the vast acreage held the email department, west tackled phone support, and where I was stationed in the south handled live chat support. Requests to chat popped onto my screen. I typically lunched at my desk, because I couldn't waste time eating when my fingers could be earning stars. This morning, while getting ready for work, I'd seriously been distracted adjusting the angle of my stair-stepper to align with the mounted television rather than the uneven wall, and after checking my watch and swearing, I'd teleported to work. And I'd forgotten to bring my lunch.

Unfortunately, the customer service department didn't pay much better than janitorial work at NBB, so the cafeteria was off limits until payday. Today's special was muskrat burger, but despite how much Andras talked it up, I just couldn't stomach the bitter patty, so I wasn't missing much. Luckily for me, my colleagues ordered takeout delivery, so someone in this vast acreage of cubicles wouldn't need their bagged lunch.

I'd helped myself to an inconspicuous brown paper bag, intending on replacing it tomorrow. No harm done. Unwrapping the parchment paper, I bit down on juicy tomato, crisp lettuce, and savory slices of chilled meats. Maybe it was my human side, but this was so much better than muskrat.

My favorite colleague—okay, the first woman I met who'd talk to me—was assigned the cubicle next to me. Heather was stuck in a chat, running late to her own lunch break. She wasn't rude to me most of the time, but she said unusual things often enough to make me wonder. Having been surrounded by human women on the surface, I wasn't well-versed in demon dating, and some demons had the ability to mess with the minds of others, so I wasn't sure if she was into me or not.

Heather was sleek and gorgeous, and very much feisty. I wouldn't mind taking her on a date.

A tomato slice fell off my sandwich with a plop, and a ringing filled my ears—the unmistakable sign of another migraine headed my way. Lights overhead consumed my eyes, and I squeezed them shut. I dropped the sandwich onto my desk and pressed my palms against my forehead to hedge the incoming pain. Images of Chris, Stella, and Dennis flashed before my eyes while a net of searing heat squeezed my skull. All three of them glared at me with disappointment, if not outright hatred. Who were these people? Did I forget to clean their toilet? Did I spill a full trash bin on their carpet? But I would've cleaned it up. I didn't know why or how I knew their names, but I never wanted to meet them. The pain radiated from the back of my neck to my forehead, and I pinched my face in agony, waiting out the hellish ride.

A hand rested on my shoulder. "You okay over there?" Heather's voice.

I held up a finger, asking her to wait. She patted my shoulder and returned to her work, each keystroke so magnified it stabbed my eardrum like a knife. But just as quickly as the onslaught of pain cranked up, it slowly receded. The ringing faded, the keystrokes softened, and lights dimmed. I exhaled a deep breath of relief. Tipping my desk organizer basket, I tapped out a couple of painkillers and swallowed them down.

"Another migraine?" Heather asked.

"The same three faces each time. Why not show me something else? It's like my brain's trying to tell me something." I shrugged. "And that sounds completely crazy."

"You'd be surprised." Heather's expression was an unreadable mix. The female was a mystery.

I finished the sandwich in quick order, crinkled up the wrappers, and tossed them into the waste bin under my desk. Break wasn't over yet, but time to get back to work. As part of negotiating the star chart, the loser earned a trip to the torture dungeon. Despite his name, Glitter had a way with pliers and retched music to make any demon want to take their own life.

I checked the rapidly growing list of names in the queue and clicked the first one, Gladys, per the chat ID. Eventually I'd should be allowed to make my own suggestions, like Heather did, but for now, my job was to copy and paste from the script library.

Me: *'Good morning, Gladys. Thank you for contacting People Support. How can I help you?'*

Gladys: *'This is my first time on this computer thing. I'm not sure what I should type.'*

Humans, man. All she had to do was spit out the problem. *'Start with the reason you need to connect to someone.'*

Time ticked by with no response. I swigged from my water bottle, wishing for a rum and Coke. Had I upset her?

Finally, Gladys typed a response. *'I think I stole something.'*

This was kind of a 'yes or no' situation. Humans liked to complicate everything. I clicked on the theft tab and started at the top. *'That's all right. No one's going to Hell for that.'*

Gladys: *'Really?'*

Me: *'Of course not. But if you want to guarantee your ticket is punched at the pearly gates, might I suggest something?'* And yep, Hell had a casual friendliness in the catalog of responses.

Gladys: *'Please. do.'*

Me: *'Did you keep the item you stole?'*

Gladys: *'I still have it, but I don't remember not paying for it. It's not in my receipt, but if I bring it back to the store, they might accuse me of stealing it, anyway. So either I do the right thing and get punished or do the wrong thing and carry the guilt.'*

On the next page of the chat transcripts, I filled in the blanks and pasted. *'Here's what you need to do—go back to the store and take another one. It has to be an identical item, though. I cannot stress the importance of that enough.'*

Gladys: *'Why would I do that?'*

Me: *'This will clear up any confusion. Trust me.'*

There was a beat of hesitation on her end before the dancing dots told me a response was coming. *'I can do that, I suppose. Then what?'*

'Then you chat me back and tell me.' A satisfied smile crossed my lips.

Gladys: *'I'll do that. Thank you, Malaikat.'*

And the smile on my face for a job well-done vanished. *'iKat. It's iKat, please.'* I needed Demon Resources to change that in the system, and now that I veered off the transcript, I had to finish the conversation without guidance. Oops.

Gladys: *'That's an unusual name.'*

'My mother had a silly sense of humor.' The humans who'd first collected me named me a translation of the word angel. I

didn't know what I was, and neither did they, so it had to have been an unfortunate coincidence.

Gladys typed a chuckle and added, '*Thank you. Goodbye now.*' She left the chat. Another soul sent down the path to Hell. Maybe one day, I'd get to watch in person as their auras changed like a kaleidoscope through the shades of gray as they made their decisions. Andras told me I was one of a few aura demons. I didn't remember seeing anything out of the ordinary at the surface, but now that I knew, I was even more motivated to return to the surface. I released a satisfied breath and scratched another tally to my count—fifty-seven. Not bad for the new guy.

Heather inhaled a deep breath. "Time for my lunch. Malaikat, yours looked good. Was that from the vending machine?"

"iKat, please. I borrowed it from the fridge."

Heather shook her head. "Just so you know, we don't do that around here."

"There was no mention of it in the employee handbook," I protested, and I would've remembered. Or at least, I thought I trusted my memory, but the electric and water incident may have knocked some things loose. "But I'll replace it. I didn't mean to upset anyone's day."

Heather rolled her eyes. "If only you heard yourself."

Again with the strange comments. "What does that mean?"

Ignoring my question as usual, Heather asked, "Want a slice of cake?"

This morning at the new coffeepot, I asked a demon named Todd for any helpful tips for getting ahead. The demon mostly grunted and then walked away. I didn't understand the mumbles, but I explicitly remembered the demon skipped any mention of cake. I loved the gym and cared very much about how I ate, but I had an unusual hankering for a slice of delectable cake.

"What's the occasion?"

"It's Todd's birthday today, so cake is served during lunch."

Guess Todd didn't like the reminder another year had passed. I didn't know why it bothered him. Demons lived for millennia compared to the super short lifespans of humans. But cake sounded awesome. "I'll take a slice. Thank you."

Just as Heather stood up, cheers erupted from the other side of the room. I rose to see over the partitions. A chef from Hell's kitchen pushed a cart with a massive five-tier cake and sparklers on top. I checked the ceiling for a fire suppression system, but there wasn't one. In a building full of demons capable of summoning fire at the snap of their fingers—or not, the snap was just for drama—one would expect some fireproofing. I shrugged to myself while closer demons sang the birthday song. The chef beat feet out of there. Either the kitchen was busy, or the chef was antisocial. I supposed those two things weren't mutually exclusive.

When Todd leaned over and blew out the candles, the cake exploded with a deep boom. I ducked from the blast with wide eyes and hands covering my hair. What the hell just happened? Did Glitter make house calls now? Did Hell have terrorists? Had the angels invaded?

I straightened. Demons coughed and waved away the billowing smoke. Pieces of demons, and even whole limbs, rained down far away from me. When demons wanted to celebrate, they sure made a bang...and a mess. The lack of crying, screaming, or panic surprised me more. One demon collected body parts and stacked them on the buckled cake-splattered cart. Another calmly made a call—probably to housekeeping. Others brushed the chunks off themselves and returned to their stations.

My eye twitched at the uneven blood splatter on the walls, and I fought a strong urge to help clean up. Heather returned to interrupt that impulse, but she was empty-handed.

I had so many questions. "Why are they collecting the body parts?"

She fell onto her seat, clearly as disappointed by the lack of cake as I was. "Once in a while the hellhounds require fresh meat, and when the dungeon is full or Glitter is backlogged, the king orders a punishment fit to solve two problems."

"I guess if I get a birthday cake, I'll run." I still had so much to learn.

"It doesn't happen often. I think Todd was the third this year. Keep your nose clean, and you'll have nothing to worry about. Of course, sometimes being bad is far more fun and worth the risk." Heather winked.

I frowned, confused by her mixed messages. She wanted me to be *bad*? Whatever that meant. Was she flirting? I wasn't bold enough to straight up ask. "I'll keep that in mind, thanks."

Andras approached, waving at friendly faces along the way. I spun in my chair, waiting for my turn. The broad demon, in his human glamour, stopped between me and Heather and leaned on the cubicle behind us. "iKat, how are things?"

"It's going well so far. How are you?" I hadn't chatted with my friend for a few days, and it was reassuring to see a friendly face. "Looking forward to a few miles at my place tonight?"

"The king wants to see you in his office."

"Me?" I stiffened. I hadn't been here long enough for that to be good news.

"Right away," Andras added.

"Um, okay." I patted my pockets to be sure I was prepared—pen, notebook, not sure what else I might need. I checked my desk, making sure it was orderly, and I locked my terminal.

Over the loudspeaker, the booming voice of The King of Hell commanded me to his office at once. The tone said I screwed up big time—like my torture session was penciled in for later that afternoon. I debated between delaying the inevitable and rushing to prevent additional punishment. Just when I thought I'd done everything right.

"iKat, in here at once!" The King of Hell repeated.

"Go," Andras urged. "It's important."

I guess I was going to meet Glitter officially. That sucks.

2

Protest

Heather

"This is an elected position," the king said in his hoity-toity tone. "I have been chosen, so my word is for all demons. If you disagree, your chance to voice that opinion is at the polls. The next one is coming up soon, but if you find yourself eying my position, fifty years isn't much time to prepare." The King of Hell was always patronizing. I hadn't considered running for his position, but after too many mistakes had been made lately, the idea was tempting.

Fifty years was a long time to wait.

"This has gone too far, sir." I said to my king, knowing such words could land me inside Glitter's torture chambers. After putting up with The King of Hell's orders far beyond a reasonable number of centuries, I couldn't stand by and watch this.

The King of Hell displayed his natural form, and I'd seen every demon breed out there. Some were so intimidating in size, one look would threaten one's bowels. The king we elected didn't have that size advantage. His natural form stood well under five feet tall with bright red skin, a swishing corkscrew tail, and a pair of curled horns no bigger than a goat's. Wispy black hairs danced on his shiny head while reading glasses hung from his sloping nose. Whenever I visited the king, I always pictured his true form even when he displayed his human glamour, which wasn't impressive either—just over five feet tall, and he walked with a limp, swinging his arm like he was swatting flies. Those of us who could, conjured our own appearances. Why not something more...intimidating? Instead, Corson used words to sway the public opinion.

Words were overrated. I believed in action.

"Glitter has an opening this afternoon. Continue to question my authority and you'll be spending time with him...again." The diminutive King of Hell raised his fluffy brow, antagonizing me.

As much as I didn't respect the way the king carried himself, he was formidable. And his warning was a valid threat. I'd spent time with Glitter, the rainbow-haired torturemaster whose outfits matched his namesake, and I had no intention of sharing a room with that demented, irrational, and obsessed freak of nature.

I squinted—and not because of the annoying fluorescent lights in the king's dingy office. Come to think of it, this office needed a feminine touch...and a change of scenery. No, not Hell City through the picture window. The city was glorious just as it was. The interior of the office needed a change.

The various breeds of demons all looked different from each other, and like our leader, I expected our military to maintain the broad-shouldered, six-to-sixty-packed, intimidating specimens ready for battle. In reality, not so much. Demons hadn't gone to war in so long, they trusted it would never happen again. But I could see it. Not on the horizon. Not some distant feeling. No. War was right here in the cubicles, putting a sticker on a chart with a proud grin.

I'd never fought the king firsthand, and others had threatened, but no one ever saw them again. Oh, there were stories. Some days, like today, I was tempted to test him myself. I believed in action, just not by my own hand. I was too smart for that, and my mani was too expensive. I had pawns to flush out the king's temper. Meanwhile, I needed to keep mine under control.

"Nick Barnes is a danger to our existence, and that was before you turned him into a demon. Did you see what he did in the customer service department—the riot for coffee and the stupid progress chart? That leadership drive, that desire to be the best, is ingrained in him, and he won't stop until he gets what he wants. But now you're letting him loose on the earth's surface in a cat's body. I can appreciate a sense of humor when I see one, but his memory block is shaky at best. He needs to be wiped fully by a properly qualified memory demon." The king's favorite pet performed the wipe instead. Whenever the king played favorites—which was most of the time—I became twitchy.

Especially since I, a contract demon, had been playing babysitter to an ego-stuffed half-human. A jewel like me—someone of true value and beauty—was flushed away for an ordinary, useless idiot who knew nothing. No one handled the purchasing department of NBB Pharmaceuticals better than me. And Nick didn't even remember any of it. My grudge wasn't solely because he'd fired me. Or the apocalypse his over-stuffed ego caused.

The king's jaw flickered with tension. "Wildabeast did a fine job activating his demon side. When Nick's ready, and we figured out how to manage his ultimate evil side effect, we'll pull him into our ranks. We can't wipe his memory twice without turning him into celery, so this is the best way to ensure he remains ready for us while harmless."

I snorted derisively. Wildabeast, the king's personal pet name for Wilda Rivers was the most powerful witch willing to work for Hell—on commission. Sure, the woman was a force to reckon with, but I wasn't threatened by the statuesque blond human.

"He needs to be destroyed." I folded my arms over my chest, wrinkling my suit coat. All demons wore the industry standard fireproof vicuña suit, which prevented accidents in public. Mine was a matching skirt set—an appropriate style for both Hell and the surface.

"I will say when and what happens around here. If I find out Nick Barnes has been killed, I'll be holding you personally responsible for putting the future of all demonkind at risk. He is never to be killed. You have your orders. Get back to work."

"But—" I protested.

"Dismissed." The big final word from the king.

In a fury, I stormed down the chilly, dank hall lit with flaming sconces, unable to calm myself enough to teleport. It was time for Hell to reorganize—top down. Screw an election. Nick

Barnes whole-heartedly embraced determination, and he was a stubborn bastard. The real Heather was ready to say hello. When I was The Queen of Hell someday, I'd turn the damned heat on.

3

Promotion

iKat

My guts swirled at the tone over the loudspeaker. Acres of demons heard that, and many of them nearby looked on at me with terror on their faces as I rushed through endless rows of cheesy inspirational posters helping productivity. None of them cheered me up. Two that I caught were 'Hang in there, Friday's coming,' and 'Together everyone achieves more'. I could've teleported to save myself from needing eye bleach, but after Heather corrected me on the sandwich fiasco, I clearly didn't have a strong grasp on the etiquette yet. The bulletin boards hadn't mentioned the rule, and Todd, rest his non-soul, hadn't been chatty. Besides, I never saw anyone teleport inside the building. Picturing Glitter and his favorite torture device of screams, my heart rattled in its cage like a lab monkey. Glitter called it The Torture Device of Screams, and that was an accurate name.

I stood in the open doorway to the king's plain office, awaiting permission to enter and meet my fate. The king, in his human form, sat behind his fancy desk with Diego, a favorite guard, at his shoulder. Diego was a quiet demon and a trustworthy soldier, who wouldn't betray his boss. I respected that, although I'd respect a bone thrown my way more (not a literal bone) about how to handle my new life in Hell.

I especially would've appreciated a bone to prevent a trip to Glitter, but hey, not everyone got what they wanted. Unfortunately, there were no wish-granting demons. I'd checked. But if I found one, I wouldn't have wished for help to navigate the demon world. No. My biggest wish was to have my memory repaired from the electric and water accident Andras told me about. Walking around with a fraction of myself was like waking up one day as a teenager: *Who am I? Where am I? Why am I here? What am I supposed to do with my life?* That was a whole mix of uncertainty and confusion I'd rather skip repeating, but beggars and choosers and all that.

What had I done wrong to earn that angry tone from the overhead speakers? I was on time for every shift, I was always clean, and I didn't think I smelled. Plus, I never abused the restroom break policy. Besides all that, I had a thirty-six percent success rate of the chats I'd completed.

I'd consider that performance exemplary for a new hire, but I wasn't the boss. A strange tingle in the back corner somewhere in my mind told me that statement was wrong. But which half? And why? I wouldn't ever want to be king.

The king was a stocky, broad demon with sharp eyes in a fine suit, but all demons wore suits. Who were they trying to impress?

I wasn't sure, but I liked the feel of this material more than my janitor's scratchy coveralls. This fireproof vicuña suit likely costed more than my year's salary. If I made it that long.

The king peeled his eyes from his computer screen and pushed away from the desk. Standing to his diminutive height, he approached the middle of the room, and the flick of a wrist commanded me to enter. The king reminded me of a mob boss, not that I ever saw one in person, but my imagination conjured the likeness all the same: commanding, intimidating, and fearless. Still short, probably a hair over five feet. Like humans, no demon had everything in life.

I squared my shoulders, fastened my hands behind my back, and entered for my fate. "Yes, sir?"

A snort of air blasted from the king's nose, like a bull about to charge. "I am offering you a promotion to Field Agent. Are you interested?"

My lips parted. Apparently, my ears were broken, too. "Pardon, sir?"

"Field Agent—you. Work at the surface. Mingle with the humans. Understood?" The king's insulting tone and little finger gestures pretending to be a person walking around were loud and clear, but it wasn't the words I couldn't process.

"But why me? Heather is a much better choice. Her success rate is higher, and she has more experience."

The king smirked. "This is what you want, is it not?"

"Well, yes, sir, but—"

Over my shoulder, the king yelled to his guard, "Diego! Bring the beast." The guard left the office, and the king leaned over his expansive desk and lifted a heavy leather-bound book. Without a word, he opened the book at a marked page.

What did I do right to get a promotion and wrong to get a punishment in one breath? Forgetting my respectful formalities, I blurted, "What's the beast for?"

Hellhound mangling was probably worse than Glitter's work. *Probably* being the operative word there. I'd never experienced the invisible claws of Hell to compare, as far as I remembered. My stomach churned, and I trusted my body's reaction to prepare for the worst. My hand slid down my suit and ocean-themed tie as if apologizing ahead of time to my trusty work clothes.

Diego, with a tight face and equally sharp suit, returned with a domestic cat under his arm—a standard-issue orange tabby. He had to be joking. What damage could this tiny cat do? And for that matter, why did the king want to carry out the punishment in his office? Demons really had no issue with gore splattered everywhere.

So strange.

As long as they replaced my suit before sending me to the surface, I'd survive. I hated cats. I didn't want to be near them, but considering the alternatives, I could suck it up. I could pick off random orange furs off my suit. I tipped my chin up.

The King of Hell cleared his throat and said, "Spell two—"

"Are you sure it's wise to do this without Wilda Rivers?" Diego interrupted.

The king shot him a glare. "Do not presume to question my ability. Besides, Wildabeast declined."

"Right, sir."

"Spell two? Like the second spell created?" I asked, both impressed at the spell's longevity and reassured it was fully tested and safe. Did the promotion to Field Agent come with a special ability?

"Today, that is correct," the king confirmed.

I smiled to myself, awaiting the arrival of this mysterious new ability. But what did the cat have to do with anything?

The king cleared his throat and said, "Spell 247,014."

My mouth popped open. *Wait a minute!*

The foreign words rolled off the king's tongue while Diego continued to hold the cat in his arm, now agitated and scrambling for release.

I tried to protest, but no words came out, as if I were smothered with invisible binds. My vision vibrated, just like teleporting, but I'd hadn't chosen to, and my brain floated—a combination of the worst hangover ever and that nauseating lightheadedness that came with a free-fall. My stomach churned harder, ready to display its protest with the tasty sandwich I'd borrowed, and when I bent at the waist, I couldn't see or touch my legs. The internal yelp of panic was silent.

The room shifted position. A loud thump turned my attention. When I looked back to where he had been standing moments ago, my body laid on the floor. I floated straight toward the cat in a forced teleportation. What kind of hinky shi—?

The next time I blinked, my color vision was sharper, sense of smell keener (unfortunately), and the desire to lick my feet way too strong. My hearing was better, too, but not by much. Another demon joined Diego in dragging my limp body by the underarms. My clean suit dragged along the filthy floor.

"Watch the hair!" I shouted. "Hey, my voice is back." And with that freedom, I focused my thoughts to calm myself and summoned my will to teleport back into my body, but a force kept me in place.

Diego's silent partner cast me an unamused glance, and the last of my shoes slid out of view.

No, no no! The king couldn't do this. He couldn't trap me like this! I focused and tried again with the same results. Trying a third time and expecting different results would appear crazy, so I refrained—barely. I gritted my teeth, caging the sassy words fighting to break free.

Shiny shoes approached my tiny new form, and I craned my neck up to see the king wearing a bored expression. "iKat, please heed the rules. I hate wasting time coming up with punishments. Dismissed."

"Why am I in this cat?" I pressed.

The king's brow furrowed at my first strike of disobedience, but I wasn't leaving until I had answers.

"His name is Mittens. Have you sampled from the break room refrigerator?"

My stomach sank. "I did, but I planned to replace it—"

The king smirked and cut me off. "I understand you're new here. With Glitter up to his eyeballs in entrails all day, he doesn't have time to set you straight...while keeping you functional after."

The king trapped me in a cat's body because I'd borrowed a sandwich? No one ever said Hell was fair. "How long is this punishment for?"

"As a Field Agent, you'll do your work at the surface until I am satisfied." The king slammed his book closed and dropped it back on his desk.

Just when I thought I'd figured out some of the rules, I got blown over again. "I want to do the best I can, but how am I supposed to manipulate humans like this?"

The king smiled. "A challenge I think you shall enjoy. Diego will escort you through the portal."

I had caught the title of that old book—the source of the spell forcing me into the cat—*Demoniška eksperimentų knyga*. Whatever that meant. Clearly it had been left out of the demon history texts. Diego approached, but I wasn't through pleading my case yet. "What if the angels find me? I'm helpless like this."

"A talking cat is a giveaway. You can still teleport." A gentle way of saying shut up and run.

Why did the king make me the mockery of the demon world? Weren't my humble beginnings and insulting name enough damage? How much harder was I going to have to work to earn some respect around here? If I had opposable thumbs and a demon blade, I'd demand my body back and complain about the punishment not fitting the crime. That news would spread quickly. Just about as quickly as my entrails on the dungeon floor, smeared like peanut butter and jelly.

Did Hellhounds like peanut butter?

"This way, iKat," Diego said.

The king nodded to his personal guard and returned to his book. Not wanting to look at the king right now, I stepped out into the hall, taking Diego's lead. The extra strong scent of moss and mildew watered my sensitive eyes. Of all things, why a stronger sense of smell? There was no use for it—especially not here.

With shoes on, I didn't have to concern myself with the ick factor of Hell, but now I was bare pawed. As Diego led us down the hall, I watched for creepy critters lurking in the crevices of the stone. Around a few turns, Diego brought me to a brightly lit hallway reminding me of the offices of the customer service department—clean, critter-free, and much more pleasant on the nose.

Pushed into the corner against the wall was a large reception desk, and behind it was a demon, doing who knew what. He ignored us.

Diego stopped at a lightweight modern door across from the desk. He leaned down. "You've read the demon history, right?"

"Of course." It was required reading, and quite fascinating, honestly.

"And you remember the hunters of interest?"

"A few." I arched a furred brow. I didn't know there'd be a pop quiz.

Diego frowned. "Look, most demons want to see you dead. There's a few who think what happened to you is an injustice." *Which part?* "So, I'm going to tell you two critically important things."

I was the new guy, and I wouldn't turn down anything for free, even advice. Especially now that I didn't have thumbs...or shoes.

After a beat, Diego glanced back at the receptionist and leaned closer. "One, we've done a spell like this before, but not on a cat, and that demon lived and died as a ferret."

"Uh..."

"Read between the lines. The king never freed him," Diego continued. "And by the time we tried, we couldn't. The spell becomes permanent."

"And two?" I was afraid to ask.

"And two, never return to Hell." That wasn't helpful.

Standing to his full length, Diego tapped the door, and it split down the middle. Glowing blue phosphorescence encapsulated the portal to the surface. Flickers danced in the waves of blue, reminding me of a saltwater reef—peaceful, enchanting.

"How did the ferret demon die?" I asked, almost afraid of the answer.

"The cat killed it." Diego lifted the corner of his lips in a soft smile and tilted his head, indicating the orange tabby I would be well acquainted with shortly.

Great. I was trapped in a *murderous* cat. With a final glance up at the helpful demon, Diego only nodded. "Oh, one more thing."

I waited.

"Keep the Hell stuff on the down low, and up there, cats don't speak."

I knew that, but I needed my body back. I wasn't going to live the rest of my life stuck in this feline at the mercy of the king's whims and dodging both angels and all the cat's natural predators. "Is someone going to come get me before it's permanent? Since last time..."

"I wouldn't count on it." Diego gestured his head, kicking me out of Hell.

Not wanting a literal boot up the ass, I walked through the blue flickering portal on all fours. While I was up there, I was so getting cake.

4

Adjustment

I INCHED THROUGH THE alley. With each step, I shook off whatever touched my paws. At this rate of step-shake-step across four paws, I was never going to get anywhere. Diego warned me that the last person with this curse, a demon trapped in a ferret, died—more specifically, was murdered by this cat, likely when the demon was roaming the halls of Hell, looking for help to break the curse. That wasn't going to be me. And two, I was never to return to Hell. I didn't want the hellhounds to shred little murderous Mittens here, even if he deserved it.

But I was not staying in this furball forever. Cat or no cat, I didn't want to be around those revolting creatures with their little clawed feet, scaly tails, and beady eyes—also known as mice. Especially now, since proportionally speaking, they were much larger than normal. I rushed through the last of the alley, having decided rotting garbage and unidentified fluids were less offensive than rodents.

At the sidewalk, a fresh breeze shifted the fur on my small body and the sun beamed down, warming me on this cool summer morning. I closed my eyes and breathed it in. I hadn't realized how much Hell was stifling—a world of darkness with no wind and too many rules.

Crowds marched along the sidewalk with a rhythmic clatter, assaulting my overly sensitive hearing. Some wore paper masks, others wore cloth masks, and some covered their mouths with ties and collars. Most didn't protect themselves at all. In the most recent demon history books, Nick Barnes released a bacterium into public. Millions were sickened. Many died. Too many returned to life. Andras explained they were called Reanimated, since they...reanimated. Zombies made more sense. But what was most unusual is they didn't take over the world. People weren't afraid to be out. The population hadn't been decimated.

Hell sent teams to contain the spread, preventing zombies from taking over the world. I was pretty grateful for that, all things considering. Without thumbs...defense against the undead would've been...tricky.

So, with a mostly normal human world, where was I supposed to go? If I couldn't talk to humans, how was I going to get help? A sharp pain blasted my middle, punching the oxygen from my little lungs, and I flew through the air. I managed to land on my feet somehow, and a woman was yelling, quite angrily. "...crawling with feral beasts. Somebody should do something..."

I glanced around and didn't see any beasts, but not wanting a repeat of that pointy-toed shoe, I boogied away with aching ribs. Footsteps marched nearby, and I winced at my receding pain. Even worse was the condition of my paws. I'd never survive as an alley cat, and the longer I stayed stuck inside Mittens, the more likely it was permanent. I needed help, and since I was cute and furry, this shouldn't be hard.

I whisked my way down the sidewalk, this time more wary of human feet, and paused when begging meows reached my enhanced ears. Two cats darted around each other in front of an alley door. It swung wide, and a human hand placed a plate of food on the ground.

Shaking off a strong sense of revulsion at the ordinary cats, I skittered down the sidewalk, as close to the buildings as possible to avoid another shoe collision. The heavenly scent of fresh baked goods stopped me dead in my tracks. A bell chimed as a door opened, and a woman swept past me with curly gray hair and curves showing an appreciation for baked goods, carrying a box. I'd bet anything it was cake.

I really wanted cake.

I ran up to her and tried that cat thing where they rubbed against human legs and got scratches for it, which was far more difficult to attempt when the human was walking. I didn't know how to purr, but I hoped my orange fluff would compensate. So I brushed against her leg and scurried over to her other leg and repeated. My fur crackled with static electricity.

The woman stopped and bent with a smile. "You remind me of my kitty at home. Who's a good girl, huh?"

"I'm not a girl." My knee-jerk answer wasn't thought out. She screamed.

Maybe she'd drop the cake? Just looking for that silver lining here.

She didn't.

The woman ran to a waiting cab, balancing the cake like a waitress, and then she was gone. I crossed the street, narrowly avoiding cars and bicycles, and on the opposite sidewalk, a glamoured demon with his telltale red essence smoked a cigarette, wearing jeans, a white T-shirt, and a black sport coat. He leaned against a storefront. A fellow Field Agent.

"Hey," I said, craning my neck up to meet the demon's human form.

The demon looked down at me with brows lifted. He leaned back on his haunches for a closer look. "You must be Malaikat riding around in Mittens. I heard about you. Tough break, man."

"iKat, please. I've been promoted, which is great, but I can't stay like this. I can't function like this."

"The ferret," the cool demon said simply.

"You heard the story?" The demon nodded. "Then you know I need help to get my body back."

The demon blew a ring of smoke in my face, and I coughed. "That's no small feat."

"I expected as much. I'll take whatever you're offering."

"Who says I'm helping?"

"You haven't kicked me yet."

The demon chuckled. "Unless you want to nest in squalor, you'll need to find a human willing to open their home to you. In this country, it's a seventy-thirty split for dog lovers to cat lovers. So, the odds are already against you. After you manage to find a cat lover, they have to accept a talking cat, which is an even bigger challenge."

"But you like talking cats."

The demon shot me a look that firmly disagreed with that statement.

"Sorry."

He rubbed between his eyes with his thumb as if a headache plagued him, and his irises turned red. The demon's face twitched and sweat beaded on his forehead. He frowned and snarled—like actually snarled—and finally he smiled, like he'd been warring with several personalities at once. His irises melded back into his normal shade of black. "I have just the target for you. The old farmhouse, just out of town. A hunter is there."

I hated to look a gift horse in the mouth, but... "A hunter? But doesn't he want to kill me, too?"

"You'll have the best luck with this particular one. Heather and she have unfinished business over the death of Ray."

"Thanks for the help..." I trailed off to prompt the helpful demon's name.

"Gremory." He took another drag. "This information is not free."

An information demon like Andras. I heard this demon could tell the past, present, and the future—someone I'd like to have as a friend. "How long have you been a Field Agent?"

"I'm not. Consider me...independent."

"Then why are you helping me?"

Gremory straightened. "There is a balance that has been disrupted. My assistance to you will set you on the path of resetting that disruption."

"That sounds...cryptic."

"Watch yourself. Most of demonkind wants you dead. Go now."

"You can't tell me that and—"

"Go."

What a strange demon. I closed my eyes to center my thoughts and pictured where I wanted to be. The familiar tugging moved my body, and when I opened my eyes, I was at the doorstep of the farmhouse. Craning my neck, I couldn't reach the doorbell, and I didn't believe any attempt at knocking would work. I'd have to bang my head against the door repeatedly...There had to be a better way.

I strolled around the old house, looking for an open window. Squeaks of a nearby mouse sent me sprinting like my tail was on fire (figuratively, because to a demon, burning didn't hurt).

I found the back door ajar and slipped inside.

5

The Slayer

THE INSIDE WAS JUST as terrifying as I imagined. Cracked
floorboards, dusty and full of splinters, lie ahead. Cobwebs were
sprinkled around the corners, and furniture was dusty, knocked
over, or broken. As horrible as all this was, it didn't compare to
the moans, grunts, and heavy panting coming from a room at
the end of the dilapidated hall. With a cringe, I crept along, on
high alert for mice, wishing to be anywhere but this disgusting
farmhouse.

Okay, almost.

But what other choice did I have? Demonkind wanted me
dead, for whatever reason. The angels, our natural enemy, also
wanted me dead, and I haven't even met one yet. Shifters,
who focused on their own special interests, wouldn't help me.
And vampires were one-track minded. None of those options
guaranteed help. In fact, most of them guaranteed death.

Daylight filtered in through dusty panes of glass, but with my
new feline vision, I saw sharper than ever. Plus, my lightweight
allowed me to move silently. A few perks, sure, but nothing

to write home about, because pungent mold and the stinging coppery stench of blood watered my eyes and burned my sensitive nose. I needed a tissue.

I stepped on a cobweb and shook my paw violently, trying to avoid causing a scene and attracting attention from those lovely sounds up ahead. The cobweb wouldn't come off. I dragged the edge of my paw over a piece of fallen debris from the ceiling. This abandoned old farmhouse should've been condemned. Why was anyone in here? I knew why I was in here, and I was regretting it more by the second.

I poked my head around the corner to the living room, bracing myself against whatever depravity considered this home. If I controlled Mittens's heart, it would've stopped. All demons had the ability to recognize other demons. We all had a red cloudiness around our hearts, visible on our chests and backs. But unlike other demons, I also had an aura vision, which I learned was quite rare. Only one other demon in recent history had the ability, but I never asked what happened to him. After seeing this, I'd really like to know.

Gremory had sent me to an option that was more suicidal than all the others—a hunter, but since the special demon could see the future, I had to trust him. But the spectacle before me included two beings, neither human nor demon. Supernaturals was a universal descriptor, but since I appreciated brevity, I liked Supers for short. And on what planet would a hunter help a *demon*? I was about to find out or die trying. (Just kidding, I'd teleport away with my tail between my legs.)

Like the repulsive hallway, dust and cobwebs coated the living room, too. At least the homeowner was consistent. To the right, broken glass from the picture window littered the floor. Furniture was knocked around, and some was broken. The only thing in reasonable condition was a crooked couch in the middle of the room with a faded floral pattern, facing the fireplace. The male and female occupying the room were in arguably worse condition. That was the source of the blood.

The female had tight black hair pulled into a high puffy ponytail. She wore a leather jacket and a healthy grimace, and a glint of silver rings along one ear. A black leather vest fitted over her cotton crewneck T-shirt showed slots for weapons, currently missing. Delightfully tight black jeans with a few slashes to the threads finished her badass ninja style. She pressed the snarling male against the mantle with a dagger to his throat. He wore jeans and a T-shirt, too, sans leather and weapons. Both leaked blood, but the stench was far greater than the mess on these two alone.

"I'm all for kink, but damn. That's a lot of blood," I said.

Both their heads turned to me. The woman spat, "What the hell are you?"

I jumped up onto the broken couch and cringed at the dust under my paws. After spotting the beheaded bodies behind the couch with puddles of blood, I wasn't sure which bothered me more—dust on my feet or the dead bodies. I twitched my rear end and leaped onto the fireplace mantle, not far from whatever these two were doing, thankful they didn't run away screaming. So far.

"I'm looking for someone," I said.

The badass ninja's keen eyes tracked my movements, like a hungry vampire, but as far as I was aware, furry kitties weren't on the menu. Her chest rose and fell with pants of exertion. I sat on the dusty mantle, and the urge to lick my feet overpowered me. Out of my control, up came the paw, and my tongue began the horrific washing process. Tastes I couldn't bear to describe flooded my mouth, while visions of microbial armies marching into my cat body made me want to heave. Gross, gross, so damned gross.

"And who might that be?" Her panting slowed down, but she held the ill-prepared inhuman man firmly in place.

The silent, ill-prepared, inhuman's shifty eyes planned his next move, scanning the open space, looking for weapons, seeking an exit. Something about him didn't feel like the man I sought, but looks could be deceiving, as I was proof.

Thoroughly disgusted with myself but satisfied my feet were clean for the moment—until I jumped down—I stood on all fours. "Well, I suppose one of you."

Which one was the question—the inhuman about to get his head severed or the woman who appeared to have anger management issues and a serious case of bloodlust?

Hmmm.

The inhuman's head slumped, but the woman propped him up, not even noticing the change in his condition.

"Is that right? When I finish with this guy, you're next. Stay there." The woman repositioned her knife to strike.

The inhuman's features twisted as if reawakened with a burst of unnecessary rage, and the hissing throaty noise was...odd. His eyes became vacant, and he decided now was a good time to snack on the badass ninja. The inhuman took that moment to chomp at her. The ninja leaped back, and the two of them tumbled all over the living room, smashing into furniture pieces and thumping against the wall. Her knife dislodged from her grasp. The male made more gargled noises.

Unless this was a scratching, or hissing contest, I was better off staying out of it. While watching the show, popcorn sounded nice. "If you two want to finish up here, that'd be great."

"Shut up!" the woman yelled.

"There's nothing wrong with wanting to play with your..." I trailed off as the throaty inhuman got a mouthful of leather jacket. A vampire wouldn't feed on someone's protected forearm, and she wasn't trying to bite him either. So that left him a... well, shit. This dude was reanimated. I'd heard about them, but never saw one. Creepy, but this one was too fresh to begin rotting.

According to the demon history books I'd studied when Andras rescued me from human land, Nick Barnes released a deadly bacterium, which spread, causing an apocalypse. Apparently, the demons hunted them in teams, keeping the reanimated contained so human life could continue. According to Gremory, I needed a demon hunter, but if Edie Randall was reanimated now, his corpse only served one purpose: allowing the woman to prove her usefulness against a hunter, a reanimated hunter.

I didn't realize that was a thing.

The woman rolled on the floor and picked up a lost blade. From the adjacent kitchen, the reanimated shuffled over to her, a partially severed limb dangling. The woman rolled and leaped to her feet, and without hesitation, she slashed with her blade. The reanimated's head tipped off its neck and fell to the floor, where it landed with a squishy thump. The woman swiped her forehead and stalked toward me with the contaminated blade. The wild look in her eye told me to back up. Among other things. So I did, not just because of the threat, but because that blade was disgusting, and I didn't want it anywhere near me. I might be a demon stuck in a cat, but since I couldn't get out of the cat yet, I needed to keep Mittens here alive. I didn't want to find out what would happen if Mittens died.

I jumped off the mantle to the floor and slowly backed into the hallway.

"What are you?" she demanded, stalking closer with the blade held in a not-so-pleasant demeanor. "Never saw a talking cat before."

My fluffy butt stopped against the wall. "And that makes two of us."

"Doesn't matter," she added, dismissing my comment. "You're not human, so it's my job to kill you before you kill us."

Threatened, heat rolled through my insides, and I focused it all into a fireball. When I had been in my human body, I launched them from my palms, (which was actually awesome), but as a cat, one at a time manifested between my jaws, like a tiny, furry, orange, flightless dragon (so much less awesome). I didn't want to set the whole dilapidated building on fire, so I tried to calm myself and center myself to teleport across the room, out of her reach. My thoughts showed me dead bodies, blood splatter, and a mouse's whiskers skulking in the corner.

The teleportation failed.

I swallowed back the fireball. The lump broke apart and tingled on the way down in a slightly unpleasant way, like a shot of vodka mixed with tomato juice and cottage cheese.

"Stop, or I'll have to make you." I didn't want to kill her, but I needed space to chat, and out of blade's reach was preferable. Instead of preparing another fireball, I allowed the flames to engulf my fur, swirling in defense, and glowing my eyes.

She gasped. "You're a demon?" She was more surprised than angry. For some reason, that reaction felt a little insulting. With her impressive display of combat and the fact that she'd slayed a reanimated by herself and knew what I was, I believed the woman was the hunter I sought.

"Did my glowing eyes or burning fur give it away?" I asked, deadpan.

She angled the knife as if waiting to swing a bat, but she stopped advancing. "Why are you a cat?"

I braced myself, prepared to handle the incoming ridicule. I'd survived years as a janitor with all sorts of colorful notes left for me in the company restrooms. I countered with an equally dumb question. "Why are you a hunter?"

She cocked her head to the side. "I can't tell if you're a smart cat or a stupid demon."

"How about a smart demon trapped in a stupid cat? Look, there's a reason I'm here. Are you...or was he Edie Randall?"

The woman straightened, but she kept her knife gripped tight. "How do you know my name?"

I smiled at my unusual luck. Ignoring her question, I said, "Call me iKat."

Edie's nose wrinkled in disgust. "I cat? Your name is 'I cat'? You sound a few rungs short on the IQ ladder. You should go with 'I'm a cat'. Makes more grammatical sense, Imacat."

I grew my flames, attempting to be threatening. "I didn't pick on your name. Back off." I growled, but in this diminutive form it wasn't as intimidating as I imagined.

"I kill evil things, you included, and it's time for you to join that pile behind me. Give me one good reason why I shouldn't add another tally to my count right now." Edie pointed her grisly, germy blade at me and stalked closer.

I understood keeping tallies on the job. If she wasn't threatening to kill me, I might like her. "If you promise to leave my head attached, I'll tell you."

"No can do. You talk, then I'll decide." She inched closer.

"Isn't it clear by now I'm not a regular demon?" I shifted my butt clear of the wall and stepped slowly backward down the filthy hallway.

Her eyes roamed my orange fur. "You're still a monster. What difference does it make?"

"I don't like you killing my kind any more than you like me interfering with yours. Can we call a truce for a minute?"

She took a step closer, and my defensive heat swirled higher, flames swaying Mittens's fur in waves.

"How's this for an answer?" Her blade split the air, but I dodged, and it jammed into the wall with a thud. Dust and plaster crumbs sprinkled down.

"Damn it, woman, can't you listen?" I dashed down the hall and outside, starting to regret some of my life's choices. I had a respectable desk job in Hell corrupting humans. I had a nice one-bedroom bachelor pad in Hell City. Kale smoothies and ten-mile jogs on the treadmill were my evenings. Occasionally I considered dialing Heather and asking her out, but instead, I'd watch demon basketball. How had I ended up at an abandoned farmhouse with a hunter on my literal tail?

I pictured Gremory cackling somewhere.

Waiting in the tall dry grass for her to appear, I engulfed myself in full flame. Edie barged through the back door and stopped, likely wondering why I hadn't fled.

So I answered the unspoken question. "I need your help, and you need mine."

She scoffed. "The only way you'd help me is by killing yourself, saving me the trouble." She tossed her own knife at my feet.

What the hell? I stepped back from it. "Look, badass ninja—"

"Don't call me that."

"Look, ass, I don't have thumbs. So unless you want to duct tape the handle to my paw, that was pointless. Two, I'll help you kill whoever you want. Name it, and I'll help."

"Did you just call me 'ass'?"

"I like brevity as much as you." Grass caught fire around my feet. With her weapon now safely out of her hand, I turned off my flames and used my tail to smack the burning patches.

Edie shook her head. "I don't need your help. I want all demons dead."

"Work with me here. I want to trade. Isn't there anyone in particular you need help with? Or are you truly a badass ninja?"

"Do you think I'm dumb enough to make a deal with a demon?"

Er, no. "It's not a deal. I'm not a contract demon. I just want to trade favors. You get something, and I get something. No strings for your soul."

"What do you want?" She squinted at me, but that was progress.

"I want my human form back. Believe it or not, I'm not actually an adorable feline."

"Why don't you just possess someone else? What's so special about this cat body you chose?"

I sighed, ready to correct a stereotype. "We don't possess humans. That's a fear tactic. We're born and raised just like you. And I happen to have a very sexy human-shaped body waiting for me."

Edie rolled her eyes. "Then how did you *possess* that cat?"

"I am borrowing Mittens here against my will...and his, I bet. He doesn't actually speak English, so I can't translate the meows in my head."

"Let me get this straight, you want my help to kill a demon, whoever did this to you, *and* you need my help to dig up your corpse?"

"Not exactly, no. The King of Hell cursed me into this furball's body. We don't have to kill him; he's far more powerful than this parlor trick. My body is in his dungeon."

"You want me to go to Hell?" she asked.

Why was it so hard to convince her to do this? Hunters, so finicky and suspicious.

I BACKED UP FROM the bloody hunter. The look on Edie's face was like daggers about to launch on my cuteness. "I literally want you to go to Hell with me, but you can come home after. You won't be dead, or anything, if you survive. I mean, you won't die just by going to Hell. This deal implies you don't kill me."

An internal war waged on her face. A hunter not killing a demon went against everything she knew, and I was asking her for something ridiculous, but still those wheels turned. Before giving me her answer, her cell phone beeped, and she dragged it from her pocket and read it. Edie's lips parted.

"What is it?" I asked.

Eyes on the screen, she read, "Corvina sends me messages of potential paranormal activity."

Hoping to win her over, I pretended to care. "What did she say?"

"Menominee, Michigan. People screaming, bitten, flames swallowing the house, but she can't find more information on it."

The biting and flames narrowed it down. "Either vampires or reanimated. Fifty-fifty shot it's a reanimated clean-up job."

"Reanimated?" Edie cocked her brow at me.

I forgot humans didn't have a complete historical recollection of all major events. An accurate one, anyway. "Humans infected with The Annihilator, who were unlucky enough to return to life, fall victim to a mindless raging hunger. Like your friend back there. They feed on live humans."

"That's not what the news says. How do you know so much about this?"

"Nick Barnes features prominently in our history books. It's all right there. He developed and released the bacterium, and named it, as far as I'm aware."

Edie stalked closer again. "Do you have any idea the damage the zombie outbreak caused—and is still causing? You saw this family. All of them are dead now! So many are dead." Edie glanced away, hiding her emotion from me, but just as quick as it appeared, she buried it. "The government isn't doing shit-all except placating people. Many people haven't encountered the zombies themselves and refuse to believe, making all this worse."

Perhaps then, I could persuade her to my side. "The demons are cleaning up the mess."

Edie glared at me. "Why? Is Nick Barnes a demon?"

"Demons don't have last names."

Edie slipped the phone back into her pocket and aimed the contaminated blade squarely at my throat. "Every last one of you needs to be wiped clean from this planet. Complete and total extermination."

Couldn't say I agreed with that, but if I had hands, I would've raised them. "If we head out, we might find some demons there. That's all."

"I hate all demons. Every last one of them. They all deserve to..." The wind in her sails sagged, and a cackle escaped her lips. She shook her head. "They all deserve to burn in Hell."

"Actually, that's not accurate." Her rage returned, and I corrected course. "But...but it doesn't matter. Whether you hate me or not doesn't matter."

Edie cleaned her weapon against the tall grass and sheathed the sticky blade. Ignoring me, she marched through the field.

I teleported to her side and kept stride.

"I'm not going to Hell for you," she called over her shoulder at me.

"It's not as hard as it sounds, and I want to help you. I do. I mean, look at me. Do you think I have loyalty to the demons after they did this to me?"

Edie stopped. Silence stretched as she stared me down like vermin, which was totally unjustified. What did he ever do to her?

"How do I know you won't betray me?"

I sighed. "There's nothing I can say that will prove anything. All you can do is take a chance on me, and I can help you."

Edie shifted her weight, considering. "Promise me. Promise me you're genuine, that I can trust your word. Because if I bring you into my home, and you betray us, it's not the demons I worry about."

Good to know. "You can trust my word."

With a grumble, Edie said, "Get in the car."

I scurried through the grass and stopped at a gravel clearing, where a silver Prius waited. I closed my eyes to clear my mind and teleport inside. Visualizing Edie changing her mind, slipping the grimy knife free, and aiming, I opened my eyes. The knife remained secured in its holster.

"Can you get the door for me?" I asked and lifted a paw. "Missing thumbs." I couldn't teleport, and after considering it, I didn't want to disclose all my abilities to an enemy.

"Are you going to be a burden the whole drive?" She opened the door, and after I hopped inside, she closed it. Fast food bags littered the floor, clothes were strung all over, and a weapon was turned blade down in the cup holder. The place was a mess. Humans were disgusting. I exhaled a shaky deep breath. Unable to help myself, I swatted litter off the seat, and with a cringe, I lifted a shredded shirt off the center console with my teeth and dropped it to the floor.

When her jeans-clad cheeks sank into the driver's seat, I said, "It depends on how nice you are to me."

"Nice? You expect me to be nice to a demon?" Edie buckled up, turned the engine over, and shifted into drive.

"What did I ever do to you?"

She ignored me while driving west.

"Menominee is the other way. Where are we going?"

"Get supplies. Are you going to strangle the demons barehanded? I'm not."

Despite her stubbornness and her mouth likely to get us killed, I liked her spunk, but Edie alone wouldn't be enough. As the trees rolled by the side window, which I could barely see out of, I wished I were back at my desk in Hell, manipulating humans, working up the nerve to talk to Heather, and splurging on a slice of cake. Despite all that, Hell was better than this mess.

I caught the coppery scent of blood again. "Did you pack a souvenir, or did you cut yourself?"

"What? I don't think so."

I followed my nose to a gash on her biceps. "You sure? 'Cause I can smell it there on your arm. It's about to drip onto the cushion."

Edie swerved as if she were about to hit a deer. Tires rumbled to a stop on the gravel shoulder, and she jumped out. In the backseat, she thrashed through old food containers and crumpled papers and tore a strip of fabric from what might've been a different shredded T-shirt. She knotted it around her gash with a frustrated grunt. Edie shut the back door and popped her head near the front seat, still digging for something.

"What are you doing?" I asked.

Edie ducked around the steering column and stuck her head down by the floor mats. She inspecting the seat cushion very closely. Edie swiped at a spot and rubbed it between her fingers. "Do you see any?"

"There's some on the seat."

"Where?"

I touched my paw to the spot.

"Damn it." Edie used her elbow to soak up the stain. "Can you still smell it?"

"Well, yeah, but I can't tell the difference between your arm and the cushion though. Why the sudden panic?"

Edie sat on the driver's seat and slammed the door. "You can sniff blood. So can other monsters. I don't need to be riding around in a target."

I didn't miss that little qualifier to the 'monsters' label, but I had her cooperation, so I'd just deal.

Buckling and shifting, she punched the gas. "It's a long ride. Tell me you won't be annoying the whole while."

I frowned, willing to sit silently. The hum of the engine, soft vibration of the cushion, and warm sunlight pulled Mittens into a catnap. I fought it. I fought with every atom of my remaining essence to keep the orange tabby awake, but the cat still curled up and slept. Humans actually liked these fluffy weirdos?

Since demons didn't sleep, I was stuck in an unconscious body, unable to talk or move, like a human awake during surgery. Just less pain...for now. Hopefully Edie didn't figure out my helplessness and whack my head off.

6

The Crew

I BOUNCED AROUND FOSTER homes when I was very young. All of them were in the city, and all the family had kept the government checks for themselves. They never took me anywhere, but I had a feeling this place was exactly what everyone had in mind they talked about 'the middle of nowhere'.

Far from the exit ramp and several turns down county roads, Edie slowed the Prius to a roll at a narrow passage between a thicket of pine and cedar trees. She turned the wheel and climbed the hill, tires crunching the gravel. A clearing at the end of the long path revealed a sad, mossy cabin surrounded by floppy green grass. An older model sedan—something typical of a high school parking lot—sat near the cabin, the only sign it wasn't entirely abandoned.

When Edie turned off the engine, Mittens finally woke up and stretched.

"Man, my jaw is sore," I said, having been kept silent for hours.

"You're an asshole," Edie said. "And if you weren't so cute, I'd slap your face off. Why didn't you answer a single question

I asked?" She reached into the back seat and lifted a black duffel bag, rattling with unknown metal and wood objects.

"The cat was asleep. Certain cat instincts and needs can override what I'd rather be doing. So if Mittens wants to nap, I'm stuck waiting until he wakes. If he wants to eat, I have to track down something edible to him. And just so you know, if Mittens gets a hairball, that's not in my control either." I glanced around her car to make the point. "Not that you'd notice in here, anyway."

Edie scoffed, clearly still miffed about me ignoring her the whole drive. "So you're a demon, cursed into a cat's body, and you can't even control the animal?"

"Most of the time I can," I retorted with a mumble, considering whether an ass-kicking hunter's skills were worth the gruff attitude. No wonder humans were beneath demons—figuratively, not literally, because demons were, in fact, under the ground.

Edie opened her car door, carrying the bag, and I hopped out on her side. I followed her up the single wooden step to the porch. Several planks were missing on the long porch, allowing plants to grow, and the windows were dirty. Edie pulled open the screen door with a screech, and a startled blackbird flew from a nearby tree.

Inside the cabin, dim light filtered on a folding card table and chairs, filling what would be the dining space. A small modular kitchenette with a mini sink sat against one wall. In the doorless bedroom, on the other side of the cabin, was a dusty bookcase and a king-sized bed covered in quilts. The doors in view were probably closets, a bathroom, and a back exit. I preferred brighter and cleaner quarters than this pigsty. But I wasn't sticking around.

A lanky woman hovered over the folding table, open books piling around her. Long strands of wheat draped down, covering her face. When the door shut behind us, she looked up, eyes bright green with surprise, and her attention shifted to me, growing the surprise further. "You brought a cat? But you don't like cats."

Edie pressed her lips tight and carried the duffel bag to one of the interior doors, opened it, and dropped the bag on the floor with a rattling thump. An organizational grid with neat rows of hangers displayed axes, picks, short swords, and smaller knives. A bow and arrow with a quiver hung on the door. Another row was dedicated to different sized wooden stakes. Considering the condition of Edie's car, I was impressed by her tool layout.

Edie called over her shoulder, "Corvina Wilsey meet iKat. That bag of fur isn't as innocent as he looks. Be careful."

Corvina's face lit up with excitement. "Oh, but he's just a cute kitty. We need a litter box unless he's supposed to go outside."

"I resent that," I said.

The young woman screeched and leaped back from the table. Books shook from the force, and one fell to the floor. "It talks!"

I sighed. "And it makes fire, too!"

"Don't patronize my friend, demon," Edie shouted from the closet.

"He's a demon? You're a demon? But you're a..." the blond picked up the book from the floor and held it up to her chest like a shield.

"Cat. I know," I said before getting the usual round of questions. "Call me iKat, and no, it's not related to what I look like."

"I'm Corvina," the blond said hesitantly but didn't offer a hand to shake. "Were you responsible for the farmhouse?"

"They were all bitten before I got there," Edie called over. "The last one turned while we were fighting. The cat arrived after."

Humans always thought demons were evil, and I couldn't keep my snark buried. "Just because I'm a demon automatically means I murdered people? How many times do I have to explain that's not what we do?"

"We don't often find...a chatty demon," Corvina said slowly, keeping the book close to her chest and feet planted firmly away from me. "And since I can't imagine an evil creature declining to take credit whenever possible, you're telling the truth?"

Frustrated with her slow-to-process questions and apparent uselessness, I asked Edie, "What is she doing here?"

The front door opened and closed behind me, but I was too irritated to pay it a glance. I needed to start influencing humans to keep the king complacent while I figured out *how* I was getting my body back, because there was no way I was staying a cat for the excessively long demon lifespan. Since hunters' souls were already earmarked for Hell, sitting here doing nothing wasted my time. "For that matter, what am I doing here?"

"Egads, it talks." A lean but obvious fellow gym rat strolled in and dropped a duffel matching Edie's on the floor. Removing his aviator sunglasses, he lifted his thick brown brows. He wore dark jeans with a thick and shiny belt buckle announcing he was a 'tool' with a capital T, a stripped polo with an embroidered logo, and work boots. Too clean for construction or hunting, and I wasn't familiar with the logo on his shirt, but I slotted this dude into the harmless but annoying category. The man leaned down to his duffel and searched for something inside while he asked, "So, what are you, besides the obvious?"

Polo Dude retrieved a fixed-blade knife from the duffel and slipped it from its leather sheath. Another hunter. Just great.

Not wanting to repeat the whole conversation again, I swirled the heat behind my eyes to glow them red in answer to his question.

"It's a demon! Corvy, get out of the way." Polo Dude rushed across the small cabin, blade aiming to strike. Well, not so harmless after all. Polo Dude moved fast, but I waited until the last moment to teleport across the cabin before the dummy struck.

As Polo Dude spun in place, confused, I asked, "You must be a new hunter. Just so you know, and this is a freebie, demons teleport. But based on your strategy of chasing a cat on foot, I'm guessing you were a solid C minus student, am I right?"

Edie finished filling her duffel and stripped out of her torn shirt, catching Polo Dude's attention. Dropping the fabric on the floor, she pulled a fresh shirt from a hanger and slipped it over her head.

My eye twitched at the discarded garment. I hated a careless mess. "Are you going to pick that up?"

Edie carried the heavy bag to the wobbly table and dropped it on top of the precariously piled books. "Garrett Ford, this is iKat. Play nice."

"Are you kidding me? You brought a demon to a hunter's cabin? If anyone else finds out about this—"

"If you don't tell anyone, they won't find out," Edie said.

"He's a demon, ergo, he's an evil asshole, and he doesn't belong here. Give me one good reason not to add a tally to my count today."

I tried to smile. If we weren't mortal enemies, I could totally hang with these guys.

"Put it away," she ordered, glancing at his blade. "The cat's harmless—mostly."

I resented that, too.

"iKat," Edie turned to me. "Demon or not, I don't know your background, but I'm warning you to treat us all with respect or I won't stop the next person who wants to kill you."

I didn't need a bodyguard, but since I did need help, I refrained from uttering the salty words dancing at the tip of my spiked tongue. Instead, I tried to be helpful. Teleporting over to the discarded garment, I asked, nicely, "Edie, are you planning on washing or putting this away?"

She leaned around Ford. "It's destroyed. I'll deal with it later."

Unable to ignore the disgusting mess of shredded, bloodstained fabric draped haphazardly on the floor where anyone could step on it, I ignited my demon fire. In moments, the shirt was history. The flames snuffed out, and I swatted any residual fire with my tail. A blackened mark on the hardwood was a small price to pay for cleanliness.

"That's it! Edie, what were you thinking?" Ford rushed me with the blade again, boots thundering along the floorboards. Not a sneaky hunter, either. The blade swooshed by my head, so I teleported to the opposite corner, and Ford spun in exasperation. "Hold still you little shi—"

"Ford, leave him alone!" Edie ordered.

Corvina stood motionless and wide eyed at the spectacle. Glad someone was entertained...or terrified. Either one was pretty okay.

"He's going to burn the place down." Ford stalked closer, slower, as if my vision only picked up movement. I was a cat, not a dinosaur.

I considered toying with the hunter. After all, what else could I do right now? This guy was a hoot. "That shirt was a biohazard. I did you a favor."

Ford's face tilted and twisted with confusion.

"Watch it," Edie yelled at me, clearly offended and inspected the edge of her blade. "I'm not contaminated by evil, unlike a certain someone in here."

"Let's not go down this road again, shall we? We've got work to do. Whenever you're ready, let's get out of here," I said.

"Good riddance," Ford muttered.

"I'm ready. Nothing's getting fixed by sitting here." Edie slung the duffel over her shoulder. "Corvy, iKat and I are headed to Menominee now, but I need more bodies."

"Should be plenty where you're going." Corvina frowned.

"You two," Edie said and glanced at Corvina and Ford. "Road trip?"

Corvina and Ford exchanged glances. After red flushed the blond's cheeks, she rushed to the table and uncovered some books, remembering what she'd been doing before our interruption. "I have class in a couple hours. We wouldn't make it back on time."

"Ford?" Edie pleaded.

"Where's Vale when you need him?" Ford mumbled. Polo Dude didn't want to play nice with me. Shame.

"Vale only helps at night, you know that. Are you in or out? I need a set of strong muscles." Edie's spicy glance took in Ford's full length.

I might've blushed if that glance was meant for me. As long as I sported four feet, I had zero chance of any action. Not that I needed yet another reason to work faster.

Ford's lips lifted. "Let me pack. I have to work tonight, though, so no wasting time."

"Pity," Edie said to his back as he refilled his duffel in the closet. Ford glanced over his shoulder with a smile.

Edie turned to the blond. "Corvy, you'll take care of preparing and organizing these weapons while we're gone?"

"I do it better than you. When was the last time you cleaned out your car?"

Edie mock laughed. "Leave my car out of this. Saddle up, Ford and iKat. We have a slaughter to investigate, and some demons to kill while we're there."

Between the disastrous car and these two flirting the whole time, this ought to be a fun ride. Humans, man, so easily distracted.

7

Road Trip

As trees flew by the windows at dizzying speeds, I glared at a tube of used lipstick on the back passenger side floor and a sweat-stained athletic outfit draped over the transmission tunnel, wishing I could ignite them both. I didn't have thumbs to pick the stuff up and throw it out, and no way in hell would I use my teeth this time. Food containers and a shredded blanket on the other side joined the mess. Did she live in here?

Highway 64 stretched on and on. Edie pulled up to a pump off the highway in the middle of nowhere—a different one this time. I was getting to see the world outside my bubble. The station was void of customers and apparently all life forms.

"Are you chipping in for gas?" she asked.

"I bought last time," Ford said. He climbed out and went inside the convenience store.

Edie stared at me through the rearview mirror.

"What, me?" I asked. "I don't have money. Do I look like I have pockets?"

"That's rich." She squinted at me. "Or, I suppose not."

"Teleporter here. I don't need the ride. You subjected me to this greasy, pungent mess back here. You should be paying me."

Edie rolled her eyes and climbed out of the car. A breeze ruffled her ponytail, and she gazed off at the farm fields while the fuel nozzle pumped. Most humans knew nothing of the supernatural world around them—for good reason. Historically, humans didn't play well with others different from themselves. What kind of life had Edie lived to consider all the monsters in the world so mundane?

After a short few minutes, she went into the convenience store just as Ford emerged. No one paid at the pump out here, apparently.

Ford ducked into the car and glanced over his shoulder at me. "You're still here? I thought you'd have left."

"Might I say what a wonderful pleasure it is to be in your company." My tail flicked with agitation.

Ford scoffed. "It's only because Edie thinks we need your help that you're here. Otherwise..." He gestured with a finger across the front of his throat.

What a loon.

Edie returned with drinks and snacks filling her arms, and Ford leaned over to push her door open. Edie climbed into the driver's seat, and Ford helped empty her hands and sort through the loot.

"I don't suppose you can drink out of a straw." She set a shallow dish on the backseat and poured water into it.

In the time between getting removed from Hell and tracking down Edie Randall, I struggled to find a human willing to listen to a talking cat, only to get kicked across sidewalks and screamed at. I'd almost got my head cut off a few times, no thanks to Ford. A lump formed in my throat at the shocking kindness—the first since arriving on the surface. "Thank you."

"You bought him food and water?" Ford asked, appalled.

"It's not Mittens's fault he's possessed. There's an innocent trapped in this situation. Plus, he's cute." Edie rubbed my head.

"You don't like cats," Ford said.

"I appreciate the thought, regardless," I said.

Ford tore into a snack stick and ignored me. "When this is over, we're not keeping him."

"When this is over," Edie countered, "he will be a normal cat."

"Are you going to give it fresh food and water every day? Buy it a litter box and scoop it? Sweep the cabin floor for tracked litter? You know...clean up after it?"

Even though the humans discussed Mittens, and not me, the offense still bubbled. "I'm not helpless. Don't worry, when this is over, I'll be long gone."

Ford made a dismissive noise. No wonder demons didn't respect hunters.

"What kind of person abandons an innocent animal?" I asked him, voice rising. "Dogs and cats aren't for me either—I'm more of a fish guy—but I would never abandon an animal just because.... Actually, you didn't give a reason. Ford, what has Mittens done to you that's so horrible you'd kick him out and leave him fend for himself? For all you know, Mittens was a simple house cat, caught up in this rouse just like me."

"Are you declawed?" he asked.

I flexed the sharp appendages attached to my paws. "No."

"Then you can fend for yourself." The idiot hunter bit off a hunk from a meat stick and chewed like a blessed cow.

I snorted, remembering Ford's attempts to kill me in the cabin. "Or what? Little girls can catch a cat better than you. Here's a hint, food always works wonders."

Ford's fists clenched, and a deep growl came from his throat. "Edie, I can't work with him. I just..." Ford got out of the car, leaving the door open.

Edie jumped out her side, and for the entertainment value, I teleported onto the vehicle's roof.

Ford paced in front of the car. "He's a demon. It's unnatural. It feels wrong. Can't you see that? At any moment he's going to jump out behind us and slit our throats." He pointed to the back seat, but a quick glance had him frantically searching around. "Where is the little shit?"

I rose and waved my tail. "Sure, whine to the momma bear. Can you make any decisions for yourself or does Edie pack your backpack?"

In a flash, Edie reached out to stop Ford from drawing the pistol at his hip. "Not at a gas station. Just stop it. Both of you. We can work together like mature adults. Right?"

Ford stayed quiet, as if still trying to contain himself.

"Right?" she pressed.

"Your packing my hunter's bag has nothing to do with this," Ford said.

Edie slowly released his hands. "I know. Get back in the car. We have survivors of a reanimated attack to investigate, and we might find demons you *can* kill."

Without another word, Ford ducked into the car and slammed the door shut.

Edie pointed a warning finger at me, silently telling him to behave. I nodded and teleported to the backseat. I was only defending myself. Perhaps I could've been nicer, since I needed the help. I'd try to remember that next time Ford blew a fuse.

Edie climbed into the driver's seat and opened a sausage stick, while keeping a close eye on Ford. She passed it to me. "We need sustenance before we reach Menominee. We don't know what we'll find there. iKat, do you eat this?"

"I can try."

She set it on the seat, and I bent down and bit into it. I shook my head to tear off a piece, but it didn't work. I gnawed at it like a bone, but still, I couldn't rip off a piece. I growled at it.

Edie chuckled and lifted the sausage stick. She tore off little bites, pooling them at my paws. "I have extra if you want more, Ford."

The hothead crossed his arms over his chest and turned his face toward the window. "I'm fine."

"You know," she said to me, popping open a bag of chips and crunching one. "Big mouth aside, you aren't so evil for a demon. Not like many of the others we've encountered, but Corvy was right, you guys aren't usually chatty."

I needed to win these people over for a little while, and being able to sleep without worrying about the status of my head and neck connection was important. "That's because I'm not much different from you."

Ford swore under his breath.

Edie shifted her head in that cute way dogs did when they heard something interesting. "Humans don't have red glowing eyes or fire covering their bodies on command. How can you be anything like us?"

Ford turned his attention back to me, hating me but still curious enough to listen.

After lapping up some water, I looked her in the eye. "Not all demons are evil. We're as varied as humans."

"Huh." She ate a few chips, stewing.

"I'll believe that when a demon buys me beer and a pizza, no strings attached," Ford said.

Edie sipped from a bottle of water and recapped it. "Beer and pizza. That's your measure?"

"Should I be insulted here?" I asked, genuinely not sure.

Ford clarified, ignoring me. "I've yet to meet one that generous."

I couldn't argue, but that was a low bar to set.

Edie asked me, "What caused you to be turned into a cat?"

"I made a mistake at work." I chewed a meat stick bite to avoid further questioning. After a long pause that said I wouldn't go into more detail, because I didn't want to be kicked out or have another entertaining attempt on my life again, Edie started the car and buckled up.

"And what? You stole out of the office refrigerator?" She chuckled and pulled onto the highway, heading east toward Lake Michigan.

I cleared my throat and said, "That was precisely it."

"Are you buying this bullshit? The cat's got a nose so long it's up his own ass."

Ignoring Ford again, Edie asked, "Seriously?"

"The King of Hell used magic to shove my essence into this cat. Diego, his personal guard gave me a demon version of an apology on my way out the door. My good friend, Andras, might know more since the king had him fetch me from my cubicle."

"God, Hell sounds like hell," Ford said.

Despite not knowing the current status on the God subject, I couldn't agree. "I like it down there, if I were in my real body. But as far as earning a paycheck, I prefer to be up here. Far more entertaining."

Ford sent me a dirty look in the rearview mirror.

"I'll never understand the demon system," Edie said. "It doesn't make sense. The punishments don't fit the crimes, whether the crimes are minor, and the punishments are way harsh—like yours—or when the crimes are insane, and all you get is a slap on the knuckles. Stealing from the office fridge really got you turned into a cat? Was it booby trapped? A fun Friday prank? Is it a Cinderella thing where you magically go back at midnight?"

"I forgot my lunch, so I borrow someone's. Since they ordered takeout, I thought I had enough time to replace it the next day."

"That's really lame."

"Why didn't you buy lunch?" Ford asked.

"Desk Agents in Hell aren't paid well."

Ford cackled.

I frowned. It wasn't that funny. "What about you, Edie? Why did you choose this self-destructive lifestyle?"

Keeping her eyes on the road as we entered the small city of Marinette, Edie answered, "My parents were hunters. I was raised a hunter, too. It's all I know."

"What about you, Ford?" I added.

Edie answered for him while merging with traffic northbound on Hall Avenue. "Ford has a vendetta against demons after his—"

"Don't tell the demon my business," Ford cut her off. "It won't help matters between us."

Edie crinkled up her wrappers and tossed them on the floor.

"You know there was a garbage at the gas station," I said. "And another one at that gas station."

"If you're willing to clean up, go for it." She paused and added quickly, "But not with fire."

"Doesn't the smell bother you?" I cringed at the greasy wrappers.

"What smell?"

"Don't bother, cat. Edie's never going to change." Ford shifted in his seat as if the cramped space bothered his long legs. If there wasn't junk all over, he'd have more room. Just an observation better left unsaid. At the light, I caught businesses here that looked fun, like Fully Loaded.

I'd like to get fully loaded myself after this conversation, but I had a feeling they didn't serve cats.

Light after light, we passed through town. After crossing the interstate bridge, where massive buildings housed naval ships in progress, the car rambled down the hill and through Menominee—a quaint town, featuring many small businesses. I asked Edie if we could stop for some edibles.

"You be better off stopping at the pet store."

I tilted my head, confused.

"Catnip," she clarified.

I frowned.

I asked to stop at the bakery instead or grab a tasting at the winery, which was a negative. I asked to roll by the marina and see the shops downtown had to offer, but Edie shot me down again.

Strictly business. Hey, I didn't get out much. And small towns fascinated me.

Outside of city limits, Edie turned off the highway and onto a small county road. Beyond the hobby farms, the forest thickened around us, and she turned onto a single lane road, which was more like a trail. So I questioned if it was a real road. At first she answered honestly—it was on the GPS. Then she scolded me for assuming she was dumb enough to drive on ATV trails.

I thought it was a fair question.

Moving slowly down the lane, driveways were swallowed by vegetation as if the whole area had been deserted. We searched for the red address plate or mailbox number, whichever appeared through the overgrown weeds and bushes.

"Here!" Edie pulled over. "According to Corvy's message, this is the place."

"Doesn't look like anything." Ford said.

"That's probably the point. No one will notice anything out here for a while...if ever." Edie steered us up a long gravel driveway, which opened to a wide clearing, just like their hunter's cabin. But unlike the cabin, the smoking husk of a ranch house stood by its lonesome. A smattering of late-model cars and a shiny pickup truck waited in front of the closed garage door. Vehicle marks dented the lawn, like someone made a quick getaway.

Ford got out and stretched. "We're too late."

EDIE POPPED THE TRUNK. "The house is still smoking, but there's no police tape. Gear up fast. We're going in. We have to eliminate any demon evidence and get out before the cops arrive."

I listened for the screams of survivors, but so far, *nada*. "I'm with Ford on this one. I don't hear anything, and the flames are out. I think there's a slim chance anything is alive in there."

Ford leaned over the supply of weapons. "Last time we thought it had just happened, we were ambushed by mice scurrying away from half eaten corpses. Remember that, Edie?"

"Did you say mice?" I asked, suddenly regretting this deal.

Ford glared at me while filling his belt with weapons from the duffel bags in the trunk. He slipped a hammer through a loop in his jeans and put a flashlight in a pocket. "Somehow a whole nest of them filled the house like cockroaches and ate the dead before we identified if they were human or not. Then they came after us like tiny savages. You get to go in first, cat. Holler if you see dinner." Ford chuckled and strapped a gas cylinder to his back.

Edie filled her belt with weapons, too. "We don't need the flame thrower, Ford."

Ford lifted the nozzle attached to the cylinder by hoses. The nozzle was bigger than me. Two could play this stupid game. I flamed on. Ford twisted a knob.

"What's going on here?" Edie spun. "You two, behave! And Ford, stop wasting fuel."

With a smirk, I extinguished my flames.

Ford turned the knob off. "I don't trust the cat, and I'm taking the flame thrower in case of rodents. Besides, we haven't used this old thing in a while. Might need to test it." Ford pointed the nozzle at me.

I said, "You could also test your cumbersome human flamethrower by *not* aiming it at the fireproof cat."

"Don't get your panties in a bunch. I was just getting ready."

Edie fisted a small pistol and closed the trunk quietly. "If demons are in there cleaning up a reanimated mess, I'm going in prepared. Not all of us are immune to the disease."

"I can sense if demons are present, so at least you'll have that warning."

Edie shot me a pointed look. "Are there any inside?"

I activated my demon vision, which showed me Hell's fire illuminated on its creatures. I scanned the premises. "No supers in range."

"Super?" Ford asked.

"Supernatural. Beyond known nature. Outside of the observable reality."

"We called them monsters, but Supers works for me," Ford said. "Makes taking them down sound like a bigger accomplishment."

I strolled behind them, paws not making a sound. "I've met demons who are nicer than you people. For example, my desk jockey cohort, Heather. She's one of the king's most trusted agents. Lovely on the outside but looking on the inside is like steel wool to the eyeball. Despite that, she still treats me better than you two. In fact, if I had my body right now, I'd be in Hell asking her out."

"It's not our fault you have low standards."

Across the crunchy gravel, we climbed the short and narrow concrete staircase to the front door.

Edie placed a hand on the grip of her pistol. "You're awfully quiet, Ford. What's up?"

"I have nothing nice to say. Let's get to work."

I reached out with my demon vision again. "I got something in the west corner. One demon."

Edie lifted the handgun, finger loosely hovering near the trigger, and opened the door. "Wait," she hissed. "If you can sense it, can't it sense you?"

Ignoring her use of the word 'it', I said, "I just gave you the warning, didn't I?"

She grunted in frustration and lifted the handgun, finger loosely hovering near the trigger. With a nod from Ford, she opened the door.

Ford gestured the flamethrower at me to lead, so I stepped inside first.

8

Massacre

THE DRY AIR SMOTHERED me like a fleece blanket. Walls and furniture, still smoking softly, had burned to char. The coppery stench of blood, speckling the carpeting and tile flooring, stung my eyes like onions. Tears filled my lids in defense, and I rubbed a paw against them to clear my vision. The crime scene cleaners hadn't come through—a good sign for the hunters' investigation. But the bodies were gone, so the coroners had picked them up. Then where were the police? Something was off about this whole situation.

I focused through my watery eyes, trying to target the lurking demon. The bright heat of the vanquished fire muted the accuracy of my vision, but a shifting shape in red caught my attention.

"He's on the move, coming right at us." I turned off my nausea-inducing demon vision. *Note to self, avoid demon vision in fires.*

Edie sidled against the wall and waited, finger positioned at the ready. Ford took the opposite side with a knife. So much for the flamethrower. I teleported to the other side of the room as a distraction, waiting for the demon to waltz into their trap. The demon stumbled through the burned debris on high heels and passed right by the humans. My fluffy mouth opened at the skirt suit set and tightly wound hair.

"Heather?"

Before my flirty colleague addressed me, Edie squeezed the trigger, shooting Heather in the back several times. The rapid pops stung my ears, and Heather's face pinched in pain. She spun on her attackers. Human bullets hurt, but they didn't kill.

"Wait, stop!" I shouted, uselessly.

Ford sprung with his short blade while Edie reloaded.

Heather snarled, and using Ford's momentum against him, she dodged and shoved, throwing Ford to the filthy floor. Heather lifted her hands ready to return fire (literal fire, she didn't have a gun).

Knowing the humans would be toast—*ha ha*—I shouted, "Stop! Everyone, just wait a minute."

With shock and confusion on her face, Heather spun, searching for my voice. "Malaikat?"

With resignation, I nodded. "It's me. Uh, down here."

She finally found me and smirked. "Orange tabby, huh? I thought the king would've chosen something vicious. It's infinitely better that he didn't...for my sake."

"You knew about this?" I backed up a few steps. She was in this...punishment?

"Everyone knows. You're quite the gossip back home."

Edie finished reloading. She'd been right when she said this punishing curse was too extreme even by demon standards.

Something beyond a sandwich was going on here. "Tell me the real reason why I'm stuck like this."

Behind Heather, Ford inched forward, and Edie held her pistol low and unsheathed a long blade, ready for a strike as they crept along the blackened carpeting. If they managed to kill Heather (doubtful), I wouldn't get my answers, and Heather would be a formidable ally in my attempt to get my body back, if she'd cooperate.

"Don't, guys. I need her."

The hunters exchanged looks of confusion. Edie shrugged. Ford gestured a clear stabbing-in-the-back motion. Edie shook her head in the negative, and Ford's face flushed bright red with his hothead anger. Under different circumstances, I would've laughed at their silent conversation.

Heather lifted a flaming hand to warn the two hunters at her back. "Stop while you're ahead. Only warning."

Ford and Edie stopped advancing, but they didn't let down their guard.

"Tell me what's going on," I pressed.

"No can do." Heather's smirk slid away. "Malaikat, whatever you're doing here doesn't concern you. If the king finds out you've been skirting around your responsibilities with these...these...*humans*, you're going to have a very bad week. Remember Glitter?"

No one could forget the flamboyant demon torturemaster, but that threat wasn't enough to stop me. "Help me get my body back. You owe me that much."

Heather closed the distance and leaned back on her haunches to meet my eye level. "I don't owe you anything."

How the king managed to get Heather to listen was a skill I had an interest in, but until then, she was useless to me. "If you aren't going to help, please move out of the way."

Heather stood, leaving her flame-free hands hanging at her sides. "So polite. That's not how I remember you."

Ford and Edie exchanged confused glances. Count me into that party. Maybe the smoke blurred Heather's memory, causing her to confuse me with someone else. "What do you mean?"

"There was a time, not so long ago, when you were holding all the power over me, figuratively speaking. It's actually quite refreshing for that power—knowledge in this case—to be on my side." Heather breathed in deep and exhaled slowly. "Yep, it feels good. I'm going to bask in this glorious moment for a while longer, if you don't mind. Ironically, if you had your memory, this would more satisfying, because then you'd know exactly what I'm talking about, and I believe it would sting just that much more."

Frustrated, I said, "Then tell me."

That stupid smirk returned. "I'm willing to cross the king, but not until the right time."

Crossing her off my short list of potential dates (okay, the list only had her on it), I growled, and taking that as a cue, Ford charged. Edie fired the pistol once. The bullet hit home, knocking Heather off balance. Ford tackled her and stabbed into her ribs.

"No!" I shouted. I wasn't done questioning her.

Edie shouted, "Go for the head! The head's the only way for sure!" She rushed up to them, tumbling on the crusty floor, and aimed, waiting for a clear shot of Heather's skull.

Ford strained to lift his blade to her throat. The demon was very strong, and apparently tired of the hunters. She ignited the flames on her body, and Ford yelped, scooting back, and patted out licks of fire on his clothes. Heather rolled slowly, trying to get to her feet, but all those rounds scrambled her.

With Ford out of the way, Edie unloaded several more rounds into the demon's head, knocking Heather with the force of each hit. I flinched from the ear-piercing pops. It shouldn't have ended like this. She could've been a valuable ally, but Heather wasn't the type to join, and I didn't expect the king to give me pointers on how to get her to fall in line.

Piercing pain crushed my skull, and I collapsed to the floor. Had Edie shot me? The rapid *pop-pops* ended. The fire near me vanished.

Edie leaned over me. "You okay?"

"My head hurts. Did you shoot me?"

"I would take offense, but you seem out of sorts."

"If you want, I'll shoot you," Ford offered, and at Edie's glare, he shrugged.

My head felt like a migraine was coming on, but it didn't. Interrupted or fought back, I didn't know. Frankly, I hated them. They only confused me and happened at very inconvenient times.

Edie holstered her pistol and stood. "So that was the demon you claimed is nicer than us?"

"Was? Is she dead?" I climbed to all fours, and Heather wasn't where I last saw her. The hunters followed my gaze.

"We shouldn't have let her go," Ford said, still holding his knife. "One demon out in the wild is one demon too many."

"She looked dead to me," Edie said. "But she must've teleported out."

They already knew about the teleporting. Good. Now I could use it when I needed it.

Ford shook his head in disbelief. "With a whole stack of metal fired into her body, she could *still* get away. That's the kind of power I expect to have soon," Ford said, puffing out his chest.

Edie tapped him on the chest playfully. "Sure thing, bub. Are you planning to ask the king to supercharge you?"

"I make my own destiny."

"You sound like an inspirational poster," Edie said. "But we can't let her get away with this."

The softest moan twitched my sensitive ears. "Hey, shush. Someone's still here."

FORD AND EDIE QUIETED at once and gripped their weapons. I used my demon vision to pinpoint the source, but I saw nothing—not human and not demon. "Follow me."

The hunters crept behind me silently down the hallway, weapons pointing into each open doorway. Photo frames hung limply off the walls, sooty from the fire. A charred decorative table held broken vases. The floor still smoldered, but I wasn't affected, and the hunters with their combat boots didn't complain.

Through the final doorway was a bedroom with less damage than the rest of the house. A twin-sized bed sat in the middle with an end table next to it, and a dresser stood on the opposite wall. Evening sunlight poured through torn and singed curtains. Floral wallpaper curled. The bedspread was clean but also singed. The whole room reminded me of a kitschy home of a grandmother. I pictured cow knickknacks all over, but I no idea why.

Smooshed into the corner, a large Super was curled into the least manly ball possible.

Edie closed the distance and aimed her pistol. "Put your hands where I can see them."

The Super didn't move.

"Is he dead?" Ford asked, approaching the motionless shape and poking it with the flamethrower rod. No movement. Ford checked the Super's throat for a pulse, and when he pressed, the survivor fell over, limp. His glasses tilted awkwardly on his nose. I listened carefully. Two normal heartbeats, one fast one (mine), and one very slow one.

"He doesn't look good," Ford said. "Blood smears all over him, but no obvious bite marks. We should cut off his head, just in case. Don't need more zombies shuffling around."

"He's alive," I said. "Put him on the bed."

Edie holstered her gun and put her hands on her hips. "This is big guy. Are you helping?"

I lifted my paw to remind her of my lack of thumbs, but I had other skills to compensate. "I can bite him in the ass to see if he wakes."

Ford stifled his laugh, and after a beat, he cleared his throat and said, "Don't threaten humans."

I was not about to correct Ford's assumption. I wanted a chance to talk to the Super before Polo Dude over here lopped his head off.

"I've got his legs. Ford, take the arms." The pair lifted the guy up and roughly dropped him on the sooty bed. Edie brushed hair away from his face and straightened his glasses. She gave him a good looking over. "Ford. Look at this."

Ford leaned over.

I jumped up onto the bed and pawed over. Groups of four slashes congealed on his massive arms and the side of his thick throat. Edie lifted his shirt, checking for weapons, but instead, more deep gouges marred his chest and the ridges of his abdomen. This was torture. Someone wanted payback—someone *not* a demon. As I puzzled the significance of the wounds, the skin slowly knitted back together. If the humans kept watching, they'd notice, too.

I swatted at the lifted fabric. "We don't need to see that. The dude is built like a tank, no need to make Ford feel less than."

Edie dropped the shirt and blushed.

Ford leaped over the bed—as best he could with a heavy canister strapped to his back—and shoved a knife at my throat. "Edie, I'm going to do it. We don't need this stupid demon to do our jobs. Talk me down or he dies."

I held still against the blade. A cut or stab from a small knife wasn't fatal, but full decapitation was, and teleporting around the room would only anger him more and waste time. Plus, Mittens's neck was...small and dainty.

"Ford, he's helping us. When I'm satisfied, we're helping him."

"You made a deal with this demon?" The knife lifted higher along with his voice.

"It's not a deal," I said. "Just a trade—"

"Shut up!" Ford yelled, pressing into my fur. "I can't believe you made a deal with a demon. You know how dangerous that is! What could possibly make you want to risk that?"

Edie calmly looked at me. "Cat, remember you asked me who I wanted help killing?"

"I do," I squeezed out, risking further blade movement.

"I want to kill Nick Barnes."

Considering the half-demon was locked in a Hell dungeon, but the humans believed he was a missing person, I could work with that. Milk it for a while until I was ready. "Done."

"And I want to kill The King of Hell, the leader of the demons. Between the two of them, we'd have justice for humankind and prevent many more crimes against us for good."

"Uh, that wasn't part of the deal."

"No deal," Ford said, pressing harder.

"Right. Trade. No deal. I didn't make a deal at all. Deal free here. But we can't kill the king. You'd need an army to try it."

Ford glared at me. "What's the price for Nick Barnes's head?"

"I want my body back."

Ford tilted his head in disbelief. "That's it?"

"It's in Hell," Edie finished. "Satisfied? Now put the knife away."

"You have to go to Hell?" Ford asked.

"It's not that big of a deal," I said carefully.

"Edie, you sure about this? 'Cause the only way out of a demon contract is to kill the contracting demon." Ford still didn't retract the blade. I assessed the post-fire condition of the dresser across the room, considering if it would hold my weight.

"It's not a deal," I insisted. "But there are other ways out of a demon contract."

"I'm not talking to you. Not a word from your mouth is trustworthy," Ford said.

"Let him go," Edie said.

A thump from across the house turned our heads—of plaster hitting furniture.

"The fire compromised the structure. This place is going to collapse. We don't have time for this," Edie said.

A deep moan interrupted the argument. The bulky Super rolled on the mattress, groaning the wooden frame, and squeaking the metal springs in agony. He sat up with a pained gasp and a hand pressed across his abdomen. With a pinched face, he leaned back against the headboard and the wood snapped. The dude was huge, like a towering, juicing gym rat, reminding me of Andras's human glamour.

Despite the new splinters, the Super declined to move. His eyes flitted around the room as if his brain wasn't processing the impatient visitors.

Ford removed the blade from my throat but left it hanging loose by his side.

"Hey, it's okay. You're safe now. I'm Edie. He's Ford, and this is..." Looking at me, her lips pressed thin. "Never mind. What's your name?"

The Super's eye caught on Ford's blade glinting in the sunlight through the window, and the hunter sheathed the unnecessary weapon.

Edie continued, "We've come to get you out of here. Was anyone biting anyone else?"

The weakened Super was dazed and confused—a dangerous recipe for limited thinking and quick action. "Lewis. I'm Lewis Gard. How are you?"

"We're more concerned with you." Edie opened her arms to assist him to his feet. "Let's get you out—"

"No," Lewis interrupted with a hand to his head. "*Who* are you?"

"Um. Friends?" Edie shrugged at Ford. He shrugged back. And they said cats were the source of copycat behavior. If I could roll my eyes, I would.

"Friends?" Lewis repeated. Those slash wounds were not demon-made, so someone—some*thing*—roughed him up good. Question was: before or while Heather was here?

More plaster crumbled to the floor, and this time Lewis heard it, too.

"Listen, Lewis," I said. "We need you to tell us what happened, ideally on our way out of here."

Lewis startled and turned toward me, but he scanned the corner as if not believing the voice came from a cat (understandable). From my time spent in Hell, that I-survived-torture look on his face was familiar. The only time I ever wanted to see Glitter was at the company holiday party, and I would bring him fruitcake, because it was always a winning strategy to be on the dungeon torturemaster's good side when staring down the glowing hot skewer.

"Where is your friend?" Lewis asked the hunters, while glaring at me, as if hoping to his eyes were playing tricks.

"You're looking at him," I answered. "Lewis, we don't have—"

And Lewis screamed.

9

New Recruit

I JUMPED DOWN TO salvage my sensitive hearing, while Lewis scrambled back toward the corner of the singed bedroom, gripping a lamp on his way. For being a Super, a broad-shouldered beast who could bench Ford with ease, Lewis was unusually skittish. He swung the lamp twice before craning his neck toward the window as if planning to escape.

I stayed put near the hunters' feet. Supers usually avoided demons, but this level of fear was something else. I said, "We only need to ask you a few questions, then we'll leave you alone while the house collapses on top of you."

Edie frowned at me and approached Lewis, open-handed. "We won't hurt you, and we won't let anything else hurt you, okay?"

Reluctantly, Lewis nodded. She rested a hand on his forearm and carefully removed the lamp from his grip. He allowed it.

"What happened?" she asked gently.

"I...I drove up here for a family reunion, but before I traversed the gravel roads of the north, I stopped for a wax." Lewis wore a healthy beard, and as Edie cringed, I thought the same thing. What did he wax? Noticing our faces, Lewis said, "The truck...my truck. I didn't want the paint damaged. And because..." His voice broke, and his face crumpled in pain. "Because I was late getting here, they're all dead."

I needed this Super on his feet like yesterday. Cops would be here any minute, assuming they weren't handling calls about zombies. "Lewis, there was nothing you could've done. If you were on time, you'd be dead, too."

Edie nodded. "He's right. Why are you still here?"

Lewis snorted back mucus. "I stepped inside and immediately called the police. Like you're supposed to. But while I searched for survivors, two men started torching the place. I tried to stop them, but they were so strong."

"Men?" I repeated for clarification. Lewis was a Super, and if this was a failed family reunion, the victims were Supers, too. All species agreed to the secrecy pact—keep the supernatural world hidden—the only thing we all agreed on. So I understood torching evidence before the police showed up. According to Lewis, Heather didn't destroy this house, and she sure as hell didn't leave those claw marks, so who did?

"Yeah, two. The firetrucks arrived first, and the men ghosted. The cops booked me for this, but after I was released—I had a time-stamped receipt for my truck wax—I came back here to mourn, to search for evidence, to...I don't know...find things to remember my family by. Those two men returned and jumped me."

"Almost like they were waiting for you," I said. Heather didn't work with others, and for a demon to stick around at all was unusual. None of this made any sense. I could sniff out a liar from a mile away, but I couldn't jump into their heads and ferret out the truth.

"Me?" Lewis said, practically squeaking. "I didn't do anything, and now I'm surrounded by a Winchester, Xena Warrior Princess, and an orange Salem."

Edie frowned. Ford crossed his arms over his chest, pretending to be offended, but I could tell he was lost, like me.

"What? I had nieces," Lewis ineffectively explained and stared off again. "I...*had*...nieces." His head fell into his hands, and he wept—all shoulders shaking and wet sniffles.

Edie patted her pockets as if searching for a tissue but found nothing of use. After a few more deep, uneven breaths, Lewis composed himself and stood with a wince.

Drywall fell from above, taking insulation with it, and landing just behind me. The ceiling sagged and groaned.

"This house is going down." I could teleport out, but they couldn't.

Lewis climbed to his feet and limped through the bedroom door. We followed him until he stopped in the living room and leaned against a wooden chairback. Lewis mumbled to himself and lifted the chair like a weapon. "My family was slaughtered."

"Slow down there, big fella," I said. "Thrashing this unstable house won't bring your family back, and those guys after you won't care—"

Lewis turned around. "You know them?" After a pause, he shook his head. "A talking cat. Are you a cat or did they just hit me that hard?"

"I'm involuntarily borrowing a cat—"

"iKat," Edie interrupted.

Lewis chuckled, the kind of sound that was neither a true laugh of joy nor the amusement of some witty quip. This was the sound of someone about to snap.

"Back up," I warned my hunter companions. Neither listened.

Lewis hurled the chair across the room. It punched a hole in the drywall and scattered dust. He picked up the hutch next and flung it at the same wall. The hutch cracked and snapped from the force and tumbled into a heap. This Super was as strong as he looked.

"That's not going to solve anything. We need to get out of here," Edie said, covering her head from the falling cloud of debris.

That chuckle came again, mixed with a sob. "I'm caught in a nightmare. I'm asleep, tossing and turning." He over-ended the coffee table and lifted it with no strain at all. "And someone is toying with my head. I'm a lab rat, and they're simulating this nightmare. I just know it." He tossed the coffee table against the opposite wall with a deep thump, and it fell, smacking against the kitchen table. More dust and drywall fell from above.

"Are you going to do something, mighty human manipulator?" Edie asked me. "Isn't that your job?"

"What am I supposed to do?" I asked. Giving the Super a heart-to-heart right now wasn't a level of therapy I could do. My job was to guide humans into nefarious decisions, and Lewis was not a human.

"A demon is cowering behind me," she pointed out needlessly.

I gave her an attempt at a cat-shaped shrug.

Ford snorted.

"Stop talking about me like I'm not in the room." Lewis barreled out the front door.

"Let's go." Ford said, glancing at the ceiling. The three of us followed the Super down the stairs and onto the gravel driveway.

"Lewis, wait. You can't just go running off," Edie said.

"I can't?" He spun on us, nostrils flaring. "And why is that?"

"The guy's broken," Ford said to her. "And safely outside. Let him go."

A loud crack came from the house, and we all turned in time to see the roof cave in with snaps of weakened wood. Blackened dust and smoke billowed into the air.

"Come to my car, sit down, and take a breath. We can talk this out," Edie said.

"I'm not talking." Lewis's hands balled into fists.

I had to say something, but I didn't want to make it worse. "They could come back, especially the...demon."

"Now those two guys were *demons*? Demons are real?"

I'd never heard of a Super who didn't know demons existed. "I don't know about the two men, but the woman who was with you in that room was a demon."

"That's enough." Lewis paced along the driveway.

"What are we going to do with him?" I asked Edie.

"We don't have time for this," Ford said, gripping Edie's upper arm. "Some of us have a paying job to go to. He's useless, and there are no zombies to clean up. No demons left to slay. Job done, now let's get out of here."

Lewis picked up a basketball sized stone and hurled it across the fading light in the evening sky. It went farther than my keen eyes could track it.

"He's really strong," Edie said, and she was right.

Lewis mumbled and grumbled under his breath. He was a well-built, tough-as-a-brick dude.

I said quietly to the hunters, "Heather works under the direct orders of The King of Hell. We've got the brains, me, and you two can...you know, wield weapons. Convince him to join us. He'd be our muscle."

Edie watched Lewis's breakdown, and her hand twitched by her blade. "Humans aren't strong enough for what we do."

"You sure about that?" I asked, feeling them out.

Edie moved to her trunk and rummaged through her duffel. She called over, "Lewis, let us help. Come here."

Lewis shook his head and kept pacing.

Risking getting kicked, I scurried over to the hulking Super's feet and matched his stride. "Lewis, we want to help you, but we need your help, too."

Lewis stopped and faced his family's destruction, now nothing more than painful memories. I didn't envy him. Of course, beyond my mother who'd passed at childbirth, a father I never met, and foster parents I'd rather forget, I didn't have family, so I'd never know that kind of pain.

"I'm hallucinating. This is all a bad dream. Something impossible slaughtered my family, gave me a good tossing around, and now a talking cat is trying to convince me to help him." Lewis chuckled and shook his head. "Somehow, I need to wake up."

"You're not dreaming. This is real. This is all real."

Lewis ignored me, continuing to scout for another large rock on the ground.

I returned to Edie's side. "He's on the verge of an existential crisis, and I don't think he's going to be helpful like this."

Edie paused with her hands full and studied Lewis from a short distance. "He's more shaken up than a Super would be, but some are very good at hiding their true natures." She approached Lewis and tossed sprinkles of water on him.

Nothing happened.

"Holy water?" I whispered. "What's that supposed to do?"

Edie flung the water on me next. I fought the urge to flee as if a tornado barreled down on me. That had nothing to do with me being a demon, more like Mittens's instinct. "Apparently, this shit doesn't work."

"Holy water does nothing to demons. You could've asked."

"And I can't trust you to give me the truth."

I pressed my furry lips thin.

Lewis picked up a fist-sized rock and faced Edie. "Why did you do that?"

"I thought you were thirsty. It was just a spill. Sorry. Here." Edie held out a silver coin. "Can you read this for me?"

Lewis held out his palm, and Edie dropped it into his hand. The Super flipped it over, but his hands didn't sizzle or burn. "I can't read anything on it. Sorry, can't help you."

Edie took the coin back. She shared a look with Ford over her non-results, who promptly removed the flamethrower from his back and returned it to the trunk. Her tests didn't seem to have any point, but then I realized they got the Super to focus.

"Listen, Lewis," Edie said. "I know all of this is hard to take in, but we've all done it. The world of angels, demons, and...Supers is real. It's my job, and Ford's job, to kill monsters or Supers, whichever you prefer to call them, to protect people. We're looking for the demon who was with you. Her name is Heather. She escaped and we need to hunt her down. Is there anything you can tell us to help?"

Lewis raked a hand through his straight shoulder-length locks. A flash of envy tore through me. I'd had windswept hair like that, and I missed it. Lewis inhaled a deep breath and blew it out. "You want me to believe angels, demons, and Supers are real. Okay, sure, why not? Then you want me to help you hunt down a demon? She got away from you already. Do you know how to kill one?"

I cleared my throat. "Actually, I'm a demon. Yes, we know how."

Lewis finally looked at me as if I were real. "You're a demon?"

Just for show, I conjured the heat behind my eyes to glow my irises red. The Super took a step back.

"Vampires can do that, too," Edie said.

"Can vampires do this?" I asked haughtily. I ignited the flame around my body, prepared to teleport away if Lewis freaked. The Super stared, and my light flickered across his shocked face. I truly couldn't believe a Super was this blind to the world.

I added, "And my job was to help people." In a manner of speaking. "But I was cursed into a cat because of a small mistake. You would be a great asset to us."

He still watched in awe.

"If you help us, we'll help you. That demon could return to finish the job," I said gently. "The only rule is you can't kill me."

"I didn't agree to that rule," Ford said, and Edie scowled at him.

Lewis dropped the rock in his fist and rubbed the nape of his neck. He stared at the smoking husk of a house. "Yesterday, I was a city garbageman. Today, I join a motley crew to destroy a demon. What's next, the apocalypse?"

I chuckled. Had he been living under a rock? "The zombies already happened. We're also going after the missing human responsible." Eventually.

10

Puzzle Piece

Edie pulled the Prius to a stop on the darkened gravel driveway of the secluded hunter's cabin. Surrounded by the privacy of woods and distant farmlands, innocent eyes wouldn't stumble upon it. If some non-innocent eyes came knocking or crashing, no one had to worry about witnesses. And being only a hop away from the city, anything they needed was accessible.

Lewis rolled up alongside Edie's car in his shiny new Silverado pickup truck and killed the headlights. Of everything Lewis said earlier, I believed Lewis's protective wax story. The four-wheel-drive probably costed more than the hunter's cabin was worth. I had wanted to ride with the Super and grill him for information, but I didn't want to raise brows with the hunters or become roadkill at the Super's thick hands. So, I suffered through hours of stinky trash and dirty clothing with occasional flirts between the hunters. My own personal hell.

I could've teleported back to the cabin and saved myself the grief of the ride, but I needed to make sure everyone arrived on time and in one piece. Getting my body back from a Hell dungeon wouldn't be easy, and I believed Lewis would be a great asset. And if he could process the world of angels and demons before finding out about a trip to Hell, that would be awesome.

Edie and Ford exited the car, and I teleported out.

"What is this place?" Lewis asked, climbing down and yawning.

"A hunter's safe house." Edie circled around to the rear of the vehicle and opened the trunk. Ford joined her.

"Does it have plumbing?"

"If you can't handle urinating on Mother Nature's terrain, you don't belong here," Ford said and grabbed his duffel.

Edie shouldered hers and closed the trunk. Everyone followed the lean and gruff hunter inside, but the screen door slapped shut in my face. Trusting where I planned to land, I teleported inside. Darkness smothered the interior, but I saw just fine by the dim moonlight.

Lewis baby-stepped across the room, hands held out as if blind. What kind of Super couldn't see in the dark? He was a fascinating puzzle.

"Got a light around here?" Lewis asked.

Ford leaned over and flipped the light switch.

Lewis's arms still jutted out, and Ford laughed. Edie covered her grin with her hand.

Face burning bright, Lewis frowned and dropped his arms. He cleared his throat, and his gaze landed on the single king bed. "So, do you all live here...and share one bed?"

Edie closed and stacked Corvina's abandoned books, and she and Ford emptied their weapons bag.

"We crash here when we have an active case to investigate, but otherwise, most of us have real lives. Like Ford here. Owns his own security company."

Ford refilled a couple of necessities into his duffel and checked his watch. "My shift starts in a few. I gotta head to the city. Thank the gods for coffee." The hunter leaned in close to Edie's ear. "Keep an eye on that one. I don't trust him."

A Super would've heard that, since most had better hearing than demons. Lewis paused for only a second.

Edie whispered back while futilely rattling wooden stakes to muffle the sound. "You don't trust anyone."

"And I'm alive because of it." Ford lifted his duffel and glared at the newest recruit. "Don't pull any fast ones, or you'll never know a moment's peace."

"Point sent and received," Lewis said, saluting.

The front door opened, and Corvina strolled in, carrying a heavy backpack. She stopped short and stared at Lewis with surprise. "Um, hi there."

"Corvy, this is Lewis Gard, the human we rescued from the Menominee massacre. Lewis, this is Corvy, our residential tech nerd, who developed an algorithm to help people like you."

"Like me?" Lewis's mouth gaped open, dumbfounded.

"I'm glad we found you." Corvina set her bag down next to the occupied table, and with a glance at me, she quickly skirted away. "You," she pointed at me. "You're still here. Okay. A demon cat. Edie, why is he still here?"

Ford patted Edie's shoulder. "Good luck."

She tossed him a frown, and he left with a smile. Edie sighed. "iKat is staying with us until we rescue his body."

"Body?" Lewis said. "No one mentioned a body."

"I'm not actually a cat, Lewis. The King of Hell cursed me into this cat's body, and he's responsible for everyone else's grief around here. You guys are helping me get my body back, and you all get—"

"Revenge," Lewis cut in. "I want a piece of that demon myself. Especially that prickly little black-haired one."

"Heather," I supplied. "In the human world, she goes by Heather Brush."

"Brush?" Edie asked. "What kind of last name is that?"

"A made up one. Demons don't have last names." The explanation rang familiar in the scrambled recesses of my memory. I jumped up on the wobbly table where Edie began the arduous process of cataloging, inspecting, and maintaining weapons.

"Then what's yours? I mean, your human last name?" Corvina asked, head tilted in curiosity.

I froze. What was my last name? To blend in with the humans, I would've picked one. I recalled my name on the computer prompt at my old desk job: Malaikat. No last name. When I worked as a janitor for the NBB Pharmaceuticals building, my last name was...

Pressure squeezed my skull like a cat-head-shaped vice. My eyelids pinched shut, and my lips clamped tight while scurrying sounds reached my ears. Foreign imagery mixed with familiar voices.

"Demons don't have last names. We just pick something when we must interact with humans to blend in."

They also had the creativity of a rock, I'd thought. Still true.

"Now remember," Heather said, *"You must be careful. Master those skills. Control your thoughts.*

"I'll try not to." I'd said and walked through a Hell portal. Why did I say that? What was I trying not to do?

The pressure slowly deflated like a leaking balloon, but a heaviness remained upon my shoulders. I remembered my years as a janitor, and none of those years meshed with whatever that was...another vision?

At the massacre, Heather had said, *'Ironically, if you had your memory, this would more satisfying, because then you'd know exactly what I'm talking about.'*

Andras had told me I had an accident with electricity and water that garbled my memories. These were garbled. But the way they trickled out in pieces suggested something more sinister: a memory demon must've played games in my head. Naturally, I couldn't remember the memory demon session. Why did the demon delete my chosen last name from my memory? I couldn't be anything as terrible as Brush or File.

Warm strokes along my fur followed the calloused hands of a human. Mittens purred without my permission, and I opened my eyes. The bright light overhead blinded me, and at once I pinched my eyes shut. "Migraine. Turn them off."

Footsteps rushed across the hardwood, and the light vanished. I blinked, regaining my senses. Seeing two humans and a Super standing over me, I first asked, "Which one of you was stroking me?"

"I was trying to wake you," Edie said. A little relief flowed through my fur-covered skin. "But Mittens ate this up. What happened to you?"

"I get these migraines."

"Cats have migraines?" Corvina asked.

"I think someone messed with my memory. Pieces of it are fighting to come out."

"What do you remember?" Edie asked.

"I was in my human-shaped body, talking with Heather." The women frowned. The Super only glared. "She was telling me demons didn't have last names. I think your question, Corvy, triggered it."

"You're a demon. Why would another demon have to explain that?" Edie asked.

Good question, but not terribly interesting.

"Do you need anything?" Corvina asked. "Aspirin or something? Can cats have aspirin?"

"I'm fine." I shifted to my feet. "I need to give Mittens here a break."

Corvina yawned. "I just got off my shift at the school library, and I'm beat."

Edie smiled. "Reading books all night is exhausting. You just proved it."

"I could read books all day," Corvina said. "Having to socialize with people in class is exhausting. People are exhausting. I'm going to catch some z's here tonight if there's room."

"The king-size is available for any and all who want it." Edie glanced at Lewis.

His face burned red. "I appreciate the offer, but I'll take the floor."

Edie shrugged, and Corvina went to the bathroom. She gargled, likely mouthwash, but it reminded me of the zombie sound. The water ran. Hey, there was water.

Lewis's head turned to the sound with relief, and he crossed to the bed and rested on the floor next to it.

Corvina crawled into bed, and Edie took her turn in the bathroom. When she finished, she turned off the light. I jumped up on the refrigerator, warming up with the humming heat. Mittens sunk down quickly. Since I didn't speak cat, I had no hard proof of my actions affecting the cat, but with how fast Mittens passed out, I believed Mittens was worn out from today's fun.

Only a few minutes passed before gentle snores filled the space. I sighed. What was I going to do to entertain myself every night while everyone else slept?

A rustling noise captured my attention. Mittens's ear twitched. Outside the cabin, shadows flitted across the windows. Supers.

I tried to jump down and warn the humans and Lewis, but Mittens was too far down to wake. With a soft rattle at the front door, a group of Supers poured into the small cabin, clubs and knives at the ready.

I could only watch.

II

Attack

I HAD WORKED TOO hard, risking my own fur, just to allow Neanderthals creeping into the cabin to slay my helpers. But Mittens, and his inconvenient need for sleep, left me trapped as a useless, silent essence.

Five Supers padded through the shrouded cabin like silent ninjas, wary of their steps. The knives in their meaty fists glinted against the filtered moonlight. One Super carried a club. Must smash food then eat! I chuckled, but no one heard it.

Various hand gestures declared the cabin secure, and the Supers surrounded the bed, weapons drawn. More hand gestures. I couldn't see which kind of Supers they were. But I already crossed out demons, and since they didn't bite anyone, they weren't vampires. From what I read in the demon history books, this wasn't the work of angels, either, and clearly they weren't zombies. Since they were trying to be quiet, they weren't ghosts. That left shifters.

Shifters could be dangerous, like bears, lions, wolves, that sort of thing, or they could be sneaky, like foxes and crows. These guys were trying and failing to be sneaky, and with that, I'd bet that most of them licked their own asses clean. Such filthy animals. Mittens's tail twitched, and I sighed.

All my hard work was about to be flushed by the hands of primitive animals. Where would I go to find replacements? There was a reason Gremory gave me Edie's name. It was unlikely the wise demon would give me another. So I'd have to track down another hunter and hope for the best. Keeping this group alive appeared to be easier. Regardless of the best choice, I couldn't move a cat's muscle.

My desk job sounded so much better right now.

The shifters dragged Lewis away from the bed by his ankles, drawing a sheet with him, and Lewis scrambled in exhausted sleepiness to free himself.

"What the—?" Lewis cut off, staring open-mouthed at his visitors.

Mittens twitched, and it was just enough for me to wrestle control back. I flexed my jaw and sat up.

Edie woke on high alert, rolled off the bed, and gripped a hidden weapon. In a flash, she had the barrel of her pistol aimed at the intruders.

Corvina sat up, lifting a quilt to her shoulders. She stared, eyes wide. "What's going on?"

"Invasion. Corvy, get down!" Edie called and used the mattress for cover.

Corvina scrambled off the bed, but the shifters paid them no mind.

The one who'd mastered the hand gestures said, "Leave us. This doesn't concern you."

"Like hell it doesn't. This is my house," Edie said. "Get out or I'm flexing my finger."

Annoyed with the threat to my humans, I teleported over to the bed and stood between them and the women. "Leave at once." The shifters glanced around, confused. "Over here. Yep, down, down. Hi, there. I scratch more than I lick. Get out."

A short shifter in the back whispered, "The cat talks."

Another shifter chuckled, and I didn't appreciate that. A third asked, "Skip, what do we do?"

The leader, apparently Skip, turned to me. He was likely in his thirties, buzzed to the scalp on top, and plenty muscular—another gym rat. But he was shorter than I used to be and shorter than Lewis, too. "Listen here, Lord Fluffybutt, this doesn't concern you. Mind your own business, and you won't get hurt."

Generic threats. "Oh, tough guy. You do know what you just broke into right? This isn't granny's vacation cabin."

The shifters glanced around again as if seeing it through new eyes.

Lewis struggled to his knees, and one shifter smashed him in the ear with the butt of his club. Lewis dropped down and grunted. What kind of shifter didn't fight back? Perhaps Lewis wasn't as useful as I'd hoped.

"Wallace, stop with the club," Skip said.

"Stop, all of you!" Edie fired a warning shot into the ceiling. Dust and debris fell.

Skip growled and his eyes flashed yellow. Oh, a wolf shifter. How cliché. "This is between me and my brother. Leave us alone. This is your last warning."

"Brother?" Corvina repeated.

Lewis returned to his knees, and the other shifters lifted him to his feet. Lewis pressed a hand against his ear, and he swayed on his feet, disoriented.

"You're in my house, and I don't want you here. Lewis is our guest, so beat it," Edie said.

"Guest?" Skip chuckled. "Lewis? You must be joking. What did this sad sack of fur do to earn your respect?"

Edie's mouth opened and closed, twice. "Fur?"

"Let's go, boys." Skip gestured their retreat and his pack dragged Lewis like a limp noodle.

Edie fired, and quick pops echoed through the small cabin. She stood, mouth hanging open. None of the shifters flinched at her gunshots. They just dragged Lewis toward the door. "What kind of guys are these? And what did he mean by fur?" Edie said to me, but she didn't leave me time to answer.

Edie rushed toward the exit, beating the pack to the door. Blocking their way out, she said, "I'm enacting my right to the castle doctrine."

If I could've plugged my sensitive ears, I would've. Edie leveled her pistol at the pack and fired at the nearest. The bullet penetrated his flesh, but he didn't flinch, and the round fell out, as if pushed away by his tissue. "You aren't human."

She fired at each one, fruitlessly, and the shifters walked right on by her.

On the gravel driveway, they dropped Lewis. Wallace with his *ooga booga* club mercilessly pummeled Lewis, who curled into a ball and made a sad attempt to protect his head with his hands. The short shifter bent over and stabbed Lewis repeatedly as if enjoying the process of murder. Another shifter partially transformed, displaying his claw and swiped at Lewis—the same type of claw that left him nearly for dead.

"iKat, what are they?" Edie yelled to me.

"Shifters. Didn't you know that, miss hunter?"

"Don't be a condescending ass. You lied to me."

"I never said he was human. You assumed, and I didn't correct you."

"Lie by omission. At this distance, there's no way they tracked the blood scent in my car. Corvy, bring me the silver bullets, quick!"

Corvina dropped the quilt and rushed to the closet, tossing equipment in the dark. "Someone get the light. I can't see."

Edie flipped the switch by the front door. Seeing her black duffel sitting near her feet, she unzipped it and gripped her own club. Like Whac-A-Mole live and in person. She stormed Lewis's attackers and whaled on them, effectively doing nothing but causing a minor disturbance and irritation. They swatted her back like a fly. Pack mentality kept them focused on Lewis and ignoring the women, which was the only reason Corvina and Edie were still alive.

Edie had been right. They couldn't track scent this far. The shifters had been deliberately hunting Lewis. What happened at the burned house in the woods? Someone wasn't telling the truth.

Corvina appeared in the doorway and yelled for Edie's attention before tossing her a loaded handgun. Edie caught it, aimed, and fired without hesitation. The pops echoed across the small clearing. I shook my head. What kind of hunter didn't know the wolf shifter silver allergy was only a fable?

With Lewis lying bloody and limp on the gravel-covered ground, the shifters turned to leave.

"Stop right there!" Edie yelled again, handgun still aimed as if trying to intimidate them to death.

Skip strolled up to her, gripped the barrel of her gun, and crunched it into useless pieces before sprinkling them on the ground. With an annoyed smirk, he returned to his pack, spitting on Lewis's body as he passed. They shifted into their wolf form and disappeared into the woods.

Corvina rushed to Lewis's side. "Did they kill him?"

Edie reached for a pulse. "I'm not sure."

"Is he a shifter too?" she asked.

"Since his brother is a wolf, it's reasonable to assume he is also," Edie said.

"What do we do with him?" Corvina brushed a blood-stained lock out of his eye. "I mean, can we still bring him inside? Doesn't that break some hunter code or something?"

I teleported over to Lewis's side. "You let a demon inside. A shifter isn't a bigger threat."

Edie sent me a crooked smile. "You're cute when your degree of evil is questioned."

I smiled. "Thanks." And I listened carefully. "He's alive."

"If Lewis wanted to kill us, he would've already. In his condition, he's harmless, and he has questions to answer. Corvy, help me." Edie lifted Lewis by the underarms, and Corvina carried his feet. They strained bringing him to the bed, and with a healthy grunt, they dropped him onto the mattress a little rougher than they'd meant to, probably. I would've dropped him from a roof if it meant seeing if a wolf landed on all fours. (If he was unconscious for the test, not my problem.)

Lewis sunk into the soft layers, but he didn't move a muscle. My eye twitched at the dirt and gravel stuck to his wrinkled clothes. I hopped up alongside and pawed at the loose bits. Each one teased and mocked me with its obvious displacement and inappropriate display of chaos.

"Are you going to lick the wolf hairs off him, too?" Edie asked.

"It's not a conscious choice to do these things. I'd appreciate some understanding."

Edie snorted. "An OCD demon cat. Who would've guessed?"

"We can't call an ambulance, can we?" Corvina asked, brows knitted in concern.

"He'll heal himself. One of the perks. Where are you two planning to sleep now?" I asked, focusing on the next pebble caught in the layers. "The top of the fridge is mine."

Ignoring me, Edie fished in the closet. She brought back a first aid kit and shrugged. "Better than nothing?"

"Assuming he lives." Corvina grabbed the pack of moist towelettes, snapped one free, and gently dabbed at his most pressing wound.

Edie threaded a needle. "Hey, cat, can you heat this needle?"

"Do I look like a blowtorch?"

Edie tilted her head and frowned at my lack of participation. I did want the shifter to join us—the more the merrier in rescuing my body—but that didn't mean I had to like the animal. I sighed and ignited my flame on one paw. Edie held the needle in the fire until too hot to touch. She waved it in the air to cool and stitched up the worst of the wounds.

Boot steps outside the cabin pricked my ears. The front door swung open, dawn casting a purple glow across the wood floors, interrupted by Ford's long shadow. Ford dropped his duffel on the table and walked over. "I missed a fun party. What happened?"

"Shifters attacked him." Corvina dabbed at the minor cuts.

"But he was here all night," Ford said. "And you two are fine"—he ignored me—"so why is he the only one hurt?"

"Lewis's brother had a bone to pick with him," Edie said, clearly skirting around the truth.

Ford pinched the bridge of his nose. "It's been a long night. Shifters attacked Lewis, one of which was his brother... I'm not a geneticist, but Lewis has to be a shifter, too." Ford glanced at me pointedly.

"Yeah, he's a shifter," I said with an attempted shrug, as if it was obvious.

"What on earth happened in the last few hours?" Ford asked, exasperated.

"We're not all that sure." Corvina threw soiled gauze and wipes into a small wastebasket by the bed.

"Well, he's alive, so they'll be back." Ford had a point there. "Either we fight off a pack ourselves, or we remove their reason for coming here." Ford removed his pistol from his utility belt and checked the barrel.

"What are you doing?" Edie asked.

"I'm making a decision in our best interest."

"iKat?" Edie asked with a plea in her voice.

For once, I agreed with the idiot, but Lewis was motivated to help us, so with a sigh, I said, "What do you want me to say? Ford, we need him alive."

"Like hell we do." Ford cocked the gun and aimed it at Lewis's body.

12

Answers

THE LEVEL OF COMPASSION humans felt for strangers baffled me. Down in Hell, no one batted an eye when a cake from Hell's kitchen exploded to feed the hellhounds demon pieces—and they weren't strangers. There was no strong bond to fight for others. No standing up for what they believed in, or to save Uncle Bob (or Todd) from becoming the next meal. Demons looked out for themselves and their own interests. But these humans were willing to risk their lives to help, essentially, their enemy. What is wrong with these people? (Well, they also agreed to help a demon, so let's not push it too hard.)

Ford—the only person in this cabin that made sense to me—aimed his pistol at Lewis's limp body, while Corvina and Edie hovered over him for protection. After I finished amusing myself with the scene, I said, "The pack thinks he's dead, so unless they find out otherwise, they shouldn't return."

"That's not the only problem," Ford said, holding the gun steady. "Because of him, the pack knows this location. Any of those feral beasts responsible for countless missing people across the globe might return for one of us or all of us. But you want to play tea party with this one? If I don't put him down now, who knows how many more humans he'll kill in his lifetime."

Corvina watched Ford's gun with a tremble.

Edie scowled at me.

"What?" I asked her.

"Do you have any witty demon deets to convince Ford here not all Supers are pure evil?"

"That's rich, coming from you," Ford quipped. "If I had half a mind, I'd lay waste to both the shifter and the demon, but considering the cat's condition, I figure he's harmless and completely unwanted by his kind. So, he gets a pass, for now. As for this thing here—there's no justifiable reason to allow him to live."

Lewis stirred on the bed and softly groaned.

"Time's ticking," Ford said.

Edie stood, palms out. "I understand where you're coming from. But sometimes the enemy of my enemy is—"

"My friend," Ford finished. "I've heard it before. Doesn't usually work out so well for the friend."

Lewis sat up with a hand to his head as if holding his brains in position. "What happened? What's going on?" Once he noticed Ford's weapon trained on his skull, Lewis held out his hands. "I've come in peace. I swear."

"You're alive!" Corvina said.

"Doesn't feel like it," Lewis said, pressing a hand against his head again.

"I can fix that disconnect." Ford shifted his finger to the trigger.

Edie approached the hothead. "That's enough. We can all talk this out like civilized people."

"Ha! People, my ass." Ford said and shifted the weapon out of Edie's reach.

"Civilized anything," she corrected. "There's a lot of laundry in this room and it stinks. Sit down and we'll talk." No one moved. "Now!"

Corvina crossed the cabin and sat on a metal folding chair, while Edie assisted Lewis. Ford kept his eyes locked on his target, and out of necessity, he followed them over to the table.

"Sit," Edie demanded at Ford.

With a huff and a roll of his eyes, Ford sat on the last chair. I remained on the floor.

"You, too, cat. Get up here."

No arguing with Edie, I leaped up onto the wobbly table.

"Now, since the three of us know each other, let's start with you, Lewis. You brought those wolf shifters to our door, somehow, so you need to explain what happened in Menominee or get out."

"He can't just..." Ford trailed off.

"One step at a time," Edie knitted her hands together on top of the table and pointedly stared at Lewis.

The shifter's eyes drifted around the room. His shoulders hunched. This docility must've been from the battering he'd taken; otherwise, it didn't make sense. Lewis cleared his throat, and his voice didn't have the usual gravelly growl of a wolf either. "It wasn't my family."

"That wolf *wasn't* your brother?" Ford asked, steam puffing from his ears (not literally).

"The slaughter at the Menominee house wasn't my family."

"Who were they?" Edie asked.

"A job." Lewis exhaled.

Ford twitched, and Edie held out a hand to remind him to back off. He said dryly, "Quite the show of grief for a job."

Lewis sighed heavily. "I didn't tell you what I was because I thought you'd kill me, too, and I needed your help."

"Your acting is top-notch," I said, but I was ignored.

"You thought hunters would be more sympathetic than your own family?" Corvina asked.

"I hoped so. There are clans of vampires around who still prefer the 'old lifestyle'. I clean up their messes. There's a ghoul farm not far from there. Look, I don't want to be their—"

"Bitch?" Ford interrupted.

Edie glared. "Stop it."

"Slave," Lewis finished on a sigh. "My family indebted me to the vampires. Okay? I'm willing to help you with your demon problem, because demons can nullify my contract with the vampires. I just need my chance to plead my case. The air is cleared." Lewis slid low in his strained chair.

Corvina's brows lifted, in complete surprise, and her mouth hung open. Edie froze, glaring suspiciously.

Ford laughed and holstered his gun. "Your family *sold* you? What did you do for that level of shame? Egads."

This was a shifter-vampire conflict, and although Heather was a contract demon, she worked with humans. Add me to the suspicious camp. "Why was Heather there? The black-haired female. The demon. You must remember her."

"I was a little too busy to notice."

"Then why were you beaten to a pulp before we got there?" I pressed. Something still wasn't right here.

Pity crossed Corvina and Edie's features, but Ford remained impassive.

Lewis hung his head low. "I screwed up. The cops found out about the party before I had enough time to dispose of the leftovers."

"Leftovers?" Ford stood from his seat, knocking the flimsy chair backward with an ear-grating screech. "People are not food, and they certainly aren't garbage. The audacity of you, a wolf shifter, walking in here, pretending to be our ally, but all you bring is danger and destruction, and you exposed our safe cabin."

"I..." Lewis trailed off.

Corvina approached Ford and rested a hand on his shoulder. "Let him finish. We don't all have perfect lives. Look at us. Sit down and let's talk this out."

Ford gripped his toppled chair and roughly placed it back in position. He fell onto it and crossed his arms over his chest. Everyone stared at Lewis.

"Because I failed to clean up the mess on time, my family—my pack—came to kill me in shame. If they discover I'm still alive, they will return and finish the job, as Ford said. I don't know how they found me here. I didn't tell them, I swear."

Ford leaned closer. "How can we trust your word now?"

Lewis met his stare. "You can't."

Unsatisfied, Ford stood. "He admitted it. I'm done here." He tugged the pistol from his belt.

Popcorn sounded good right about now.

Corvina rushed to stop him. "That's not fair. He's just being honest."

"Life isn't fair, Corvy. Or haven't you figured that out yet?"

The condescending tone dropped Corvina's head. If Ford made the girl cry, I might have a problem with that. (I hadn't decided yet.)

Edie flew from her chair and shoved Ford backward, tipping him off balance. "Enough! We all agreed to work together on our demon problem. This Heather is involved with Lewis's mess. She works for The King of Hell, who we're going to invade to get the cat's body back. Corvina has her reasons for helping, and you, Ford, are the best soldier we have. But if you can't be a team player, get out."

Ford crossed his thick arms over his chest. "We had a pact. No Supers are left standing, and now you want to let a shifter and a demon into our circle? How can you be so sure they aren't scouting our weaknesses? How can you trust this cat won't call in the cavalry to destroy us?"

"If I wanted to kill you, I would've done it already." I stood up, tail reaching skyward. As much as their bickering entertained me, time ticked away. I pointedly glared at Ford. "I can speak for all demons—well, all normal, well-adjusted demons—we only want to influence your actions, so Hell earns your soul when you die. Since the vast majority of the human population is good enough to punch their tickets at the pearly gates, we *don't* want to kill you. And since we have a common enemy and we're all adults here, we can work together for all our benefits."

"Let's vote," Edie said. "Raise a hand to stay, agreeing to work together to kill Heather in Hell and get iKat's body back."

I waved my tail. "Missing some hands here, but I vote to stay."

Edie's hand raised. "I need to kill a high-ranking demon for my family's sake."

Lewis lifted his hand. "The demons can fix my contract, but I don't know why Heather was at the massacre. I need to find out why and get out of this deal. And, yeah, kill her after is fine with me."

Corvina left her hand on the table. "I'm no good to you in a fight, unless you need a decoy."

Everyone turned to Ford, whose arms remained crossed over his chest and a scowl twisted his features.

"An extra set of guns might be the difference between who returns home and who doesn't," I said. That squishy human stuff usually worked on them.

The front door opened on a squeak, and in walked a stranger carrying a large brown paper bag. Since no one in the room screamed, I believed the striking man to be friendly. The newest hunter wore a calm strength, like a man who'd seen too much but continued fighting to keep his head clear. His pale skin and light gray eyes contrasted sharply to the shaggy black hair on his head. I checked him with my demon and aura visions. I got a negative for the demon and for the human. This handsome fellow was another hunter.

"What happened here?" the pale fighter asked.

"Vale! Where've you been?" Edie rushed over and gave him a side hug. "We missed you."

Ford approached with a broad grin, freeing the bag from Vale's pale but cut arms, and brought it to the kitchenette. Ford lifted out a can of sauce and a box of noodles and kept digging, filling the small counter with food. "Oh, I can make a proper feast tonight."

Vale stuffed his hands in the front pockets of his jeans. "A small horde of zombies attacked some teens in the park downtown. I don't know how humans can ignore the dangers right in front of them. And I still haven't figured out why they randomly appear in pockets."

"Are you bit?" I asked.

Vale noticed me and his brow furrowed. "What's a demon doing in here? Furthermore, why is it alive?"

Ford stacked cans in the upper cabinets and faced his friend. The hothead squinted. "How do you know it's a demon?"

Vale darted Ford a look. After a beat, he shrugged. "It talks."

Ford visibly relaxed and asked, sticking his nose in the bag, "There isn't a laser pointer in here, is there?"

"Are you going to eat this time?" Edie asked Vale. "You always bring the food, but never join us. It's like you hate the American diet. Why not bring something you like?"

With that information, this Vale fellow wasn't just a hunter. He was a Super of some sort. But what kind didn't eat human food? Vampires. Now that was interesting.

"I'm good. Anyone care to spill the beans here?" Vale assessed Lewis's condition, likely noting just as I had, the wounds were rapidly healing.

"Wolf shifters tracked us down, somehow, to kill Lewis here," Corvina said. "Those three are going on a suicidal mission to kill Heather, one of The King of Hell's minions."

"And rescue by body," I added, so no one would forget.

Vale snorted. "I sure missed a lot."

"Will you come with us?" Edie asked.

Vale glanced at each of them. "All of you are going?"

"Everyone but Ford and Corvy, so far," Edie said.

Ford lifted a jar of sauce and skimmed the label. "As she said, suicidal."

Corvina glanced at the table and rubbed her arms. "They can't do this, but I can't stop them. Can you, Vale?"

Vale's back stiffened. "I protect humans. It's against my nature to seek out destruction. I do not condone a suicidal plan, but I also cannot stop them from going."

"But stopping them is protecting them," Corvina pleaded.

"We can't do this alone," Edie added. "We need you all. Please?"

Vale stood still as a statue, and Corvina played with her cell phone, failing to meet the mother hen's gaze.

Ford folded the empty paper bag flat. "What about Nick Barnes? He's the human you wanted to track down. If you want your body back, cat, Nick Barnes's head was the non-deal. He's the guy behind the zombies. Vale, you could help with that, right?" Ford asked.

I didn't want them chasing after a ghost. But if Edie failed to convince her *friends* to join us, how was I going to convince *enemies*?

13

Chase

CORVINA APPROACHED ME CAUTIOUSLY, and I backed up
a step. The young woman didn't support Edie's plan to hunt
Heather, and she was afraid of me, so I didn't know what she
was going to do. Although I wasn't afraid of the lanky blond, I
didn't want to hurt her by accident either and lose the support I
did have.

"I found something interesting," she said, turning her phone
screen to me. "According to articles on Nick Barnes, Dr. Tyler
Gibson was the creator of The Annihilator. And this is the
microbiologist's last known address, but it's pending sale. If you
want to question him, we should go before he's gone."

I didn't want the hunters tracking Nick Barnes at all, but if
they had a way to stop or reverse the zombie epidemic through
this doctor lead, I was all in. Maybe The King of Hell would give
me my body back if he learned I ended the zombies. Corvina
just leaped ten points in my book. I eagerly read the screen—a
residential address that didn't sound familiar. "Edie, up for some
reconnaissance tonight instead?"

Edie slipped her phone out of her back pocket. "At this hour? The guy's going to be asleep."

"And that's a good thing," I said. "If he leaves, we might not find him again, and things tend to go missing during moves. This might be our only chance on our only lead to stop the zombies."

"I need the demon, but chasing one in Hell sounds horrifying," Lewis said. "So I vote for zombies." Lewis tossed a black duffel over his broad shoulder and pushed his glasses back up his nose. "As much as the zombies did me a favor by biting my ex-wife, their random occurrences are hurting a lot of people, like those teens, Vale. And no one knows where they're coming from. Ending this thing is in everyone's best interest."

"My burial plans include staying in the ground, so I'm in," Edie said.

"I'm coming too." Corvina shouldered her backpack.

"You have class in the morning," Edie countered.

"And you only have tonight off. So we go while we can. I can brew some coffee. It's no big deal."

Ford sighed. "Vale?"

The pale Super said, "I have to open the shop in the morning."

Ford nodded. "Well, can't chase after the big bad alone, so, yeah, I'm coming too. Let's go."

Everyone collected gear and piled into vehicles like soldiers deploying for war. Almost seemed like overkill. How much trouble could one sleeping human cause?

Outside the two-story townhouse stood a real estate sign with a smiling agent and her phone number in bold blocky letters, in case passersby had the sudden desire to sell their homes. In the driveway, a pair of rental moving trucks waited. Streetlights showered orange light on the sidewalks, and through the bushy trees, narrow columns streaked the front yard. The cool air was comfortable and low in humidity, but not so low that I risked static electricity in Corvina's lap. She was nice enough to not pet me on the drive over.

"This is the place." With her thumb, Corvina scrolled the phone screen shining in her face.

The stinky Prius, Lewis's shiny Silverado, and Ford's SUV marked with a security company's logo, all parked at the curb, and everyone poured out. I teleported out of the car and waited. The house was too small for all of us to fit. Ford's mood swings were unpredictable, and Corvina wasn't the type to jump into fire with guns blazing. Besides, I needed lookouts. I picked out the two I wanted to help me. "Edie and Lewis with me. You two, keep an eye out for zombies or cops."

"Wait!" Corvina whisper yelled. "You're a cat. You can't just go knocking and talk to this guy."

"Who said anything about knocking or talking?" I attempted a smile. "Edie, door please."

Edie approached the townhouse with her hands empty while Lewis followed, carrying a duffel over his shoulder. On the top step of the porch, Edie peeked through the windows, shrugged, and tried the doorknob. "Locked."

"Can you pick it?" I asked.

"What do I look like to you?" Edie asked. "Ford can."

"I can break it down," Lewis said.

"Just wait here." I didn't want Ford butting in, and I definitely didn't want to leave behind obvious damage. I centered my thoughts, clearing my mind to focus on the location where I wanted to go. The tugging of my body warned me of the upcoming shift in location. When I blinked, I was inside the house, facing the darkened interior half full of boxes. I turned around and leaped onto a table beside the door and swatted the deadbolt over. With my teeth, I turned the knob lock. Being a cat wasn't entirely useless.

Edie swung the door wide, and Lewis entered on her tail. When the door closed behind them, Edie clicked on a flashlight. The beam danced all over the living room. "They're in the middle of packing. Come on." She nodded her head for us to follow her.

Room by room, we searched for anything useful. Furniture filled a few rooms, boxes climbed the walls, and piles of unsorted belongings sat on the floor.

Up the narrow stairs, I strolled into an office. A wooden desk filled the small space. Cases of books lined the walls. Nothing in here was packed for moving—not even the photo propped on a shelf. My excellent vision allowed me to see a smiling man with his arms wrapped around a happy woman's shoulders at a park. Something about the man's face—his eyes, in particular—looked familiar. I didn't know any Dr. Tyler Gibson, but maybe I'd seen him in the halls at NBB.

With a shrug, I approached the desk. I pulled out the drawers one by one and found paperwork. Hmmm. A plain folder with NBB stamped on it. My tiny heart galloped in my chest. I bit the folder and dropped it on the surface. With a paw, I pushed the top open.

Page after page of photocopies of scientific reports full of nonsensical diagrams and shorthand scribbles. Well, crap. With a background in scrubbing toilets, my chemistry experience stopped at the classic yellow dish soap trick, where a flush caused urine-colored bubbles to overfill the bowl. And I was the poor sap who had to clean it. Every. Single. Time.

I skimmed the foreign pages. "Edie, Lewis? I got something."

Shushes followed, and Edie entered the office with Lewis behind her. "There's a woman around the corner sleeping. Her phone was unlocked. You need to see this." Edie swiped at the screen and held it out to me—a photograph of a casket. In front stood the woman from the shelf photo, holding a tissue. Beside her was a large, framed photograph of—the man from the shelf photo. "That's our guy, isn't it?"

"It appears our Dr. Tyler Gibson is recently deceased. After rummaging through her phone, I believe he's at the Riverside Cemetery on Webster."

Well, that was just the wrinkle I didn't need. "I have a problem, too. Can you read these?" I pushed the documents closer to Edie. Lewis read over her shoulder.

"You can't read?" Lewis asked, brows lifted.

I snorted. "Of course I can read, but chemistry isn't my language. Either of you know anyone good with the chemicals?"

Edie closed the folder and tucked it under her arm. "Corvina might be able to help. Let's go. Lewis, return this."

Skeptical about the biggest shifter's tiptoe skills, I asked, "Are you sure he's the sneakiest one of us?"

"He's quiet as a mouse," Edie said, holding out the phone and encouraging Lewis to take it.

The shifter gripped it tight, pressed a button to turn off the screen, and disappeared out the door. Yeah, completely silent as a mouse.

I shivered. "Don't even say that word. Gives me the creeps."

"You're afraid of mice? But you're a cat," Edie whispered and led the way down the hall.

I ignored that comment and listened for heavy footfalls and creaky floorboards, but not a single sound reached my sensitive ears. Impressive.

Out of the front door, Corvina sat in Edie's car, while Ford leaned against his SUV. If they were trying to be nonchalant, they'd failed. In the grassy yard, Lewis waited alongside a tree.

My jaw slackened. "How did you get out here so fast?"

"What took you guys so long?" Ford asked, standing up straight.

Corvina climbed out of the car. "Did you find anything?"

Sirens wailed in the distance. I craned my neck. Light glowed from the second-story window across the street, and the curtains shifted. Just great. Some nosy neighborhood watch was going to stand between us and saving the world from Nick Barnes's bacterium. The last thing we needed was to spend time behind bars—not that bars could hold me, but I needed the others to do the work for me.

"We can't all get caught, and I have my company vehicle," Ford said.

"Well, someone saw us," Edie said.

"We got what we need," I said. "Let's get out of here. Scatter and meet back at the cabin."

I slipped into Edie's car with Corvina. Lewis climbed into his pickup, and Ford roared the engine in his SUV. Tires blasted down the road. At the intersection, we all took a different turn. Edie handed the folder to her cohort.

"What's this?" Corvina asked.

"Hopefully something helpful." I said.

Corvina held the folder of documents against her chest. Not so much like a shield this time, but like a protector needing to coddle the answers to saving the world.

Edie slowed to a stop at a red light. The ramp to the freeway was right ahead. No sign of the shifter or the hothead—hopefully a good sign.

A distant, muted buzzing alerted me. "You hear that?"

"Hey, none of that." Edie yawned, ignoring my alarm. "But I'm beat, too. Didn't get any sleep during the day."

"Seriously. Do you guys hear that?" I repeated. Something was coming in hot.

Flashing lights reflected off nearby buildings.

"What?" Edie lifted off the brake, and the car rolled forward into the intersection.

"Incoming!" I said.

Taking a corner too sharp, an SUV screeched tires and flew in front of Edie's Prius. In a blink, it turned down the way we'd just left. Edie stomped on the brake. A police car with its reds and blues flashing stuck close to the SUV's tail.

"What time is it?" Corvina asked. "They don't have their sirens on."

"Must be late. Was that Ford's SUV?"

"I think so," Corvina said.

"Well, he's going to be late getting back to the cabin."

"Yep." Corvina leaned back in her seat.

Edie pressed on the gas through the green light.

"Why don't you care if he's caught?" I asked.

"He owns a security company. He's not going to get caught because he's not going to stop."

"If the cops identify him by his plate and the fancy logo stuck to the door panels, and these documents are discovered missing by Dr. Gibson's widow, who do you think they'll throw behind bars?" I asked, leading her to assist Ford.

"Oh..." she trailed off, considering her options. "I don't want us to get caught, either. We have the formula. Nothing says 'guilty' like holding the evidence."

"We won't," I insisted.

"You sure?" Edie glanced in the rearview mirror as if expecting a cruiser hunting us, too.

"I'm sure. Just go!"

"Okay. Hang on." Edie turned the wheel and punched the gas, roaring in the direction of the chase.

"Get us close enough for me to see the cruiser," I said.

"Can do." Edie made a U-turn and flew east on Shawano Ave, headed back downtown. "Ford's not going to turn into the residential areas—too many eyes and too quiet. Downtown is the way to lose them. I think I know where he's going."

Blowing through red lights, Edie made a sharp left, and I tumbled over. She didn't have a pet seat, nor would I accept a leash, so I would deal with the bruises tomorrow.

Up ahead, the red and blue flashers said we were on the right trail.

"There!" Edie pointed, as if I couldn't see the blindingly bright lights in the dead of night. "What do you want me to do?"

"Get closer. I need to see the gap between Ford and the cruiser," I said.

"I can't believe we're chasing a police chase," Corvina said, bracing herself.

Edie closed the distance to the police cruiser. While Ford's SUV hung a corner up ahead, I said, "Stop here and turn around."

"What? Why?"

"Just do it," I said, concentrating on the location while the vehicle slowed. I teleported from the Prius and reappeared in the middle of the lane, a full car length from becoming bumper damage.

I sat neatly on the asphalt and flashed my glowing red eyes, daring the cruiser to hit me. The vehicle slammed on the brakes and swerved just enough to lose traction on the back tires. The rear quarter panel slammed into the nearby ancient light pole, cracking it enough to tilt on its axis, and shrouding the nearby blocks in darkness.

The Prius silently idled where I had teleported out, its headlights off. Edie backed up the car and turned around, quickly leaving as directed. Up ahead, Ford's SUV stopped, red taillights glowing. I gleefully ignored whatever my paws might be touching and teleported into Ford's vehicle on the passenger seat. Polo Dude held a cell phone to his ear.

"Single vehicle accident on Shawano. A reckless police cruiser struck a pole. Yeah, ambulance. Please hurry, the officers look hurt."

A tiny voice said to stay on the line, but Ford swiped the call away.

I asked, "Didn't you just give away your involvement?"

Ford startled with a yelp. "Damn it, cat. Warn someone next time. I'm not so heartless to leave their lives to chance. Did you see what made them crash?" Ford shifted into drive and slowly accelerated to avoid attention.

I braced myself. "I teleported in front of them and smiled."

Ford chuckled. "Sounds terrifying."

Headlights showed the yellow dashed lines zipping along, and Ford merged onto the highway. "Thank you, by the way, but this doesn't change anything between us."

I sighed. "Understood."

14

The Destruction

I COULDN'T SLEEP, WAITING impatiently while Corvina read through the documents we'd taken from Dr. Tyler Gibson's house. As soon as Mittens woke up, I darted over to the table, and it wobbled under the force of my vicious paws.

"So, what did you find out?"

"It's a formula for something called Bacillusly 666 version 47." Corvina flipped pages carefully, and then she gasped.

"What? What is it?"

The shifter flew off the floor to his feet, arms framed to fight, wearing nothing but socks and boxers and squinting without his glasses. Less awkward was him stripping down to sleep; more awkward was the shape of his boxers standing up. I looked away.

Edie woke up next, drowsily squinting into the breaking morning dawn.

"What's going on?" Edie asked. Her eyes tracked to Lewis's excessively trimmed and enormous form. Nothing like showing off for the ladies. Jerk.

"This bacterium, if I'm reading this right, is like nothing currently known to science."

I leaned close. "What's special about it?

"These tests. The Gram stain. It makes no sense. Maybe this is a failed experiment."

"We need to get to NBB. Dr. Gibson could've stolen this formula. NBB could be missing it." Perhaps this little effort could put us on the path to fixing the zombie outbreak. And then, I could see great things for myself.

Lewis relaxed his defensive position, making his tented boxers more pronounced. That was the only thing I didn't miss about being man-shaped.

"I can't." Lewis checked his watch. "I have a shift in the city. Garbage doesn't pick itself up."

Corvina checked the time. "I have class, or I'd go."

The front door opened. Ford stood in the entryway fully clothed and armed, ready for anything, but he looked exhausted. "What's that noise? Everything okay?"

"We're going to NBB. Are you coming with?" I asked.

Ford strolled inside to check the cabin over. Lewis, still half-masted in the bedroom, scratched the nape of his neck. Ford turned away. "Think you could get some clothes on there, buddy? We don't need to see that."

Edie chuckled. "It's not every day we get a nice show." She purposefully stared at Lewis before winking at Ford.

Ford's cheeks burned red, and he cleared his throat. "I have to head to the office, so if everything's okay in here, I'm out."

"I'll be behind you," Lewis said.

"Not like that you won't," Ford said with a warning tone.

Lewis looked down, covered himself with a broad palm, and scrambled for his pants. The women dressed, taking turns in the bathroom, and Ford left, followed by Lewis.

Covina shouldered her excessively large backpack and waved to me on her way out. Guess the young woman wasn't afraid of me anymore. I wasn't sure how I felt about that.

Edie came out of the steaming bathroom, protected hair wrapped. Her T-shirt stuck to her chest, and I couldn't stop staring. It had been way too long since I'd been with a woman. How much longer before I got out of the cat?

"Ready?" Edie asked, picking up a restocked duffel.

"So very ready." I teleported into her car, and Edie drove us into the city.

In the heart of downtown, Edie pulled to a stop at the curb and craned her neck over the steering wheel to see the top of the twenty-story steel and glass structure. The top floor had cracked glass that only my superior cat and demon vision could see at this distance. What happened up there?

"This is the place, but no one's coming or going." Edie unbuckled. "Not seeing any zombies, either."

While I worked here, I remembered the sidewalks having more foot traffic. Things were quiet now. "The company doesn't sell directly to the public, so it's normal they don't have lots of people coming and going. Let's check it out."

"Wait." Edie held her palm in front of my face, as if that would stop me. "You can't waltz in there."

"I'm sure you can't either. Don't be so judgmental."

Edie chuckled. "No, I mean it. You're a cat to everyone else."

Well, damn. "You can't leave me in here."

Edie hummed a tune and strained to reach the messy backseat. She rummaged through debris that curled my lip. "Ah, ha! Climb in." She opened a large purse, reminiscent of the tiny dog carriers from long ago.

A shred of dignity forced my paws to stay put. "No way am I getting into that."

"What are you going to do instead—glamour everyone into thinking you're a human? How would you shake hands? And me holding the door for your glamoured image would be weird."

Many demons could glamour, but I was the only one who had a natural human look, and I couldn't. Likely had something to do with my half-demon heritage. With a grumble worthy of a stubborn old man, I climbed into the pink polyester and polyurethane monstrosity, wondering why I knew anything about the materials at all. Vanilla soy latte assaulted my nose. "Not a word about this. Understood?"

Edie snorted. "Trust me, you climbing into my old purse is the last thing I'd tease you about."

"You don't seem like the type to choose pink." I ducked as she closed the magnetic clasps overhead.

"Why do you think it stays buried in here? My cousin bought it for me one Christmas. I think she hoped I'd say 'thanks, but no thanks,' so she could take it back. Jokes on her. I carried my gym clothes in it, and I made sure to put a stick of vanilla bean in a pocket to help with the smell."

I groaned. "I think it's still in here."

"Hang on to your fur." Edie climbed out of the Prius and swung me over her shoulder. How freaking humiliating. The ride was bumpy as she crossed the calm street, hopping over potholes and avoiding trash. A vehicle, burning oil, rolled by, helping to dilute the pungent vanilla.

"Front door's open. I'm going in," she whispered.

A smacking of glass followed. "The rotating doors aren't working."

Edie opened and closed a side door. I couldn't hear anyone inside—no voices or footsteps. A humid, mossy smell—like wet carpet—filled my nose—strong enough to overpower the vanilla bean crammed at my feet. To be on the safe side, I waited for Edie to tell me what she saw. The bag bounced against her side as she strolled across the floor. The clatter of her shoes told me the floor was not carpet, perhaps tile.

Edie jabbed a mechanical button. "The elevator's out. Where is everyone?"

"If the coast is clear, can you open the bag for me?" I could've teleported out, but I didn't want to shock some wayward security guard.

The magnetic clasp overhead pulled open, throwing light all around me. I popped my furry head out of the bag. A circular glass door remained still. The overhead fixtures were off, but the glass wall allowed in enough light to see. "The weirdest thing is I know this place, but I can't picture when I was ever in the lobby. What kind of janitor never cleaned the lobby? Does that make sense?"

"No," Edie said, still looking around.

"The stairs are over there."

"Where?" she asked.

I tilted my head to the area across the abandoned lobby. "Do I need to point for you?"

"Just wondered if you would." She crossed the empty space and pushed on the door. It gave way, and Edie entered the stairwell. "Now where?"

"The most important man is always on the top floor. Let's check that out first, and if he's not home, maybe he left something behind we can use."

Edie sent me a look of exasperation. "I'm not carrying you up twenty flights. Get out." She set the purse on the floor and held the straps apart for me.

For my own amusement, I said, "I can teleport. Meet you at the top!"

"Whoa, whoa, whoa. Hang on there. I'm not climbing my ass all the way up there alone. This was your idea. You can suffer right along with me."

Mittens was in plenty good shape and well-rested. "After you."

Ten stories later, Edie's climbing slowed. Her back leaned forward into the steps, and her panting showed her inferior stamina. She stopped and flexed her Achilles tendon. "Can you teleport me with you?"

"Never thought of that." I leaped three steps in one bound and waited for Edie to catch up. "Or tried it."

"How about you try it, yeah?"

"Stand still." I closed my eyes and pictured myself moving to the place where I wanted to land. I added a visual of Edie standing next to me in this new place. When the tugging sensation ended, I opened my eyes, and I was alone. With a sigh, I teleported back to where I'd left her.

Edie's arms were crossed, and her lips twisted with annoyance. "I half expected you to not come back."

"Oh, come on. You think so little of me?"

"Yes."

A stairwell access door opened on the floor beneath us. Edie's eyes opened wide, and she bent over, shooing me into the purse.

I shook my head. "Can I just hide behind your boots until whoever it is passes? They might not even come this way."

Footsteps took to the stairs, and a man in a suit, carrying a sporty duffel bag, appeared around the bend. Well, shit.

I STARED WIDE-EYED AND confused at the random visitor trudging through the abandoned NBB building. "Andras?"

The bouncer-dwarfing demon tipped his head up and lifted his brows while slowing his ascent. "iKat, what are you doing here?"

"I'm going to ask you the same."

"A demon! He's a demon, and I'm not armed." Edie patted her pockets, frantically searching for a weapon.

"It's okay. He's a friend," I said.

Her patting slowed to a stop, but her rapid breaths from an adrenaline rush heaved her chest. "Friend?"

"It's fine." I assured her, not that she'd stand a chance against Andras if he wanted to obliterate her in flames. "Calm down."

Edie's face pinched in unspent energy. "Don't tell me to calm down!"

"Wrong words, iKat." Andras shook his head with a small smile.

I never had much luck with women, as far as I remembered. "I told you it's okay. He's not going to hurt us, and since he's a friend, you aren't going to hurt him. So, can you just be quiet while we talk?"

Andras's shoulders shook as he silently laughed. Just great.

"If it weren't for cute little innocent Mittens, I would've smacked your fuzzy ass down the stairs." Her finger jabbed toward me with her words, driving the point home. "Don't ever speak to me like that again."

"Got it. I got it, okay? Andras, why are you here?" I shot a look at Edie, waiting for her to repeat her outburst, but she only folded her arms across her chest, the gaudy bag hanging by her side.

Andras thumbed back down the stairs. "Hell portal. On my way to the gym. You?"

I had no reason to lie to my friend. "We're looking for the big bossman upstairs. Hopefully, we can find some answers about this zombie issue. We found what looks like a formula, and since it was hidden in a doctor's desk drawer, it must be important. We just don't know why."

Andras nodded his approval. "Well, sounds like you're on the right path. Just be careful. Not everyone is friendly out there."

I chuckled awkwardly. "Thanks." I wanted to ask the demon about my memories and the electricity-and-water accident I couldn't remember, but before I opened my mouth, Andras teleported away.

Edie's head whipped around toward me. "If he can teleport with a bag in his hand, then you can bring me up there. Do it, and don't give me any lip."

"I'll try again. No promises." Since I'd tried not touching her and it didn't work, and Andras touched his bag and it did work, then touching her sounded plausible. Pressing my furry eyelids shut, I leaned against her leg to make contact. I repeated my thought process, and the tugging on my fur *whooshed* me back to the twentieth floor.

This time, Edie stood next to me, wobbling with a loss of balance. I smiled but didn't bother to help her. What? She'd just crush me, anyway.

Edie fell over. When she stood, she rubbed her hip and frowned. "Uh, thanks."

I took a step toward the only door on the penthouse floor, but my paws gave out. I crashed to the tile, hitting my jaw first.

"You have four feet. What's your excuse?" she asked.

I shook my fur from shoulders to tail. My head felt fine, but my legs had no strength. "I never teleported another person before. Didn't know what would happen, but so far, I'm not liking it."

"Then don't do it again."

I scowled at her. "No problem."

Outside the only door, there was a keypad for electronic access. "Technology for the loss. How do we get inside? Call Ford to use his 'tool'? The owner of a security company has to have some tricks, right?"

My cohort gave me a look of annoyance. "I'm not calling Ford over here just to wave his magic fingers. Teleport in. Unlock the door. How is this not obvious?"

"First, I don't want to hear about Ford's magic fingers, just no. Two, I can't just teleport somewhere without having a reasonable expectation of where I might end up. Once, I teleported into—" conjuring the memory of my first attempt to teleport caused a massive squeeze to my brain. I fell to the floor as the memories ripped from their cage.

> *I tried to wade through the trash to climb out myself—ready to shower in bleach—but my feet wouldn't move. I turned on the flashlight feature of my cell phone and shined it at my ankles—or where they would be if the dumpster hadn't severed them at its raised floor.*

> *Hot, searing pain radiated up my legs. I shoved the overhead lid open and concentrated on moving, but the pain demanded my attention. Bacteria crawling inside here, touching my legs, must've numbered in the billions. Tiny invisible critters snacking and defecating all over my skin, trying to invade my eyes and mouth. My heart thundered in its cage. My breaths quickened. Think, think, think, I told myself. Outside the dumpster. Feet on the asphalt. One, two, thr...*

I shook my head. If that was a memory...? What kind of janitor was afraid of germs? Fear of mice made sense. They were creepy, crawly things sneaking into your house and eating your food.

Pooping in your clothes and climbing all over your body. And the weirdest part, that teleporting test had happened on the surface.

"What happened? You okay?" Edie asked with a hand on my fuzzy shoulder.

"A memory. I remember my first time teleporting. I severed my ankles."

"Eesh. Well, teleport inside that door without cutting anything off."

"Thanks, genius," I said with sarcasm and straightened up onto my paws. My strength had returned, and my head was back online. "Here goes nothing."

I concentrated on landing just inside the door. It had to be a safe location—free of obstructions, just waiting to cause painful damage. Unless zombies attempted to break in and the door was barricaded.

Could zombies climb stairs?

Taking a figurative leap that they couldn't, I teleported inside. My jaw dropped in horror. A massive reef aquarium had shattered, rippling the floors with water damage. The corals were all white, bleached from death. No fish remained, if there were any, but the smell of decayed and moldy sea life stung my eyes. Recently, I'd gotten into aquariums, so I knew what an investment in time, money, and love a tank of this size would take. I hadn't set up my first aquarium yet, thankfully, otherwise I'd be down in Hell watching out for my finned friends.

And yes, that massive exterior glass wall pane was cracked. What the hell happened here?

I spun around and leaped up to tip the deadbolt over with my paw. Up and down I went, paws thumping on the spongy wood floor. After my third try, Edie said through the door, "I'm not getting any younger over here."

"Aren't women like a fine wine, anyway?" With a grunt, the lever flipped over, and Edie entered at once.

"Say that to my face." She scowled.

"I guess not every proverb has truth to it." I shrugged.

She glared at me for a moment before returning her attention to the task at hand. Edie scanned the damaged room. "What the hell happened in here? Anyone around?"

"Not that I've seen in the two minutes I've been wrestling with the doorknob for you."

The scowl returned.

"Doesn't look like anyone's been around for a while," I added. "Let's see what we can find."

Edie split from me as we took separate areas to inspect. A lucky guess brought me straight to a home office.

Edie wasn't as lucky. "Oh, this is nasty. What is all this stuff?" Since I was nowhere near her, I figured she spoke to herself. A fine quality in a hunter who needed to be stealthy as a prerequisite for the job.

I leaped onto a padded leather chair and pawed at the drawer handles. A pen sitting on the surface caught my eye. I tried fitting a paw around a handle again when my eye returned to the pen. A need pulled me. Unable to help myself, I jumped onto the desk surface and swatted the pen off the table. I leaned my head over, tail swishing, watching the pen clatter to the floor.

"Everything okay in there?" Edie called.

From the new angle, I pulled at the drawer handle again. It opened. "Yep. Yep, it's fine. Nothing to worry about here."

"You're sure?"

Stacks of paperwork filled the tight space, and I pawed, lifting a side, and I bit the files. Dropping them on the desk surface, I swatted open a folder.

Edie walked through the door. "It's unlike you to stay silent. What did you find?"

"A marketing plan for Heromycin. What an on-the-nose name. Come see."

Edie leaned over my shoulder to read. She flipped pages as I scanned them. "Chris Barnes put this package together. If the owner is missing and the scientist is dead, maybe we can find this Chris guy for help."

"I know a Chris," I quipped, remembering Chris, Dennis, and Stella, but not who they were or what importance they might have.

"Really?" Edie said with a mocking tone. "I know a few myself."

Squinting at her, I said, "Take the files. Something tells me no one's coming back for them."

Edie tucked them into her pink purse without hesitation. "There's nothing else we can do here."

"Agreed. Meet you in the car." I winked.

"Hey, wait!"

I teleported down to her Prius and sat comfy on the passenger seat, basking in the sunlight. It was going to be awhile before Edie climbed down twenty flights. Mittens napped. See, I could treat my host well. Hopefully, the borrowed cat woke up before Edie returned, because something told me she wouldn't be happy.

15

Dead End

I LEAPED UP ON the rickety card table in the hunter's cabin. Mittens's nap took longer than I preferred, but Edie was too tired from marching back down twenty stories to do more than grunt at me and give me the silent treatment. I wasn't going to help a hunter who threatened my life every four to six hours. Besides, she explicitly said not to teleport others again.

Corvina strolled in the front door, an overstuffed backpack threatening to crush her flat. She dropped it to the floor with a thud and crashed into a chair. "Hey, guys. Did you get any answers?"

Edie slipped the folders out of her stinky pink purse. "What do you make of these?"

Corvina turned them around and opened the documents, while Edie explained, "The building was empty, except for one guy, a demon friend of the cat's apparently." She avoided looking at me or speaking to me. Her resolve for the silent treatment was strong. "Whatever was going on there has long since ended. We have a lead, this Chris Barnes guy. He has the same last name as the missing owner, and the owner had his marketing documents."

Corvina unzipped her backpack and pulled out a laptop. Setting it on the table, she opened the lid. Her finger tapped and slid across the trackpad, and she typed away. "Well, I found him."

She was a genius with the technology.

"That was easy. Where?" Edie asked.

"Chris Barnes is currently occupying a small space next door."

"Next door? We're in the middle of the woods. The nearest neighbor is...oh," Edie said, disappointment in her tone.

SITUATED BETWEEN OTHER UNREMARKABLE headstones at West Lawn Cemetery was a squat granite marker with an etched name that meant another dead end. Just like the mysterious doctor, Chris Barnes expired. Permanently.

"The dirt's been disturbed," Edie said, pointing to the freshly dug grave.

"They did have to bury the casket," I said.

"Those marks there." She pointed. "Don't look like a shovel or a backhoe."

"Claw marks." I chuckled. "Maybe the ghouls escaped and found themselves a snack."

Edie scowled. At least she was speaking to me again.

Corvina opened her laptop and balanced it on her arm. "Listen to this: Chris Barnes, 45, passed away at Mercy Medical

Center with his wife at his side. Chris was born to Dennis and Stella (Janowski) Barnes. Chris graduated East High School blah blah blah. Married the former Cyndi Hanson yada yada—"

"Did you say Dennis and Stella?" I interrupted.

"You know them?" Edie asked.

"No, but the names are familiar." The names and faces that appeared in my head, but I didn't know if they were premonitions or memories or just a movie I'd watched in Hell. Anything was possible. Since one was dead, guess they weren't premonitions or movies.

Memories?

Edie frowned. I wanted to say if she spent so much time scowling and frowning, the lines would become permanent, but somehow that tidbit of helpful advice might be construed as wrong.

"Oh, here," Corvina said, eyes still on the screen. "He worked at NBB in marketing. Loved his job." She hummed while skimming. "Loved working for his little brother, Nick. That's sweet. It sounds like they had a great relationship." Corvina looked at the gravestone. "But it didn't end well."

"Chris and Nick are brothers. Dennis and Stella are Chris's parents, and therefore, Nick's parents. We got that much. Is it useful? I don't know, but if Chris enjoyed being part of what Nick Barnes is responsible for, then this Chris dude is just as bad as Nick. I wouldn't call it sweet." Edie pressed a hand on top of her hair and paced the grass, careful to avoid stepping on flat markers.

She ticked off the information on her fingers. "The owner, currently to blame for the zombie outbreak, is missing, and so far, two employees—his brother, the marketing guy, and the evil genius doctor—are dead. The whole building is empty, besides the demon friend, who didn't appear to belong there, anyway. A formula, important enough for the doctor to take unauthorized copies, was sitting in his home desk drawer. Oddly named, with a number known to be evil. The marketing details of something called Heromycin penned by the brother were sitting in the missing owner's desk drawer. NBB is as mysterious as the recurring pockets of zombies appearing out of nowhere," Edie said, frowning at the headstone. "But I have a feeling it's all connected somehow."

"I don't know about you guys, but after this, I have no interest in finding Nick Barnes." Corvina closed the laptop. "He sounds like an awful person, and the city is better off without him."

"The non-deal was for the cat to help me track down the bastard, wherever he's hiding, and kill him. And he's going to pay." Edie's fists balled with her memories.

"I think we're better off focusing on this thing called Heromycin instead of trying to kill a single missing human, no matter how guilty." Corvina shoved the computer back into her schoolbag. "Nick Barnes is human, right?" She glanced at me.

I recalled what I'd read in the demon history books. "Nick Barnes is an eccentric megalomaniac. He was rich, and he loved attention, but he suffered. His family treated him terribly, and he lost everything. According to the demons, the zombie outbreak was his creation, but I'm guessing the real creator was the doctor who died from his passion. The egotistical asses always take the credit. But Nick was responsible for releasing it. In my opinion, he's a worse demon than some demons I've met, but not necessarily more powerful."

"If the demons know all that, where is he?"

I'd wanted to milk these hunters' skills until I got what I wanted—finding enough lackeys with opposable thumbs brave and dumb enough to infiltrate Hell for me. Despite her involvement with Lewis's vampire contract and her being a high-ranking demon to The King of Hell, Heather might not have been a big enough carrot. But if they insisted on tracking down Nick Barnes, then this could be a two-for-one deal. "If you really want to find him, I know where Nick Barnes is."

"Where?" Edie asked, clutching her keys to go now.

"It used to be called Corson's Correctional Facility," I said smugly. The technical term wasn't used anymore. And I flaunted my superior knowledge for a few minutes. At least until Edie's patience ran out.

Corvina dug out her cell phone for a quick internet search. I said, "You won't find it on there."

"Everything's on the internet." Corvina worked her techy magic, but the look on her face said she wasn't successful. "Or not. I don't have a passport, so if it's not in the USA, I can't go," Corvina said.

"You won't need a passport for Hell," I said. "You only need me to get you through the portal."

"Hell? Nick Barnes is in Hell?" Edie's fists balled up. "At least he's where he belongs."

No, no, no. They can't back out now. "I have a deal for you," I said.

The two women turned their attention to me. Edie said flatly, "No deal."

"Right, I know. No deals. This is a non-deal deal. Okay?"

Edie nodded.

"As I explained, demons don't want humans dead, so this Annihilator is throwing a wrench into our plans. Likewise, humans don't want to die, come back to life, and attack their loves ones as mindless, mouth-breathing idiots."

"What's your point?" Edie asked.

"We go to Hell. After I get my body back, I'll be far more functional and powerful. I'll help you track down Nick Barnes. And bonus! If we happen to come across Heather, then I can negotiate something for Lewis."

Maybe.

"Yeah, you know what? Yeah, I'm in." Edie spat her words with the malice she intended to unleash on that poor bastard. After seeing her single-handedly decapitate a house full of zombies, I would hate to be that guy.

"Let's get the others. We're going to need them," I said.

Getting back into my body was finally within reach. I teleported into Edie's car and waited while the women joined me. I was so excited I could explode like Todd's birthday cake.

I still wanted cake, but I had a feeling Mittens couldn't handle it. And note to self: Avoid demon birthday cakes.

16

The Plan

NIGHT FELL, AND EVERYONE collected back at the hunter's cabin. The women and I updated the males, and five faces waited for my plan. I stood on the wobbly table, moving around to address them all. "We're going to Hell."

"Please tell me that's a turn of phrase," Ford said dryly.

"Like actual Hell is real?" Corvina asked.

"Of course Hell is real. Seen a map? It's a village west of Detroit," I quipped. A great little spot to visit, but no one laughed. Tough crowd. "The Hell I'm talking about is generally used to scare people. I assure you, it's real, and depending on where you go, it is scary."

All five of them listened intently, but Ford remained impassive.

"Now, as I promised Edie, you can go there, and you can come back." If they survived. "It's not like your soul will be trapped and burned for all eternity."

"What's the catch?" Ford asked.

"Hell, like any facility that has things others want, has security. The plan is to infiltrate Hell through the portal. We'll get by the guard on desk duty."

"How?" Ford asked.

"With my charming smile and a bribe."

Ford snorted. "Figures."

I attempted to roll my eyes. "First, we head for my body. When I'm in it, we'll track down Nick Barnes. Edie will get to work her magic on him."

Edie grinned mischievously and nodded.

"At which point, we'll search for Heather. Lewis, I'll see what I can do about your contract."

Lewis nodded in appreciation.

"And then we all get the hell out of there," I finished.

"That's it?" Ford asked. "Sounds like a lot of work, but too easy."

"Well, if security is tripped, then I'll need the four of you, Edie, Lewis, Ford, and Vale, to distract the incoming demons while Corvina helps me find my body. If I already have it, then the three of you distract while Corvina, Edie, and I finish the Nick business. From there, I'll see what I can do about Heather. We'll have to do a little improvising. But at that point, our alliance here will be complete." I glanced at Edie. "And I'll be out of your hair for good."

Ford squinted. "A small army of Hell's own bodyguards..." He spun a finger in the air, indicating their misfit group. "And you expect us to 'distract' them? What kind of bullshit plan is that?"

"I really want to help," Lewis said, pushing his glasses up his nose. "And I think the plan is great, but all of that hinges on a whole lot of things out of our control."

"Corvina?" I asked. Bringing her along was close to suicide for her. With no supernatural abilities... I realized I'd never checked the lanky blond woman. Switching on my aura ability, I scanned the human. No cloudy shade of gray—or nearly invisible cloud of white. *Well, I'll be damned.* She was a Super, too. With her physique, and lack of blood drinking, I couldn't imagine what.

"Why not go through the portal and teleport back into your body?" Corvina asked. "That would save a lot of time and slow down the security response."

Having tried that in the king's office with no luck, I expected the answer was the same as teleporting. I had to touch my body to get back in. "The cells are locked. If I did that, I wouldn't get back out, so it has to be done the old-fashioned way."

"Why not teleport out of the cell?" Corvina asked.

"You think Hell's dungeons allow prisoners to escape that easy?"

"I suppose not. I'm in," Corvina said with an unusual show of confidence.

That was good enough for me. "Perfect. How about you, Edie? How badly to do you want to kill Nick Barnes?"

Edie snorted. "Was there ever a question about my loyalty to this mission? Of course, I'm going. The bastard's going to pay, and I look forward to it."

"We're talking about an army, and it's demon territory. Don't you think this all sounds a little crazy, even for us?" Ford said, still not swayed.

"Ford, you always have my back on this stuff. Why are you copping out now?" Edie fumed, murder glinting in her eye. I never wanted to be on the death end of her blade. "We need your lock picking skills."

Ford said nothing.

"Pia would want you to do this," Edie added.

Ford's nostrils flared. "Don't bring her into this. I'm warning you."

"Then join me," Edie said. "Let's kick some demon ass and get justice for humankind."

Ford glared, considering, and glanced from Edie to Corvina and back. "Fine. Okay, fine. But if you"—indicating me—"stick a toe out of line, consider your expiration date stamped."

"Threat to my life understood," I said.

"What about you, Lewis? In or out, wolf?" Ford asked.

Lewis ducked his head toward the table.

"If I can do this, there's no reason why a strong, efficient dealer of damage with massive claws couldn't," Corvina said softly, with a friendly smile.

Lewis puffed his cheeks and blew them out forcibly. "Fine. Alright? Fine. I'll go, too."

"Hey, don't allow anyone to pressure you into this. I mean, if iKat sucks, we could all die." Ford rested his hands on the top of his head. "So make the choice for yourself, not because we need you."

I took no offense. Instead, I chuckled. No wonder the demons avoided manipulating hunters and other non-humans. They were fully capable of degrading their own souls. No help needed.

"I'm going, and you aren't making me. Got it?" Lewis said with an unusual irritation in his voice.

Ford lifted his palms. "Vale, you're quiet. You in on this one?"

The broody Super finally spoke, uncrossing his arms from his chest. "I'm afraid I cannot. I am bound to protect people, not go charging into an assassination plot."

Ford tilted his head to face Vale. "Don't give us the moral high ground crap. After all these years we fought together, you can't do this for us?"

How had the Super fought with humans without them knowing he wasn't human? This group of misfits was blind to each other.

"I've spoken. I must be going. Enjoy the food." Vale bowed and left.

"That's weird," Edie said. "Usually he's there helping us. He's a great fighter, too. Should we replace him, or can we do this ourselves?"

"We can do this ourselves," Corvina declared with a smile.

Ford smiled. "Where did this new Corvy come from? I like it."

Corvina glanced at the floor and stroked her hair, a smile playing at her lips.

"Watch how close to the edge you get, Ford. Once you dive into the deep ocean of Corvy, there's no coming back up for air," Edie warned in a playful tone.

Ford's turn to blush. Seriously, these people couldn't stay focused. "Let's pack up. Bring whatever weapons you can comfortably carry. I want water in the car, a first aid kit, and if you need it, bring some food, too."

"We're not going camping, cat. A gun and a blade are all I need," Edie said.

Eh, Ford wasn't too far off about the army of demons. And they certainly wouldn't be lenient to this group. "Actually, we need something else. As a demon, I can get you through the gate, but to give us the best head-start, you're going to need something to disguise you from upper management."

"Like what?" Edie asked.

"You hunters have a grimoire?" Blank stares. "A spell book?" Any decent hunters would have magic in their arsenal because blades and bullets were not enough against the Supers.

Edie's face twisted with confusion.

Guess not.

"Yeah, on the shelf." Ford crossed the small space and bent over the bookcase, finger skimming the titles. "Ah, this one." He pulled out a dusty blue book, and Edie tracked him with wide eyes.

"Since when do you know anything about spells?" Edie asked him.

"I've dabbled. It's not much different from cooking. Recipes listing ingredients, a string of procedures..." Ford trailed off as everyone stared. "What?"

Corvina chuckled. "You just don't seem like the type."

Edie laughed. "Not by a mile. A big tough security guard, packing heat in case the ice cream parlor is robbed, and you dabble in *spells*?" She emphasized her word with a mocking tone. "Magic Fingers sure has a new meaning."

Ford shot her an annoyed look.

For once, I was compelled to step in and defend the hunter, knowing precious time ticked away. "Hey, newsflash. How do you think I ended up in here?" I lifted an orange fluffy paw in demonstration. "Magic isn't a joke, and it's certainly not something to take lightly. I have demon friends who are pagan." I paused to let that tidbit sink in. "You're submerged in the world of the supernatural. You hunt what you call monsters as a hobby, but magic is the unbelievable part? That being said, Ford, are you sure you can perform the spells with absolute accuracy? Because anything less can be disastrous."

Ford frowned. "Don't question my skills, cat, unless you want to see them firsthand. It's my duty to fight against evil. So what kind of spell do we need?"

"A veil. The more time we have before the demons discover what you are, the better our chances of success. And by success, I mean getting out of there alive."

"Is there anything that's not life and death?" Lewis asked.

"No. Not really." I leaped down onto the floor.

Ford opened the worn hardcover. "I think I saw something like that before, but I've never tried it." Pages turned with speed but care. A witch's grimoire was nothing to trifle with. "Here! Shrouded in Safety. I have all these ingredients." His finger slid down the page. "But we can't do it."

"Why not?" Edie asked.

"It's not Tuesday. It won't be right if it's not Tuesday."

"We can't wait five days to do this," I grumbled. Even one more night trapped like this was my own personal hell. "Is there one that would work tonight?"

"Not that I recall." Ford turned more pages and skimmed. At the end of the book, he said, "Tuesday or nothing."

"What do we do now?" Corvina asked.

"We do the spell tonight," I said.

"But you just said...?" Corvina leaned forward, face drawn with concern.

"Forget what I said," I interrupted. "You three, pack up the vehicles. Man-witch, start setting up." No one moved.

Ford slammed the book shut. "Call me that one more time and consider half of your nine lives over."

"Uh, point taken." Note to self: ixnay on the man-witch. "Look, if I'm in this cat too long, it's permanent. How would you like to ride around in Mittens for all eternity?"

"The cat's not immortal," Corvina said quietly.

"Precisely." Someone finally understood.

Oh, shit.

Frowning, Ford said, "Assuming I can do something of this veil spell, which might not work, how do we get into Hell?"

"There's a portal downtown. I'll give directions."

With a sigh, Ford headed to the kitchenette and opened and closed all the cabinets, collecting his stash of spices. "These aren't enough, but good thing I have my own." Ford headed out the front door.

Performing a Tuesday-only spell on a non-Tuesday was a recipe for disaster—pun very much intended. Whatever went wrong wouldn't affect me, so all that was in store for me was some eagerly anticipated entertainment.

As long as I got my body back.

17

Magic Fingers

Lewis, Edie, Corvina, and I lounged around the cabin, watching Ford brush the floor clear of debris with a broom while mumbling in Latin. Witches used their current native language, not the ancient language. So my trust in this man-witch was diminishing by the minute. I leaped down from the refrigerator and stalked up to the cleared space where Ford began setting up an altar.

"Hey, magic fingers, what's with the fancy words?"

Ford stopped his chanting, pulled a knife from his utility belt and angled it at my throat. Thankfully, he seemed to remember our chase around the cabin, so he didn't try that again. "What did I tell you?"

"You said negative on the man-witch."

Ford closed his eyes in frustration. "Once more and I'll have myself a new pair of slippers."

I looked down at Mittens. "His diet's been crap lately. They probably won't be very soft."

"Can you just shut up? I have to concentrate," Ford said, putting the knife back. The man was twitchier than usual. Not a good sign for delicate spell work.

"Don't interrupt a spell, iKat. It's dangerous," Corvina said, looking up from her phone. "Besides, it's nice to quietly watch a man clean for once."

"I don't need you to defend me!" Ford yelled at Corvina. Everyone flinched at his outburst. Okay, more than twitchier than usual.

Corvina recoiled as if struck, face turning ashen with genuine horror. I had the urge to scratch the shit out of Ford, but Edie beat me to it.

The hunter removed her feet from the table and got up in Ford's face. She pointed backward at Corvina. "Don't yell at her like that. What's wrong with you? Look what you did to her."

We all looked at Corvina. Her face flushed bright red in embarrassment, and she cradled her phone and jogged out of the front door. At least her phone would be spared the inevitable frying from the spell.

"You want me to do this intricate spell on a night it isn't meant for, and you're interrupting me?" Ford stood, jaw working hard on destroying those pearly whites. "You should know better than that. And I don't need a cat babbling nonsense, and I don't need a girl defending me."

"You're an asshole to her so often. Can't you see what damage that's doing?" Edie held up her palms in surrender. "She's a woman, not a child. Seems like the Ford I knew died with Pia."

Ford's muscles tensed with contained aggression. Turning away from her, he approached the rickety card table. Ford propped open a tackle box full of various herbs and ritual tools with more force than necessary and mumbled, "Dew of the Sea, check. Cat's Milk, check." He sent a pointed glance at me, but I wasn't afraid. Mittens wasn't female, so if one had to be milked for the spell, no skin off my back. "Bloody Fingers, and Swine Snout."

Ignoring Edie, Ford set the ingredients around a chalice on the floor and drew a white chalk circle counterclockwise on the hardwood planks. An amulet rested in the center, and a different colored candle was placed in each cardinal direction and lit with a long-stemmed lighter.

Edie left the cabin to find her distraught friend.

The apprentice man-witch stood on the eastern rim of the circle, pointing the shiny dagger at the floor. He closed his eyes and chanted in Latin before walking around his chalk circle, still pointing the dagger at the floor. Finished with his revolution, he raised his arms to the ceiling, and the point of the dagger scratched the wood beam. Ford frowned and then grunted at his own disruption. The odds of this spell working were about as good as me strolling into Hell, being greeted with a fat can of cat food, and getting pats on the head while they unlocked the bars to my body with glowing angels playing music.

Harpsichord or not, less than zero. (I didn't know if the harpsichord thing was a stereotype, but considering how many stereotypes were out there for demons, it probably was.)

Lewis sat on the bed across the room, munching on popcorn. I would've rolled my eyes if I could.

Ford scooped out a measure of each ingredient (the Bloody Fingers weren't actually fingers) and dumped them into the chalice of rose water. He lifted the mixture high, spoke more ancient words, and dipped his fingers into it, flickering the water around the circle.

Completing the revolution, Ford paused.

Not a bird whistled, not a leaf rustled. The women outside were silent. Lewis froze mid-bite. Cars rumbled off in the distance, but nothing else happened.

"Was something supposed to change?" Lewis craned his neck around as if trying to see the spell's effects.

Ignoring the interruption this time, Ford kneeled at the eastern edge of the circle and snuffed out the first candle. He bent over the other three, repeating the gesture, and when smoke drifted from each wick, he swept the dagger across the chalk. More words followed, and Ford stepped out of the sacred space. "Now everyone needs to drink. Lewis, you're first."

"Why me?" Lewis popped the last bite into his mouth. "I don't want to be your lab rat."

Ford sighed. "Edie! Corvy! Come in here." The two women returned and crossed their arms over their chests, clearly still miffed. "Drink from the chalice and the spell is complete."

Edie glared at it. "Did you drink it?"

"Not yet. You're first."

"I'm not going first," Edie said. "It's your spell."

Tilting her chin up and glaring at Ford, Corvina said, "I'll drink it."

"Are you sure?" Edie placed a hand on her forearm, stopping her. "You don't know if it'll kill you."

"So much faith you have in my skills, Edie. Nice." Ford quipped.

"I said I'll go first," Corvina insisted, gazing into Ford's eyes in a confident challenge.

Edie released her, and Corvina closed the distance. "This doesn't change what you said to me."

Ford didn't reply. He handed her the chalice, and they held each other's gaze while Corvina lifted it to her lips, as if daring him to harm her. She swallowed and winced.

After an observational beat, Ford asked, "Feel anything?"

"I bet she feels like kicking your ass," Edie said.

I chuckled.

"Nothing. Am I supposed to?" Corvina handed the chalice back to him.

"I don't know. Who's next?" The man-witch (yep, that was never going to die), held the chalice in the air.

Edie barreled her way up to Ford. "If this kills me, I'm haunting you for the rest of my life."

Ford chuckled, all sense of anger and frustration having drained away. The swirling heat in my eyes returned. Ugh, humans flirting. "Promise?"

With a glare, Edie sipped and grimaced. "It needs seasoning."

Ford took the chalice back from her and swallowed his own sip without reacting. He offered it to Lewis. "Trust me now?"

The shifter stood tall, brushing his hands clear of popcorn residue, and punched out his chest like the big wolf man should. He gripped the small cup in his meaty hand. "What she said." He nodded to Edie.

"Got it. Loud and clear. Everyone will haunt me until I die." Ford watched as Lewis sipped.

"It's good. No wonder you're the chef." The shifter's brows lifted, and he eagerly swallowed down the rest.

"Well, that's the best it's going to be." Ford wiped out the chalice and returned it to the table. He lifted an amulet he'd placed in the center of the casting circle and pulled it over his head. "Can you see if anything happened to us, cat?"

Using my demon vision, I inspected the crew but didn't see any red essences. "No. How about you Lewis?"

"Me? Why me?" Red crawled up the shifter's concerned face.

"Magic destroys electronics. Is your phone working?"

Lewis frowned. "Why are you only telling me this now?"

I shrugged. Wasn't it common sense?

Lewis slipped his phone out of his pocket. "Well, it works."

That wasn't good news for the hothead.

"I guess we won't know how the spell performs until we get there," I said, not wanting to start over. "Now we need to pack up everything else."

Edie crossed the small room to the closet, and she collected and prepared black duffels and a few extras. Lewis hoisted bags over his shoulders and carried them like the good pack mule he was. Corvina dumped her backpack empty of schoolbooks and went to the bathroom for first aid. And Ford packed up his ritual tools and supplies and stuffed a few choice witchy things into his pockets. He set the tackle box on the floor next to the bookcase.

Just like old hat.

Now I had my motley crew, and we were going to Hell. Which part was the harder one?

We were going to find out.

18

Ambush

STANDING THE HEART OF downtown, there was surprising noise pollution behind us today—a few honking horns, a couple of rumbling engines, and a handful of humans on foot walking down the sidewalks with purpose. I was sure most were pedestrians armed these days in preparation for a zombie ambush. The rest, well, they'd be food.

I inhaled, puffing out my little chest with the pride I'd have to swallow and abandon. After life shit on me again and again, I had a feeling one day I would get my break, a chance to show the world I could do more. Be more. As an abandoned and neglected foster kid and half-demon, no one expected much out of me. But I'd promoted from lowly janitor, kissing human's asses, to Desk Agent in Hell, where I manipulated human's asses. I prepared to climb Corson's corporate ladder until I choked on clouds. Getting trapped in a cat's body wasn't in the plan, but once I resolved that small inconvenience here soon, I planned to soar with arms wide open.

And I knew exactly how to do it. This zombie apocalypse was really angering the king. While I was up here, I could find my dad and solve Nick's negligence. The former being personal, and the latter being the secret to choking on clouds. Unfortunately, to achieve my sky-high plans, I first had to eat the humblest, most shameful pie by asking the most humiliating favor from my sworn enemy.

"Edie?" I swallowed a lump in my throat and squeezed my eyes shut. "Can I... Can I ride in your pink purse?"

"What? Why?"

I opened my eyes to see all of them staring at me like I was a leper. I whispered, "Alleys freak me out."

"What?" she repeated.

"Alleys freak me out!" I shouted on a high-pitched panic.

Lewis didn't move a muscle, holding as still as a blade of grass in a dead field. Ford snorted and displayed a satisfied smile. Corvina was polite enough to hide the curve of her lips.

Edie barked laughter. "Why? There's nothing here but garbage and various indistinct fluids."

"And mice. I also don't have a fondness for cats, believe it or not."

Ford shook his head. "Do I have to find some kitty booties for you? I'm sure someone's grandma wouldn't mind knitting a couple of pairs."

Corvina laughed and covered her mouth. "Sorry."

I growled. "Look, the portal is just down this alley. Let me ride across the scourge of the city, and I'll be forever grateful."

"It's him!" A man's voice lifted above the noise of the city around us. That couldn't be good.

I turned my head. "Did you guys hear that?"

"Hear what? A mouse skittering on the ground?" Ford's shoulders shook with silent laughter.

"Get him now!" The same voice, now much closer, crawled down my fur. Something was very wrong.

Humans and their shit hearing. Craning my neck around, I searched the sidewalk for the voice's owner, expecting to see a man charging at full speed. No such luck. I searched faces. None I recognized, and none paying any attention to me. Not much different than when I'd pushed my janitor's cart down the nearly empty halls, ignored as a piece of equipment, an eyesore to behold, an inconvenient hamper on the walking space for the more elite employees of NBB—those who stuck around after hours.

I had plans, and I wasn't going back to that life. Switching on my demon vision, I scanned the busy intersection filled to the brim with gray-clouded pedestrians. But on the south side of the street, cutting through the crowd with a calculated speed to not alert humans, a pack of Supers prowled closer. One broke away from the group, disappearing into the sea of fog.

I recognized those faces. "Incoming! Shifters, six o'clock."

Lewis and Ford immediately zeroed in on the targets.

"They're back," Lewis said, digging into his pocket for a weapon.

Ford searched for exits. "I don't know about you guys, but I'm not about to scale a ten-foot chain-link fence down this alley. Cat, get us into Hell now, or it's going to get messy."

"We can't go storming in there in a panic. The front desk demon will trigger all the alarms, but if you were looking for suicide, that's an efficient way to accomplish it. There's an alternative portal we can take."

Edie flashed a short dagger as the incoming wolf pack closed the distance.

"They know I'm alive now, and they won't quit until I'm not," Lewis said, fighting back tears. "Get out of here before it's too late. I can't let you get hurt for my troubles."

"You're helping us, so we were helping you," Edie said, gripping the handle.

"Are we really going to do this in view of the public?" Corvina asked, clutching her backpack to her chest. "Aren't there rules about that kind of thing?"

"Cat," Edie said. "Teleport us out of here."

"I can't do that! Remember what happened when I tried to bring only you? I collapsed, and you were a disoriented mess! We fight or flee. Take your pick."

"Move and I'll take your head," a gravelly voice startled me. The shifter who'd broken from the group had circled back around, catching us all off-guard. Standing behind Corvina, the shifter pressed a short baton with blades embedded through it against her throat. Not exactly the same ooga booga club.

That was a bad sign.

Corvina whimpered. "Don't hurt me."

Ford tensed, ready to throw down, but he held firm with his jaw working out his tension, respecting the orders to protect Corvina's life.

"One shout and you'll have dozens of witnesses," Edie threatened.

The wolf shifter, in his upper-hand position, took on a mocking tone. "And those ordinary humans will be so confused. Was it a coyote, a fox, a wolf? Why was it in the city? Where did it go? It couldn't have been an animal here. I've been watching too much TV." His smile curled into something sinister. "You'll have a dead girl, and I'll scamper away free."

Begrudgingly, everyone waited, tensed and ready to fight at the drop of a sneeze. The remaining shifters approached casually, drawing no public attention.

"Lewis Gard, my elusive younger brother." The leader, Skip, nodded in acknowledgment. "For someone who would've been better off dead, I'm surprised you continued your garbage route. The audacity to think we wouldn't find you. But I'm actually glad to see you again. It means I underestimated you twice, but it won't happen again."

"You can't hurt him here," Edie said with a scowl.

Corvina's fear, with the blade pressed to her throat, was palpable.

"Oh? Why do you think that?" Skip asked her.

"Those people"—Edie nodded to the passersby—"may not understand what they'll see, but we will identify every one of you."

Each of the shifters glared at each of my crew.

Skip laughed. "If that's the way this goes, then none of you will be left to identify us."

Out of ideas, I asked, "What do you want with us?"

"Oh, look. It's Lord Fluffybutt." Skip strolled around the crew, but the tension among them held firm, ready to snap. "With you? Nothing. But little old Lewis here needs to come with us. If you insist on inserting yourselves into our business, then that's a different matter."

Lewis shook his head to stop Edie from saying anything, but she didn't listen, as usual. "Walk away, Skip. I'm only going to warn you once. Just go."

Two of the wolf shifters chuckled, and Skip darted them a warning look. "Is that so? What are you going to do?"

Ford reached into his pocket and pulled out a corked glass vial. He opened it and slammed the glass to the alley floor. It shattered on impact and yellow smoky plumes danced around their feet. The shifters coughed and coughed, harder and harder, as if under an asthmatic attack.

Lewis coughed, too.

Giving up, Skip gestured to the others to flee. Corvina was released, and she ran to Edie's side. Lewis staggered in the opposite direction of his brother's pack, trying to reach clean air.

In a downtown alley strewn with garbage? Good luck with that.

With the gas creeping around, I said, "We can't go through the portal now. A hostile attack at the door will also trigger alarms. We have to take the alternate entrance."

Lewis came back, having decided to not scale the ten-foot chain-link fence for fresh air. He waved his hand in front of his face. "What was that?"

"Wolfsbane," Ford said with a sly smile.

"You turned wolf poison into tear gas?" I asked.

"It worked, didn't it?"

Lewis coughed and swiped at his eyes. "It burns like hell but thank you. I owe you my life."

Ford's smile slid away, and he stiffened, as if not wanting to make friends with the enemy.

"Cat says the door's compromised, so we're going to the other portal. Let's go," Edie said, wrapping her arm around Corvina's shoulders.

"Where's the other portal?" Ford asked, following in their footsteps.

"Not far. I'll show you." I took a few steps forward. "Uh, about that ride?"

Edie groaned. Releasing Corvina, Edie leaned over and opened the pink purse. She whispered, "Baby."

"That's Lord Fluffybutt to you." I hopped inside and tried to ignore the pungent stink.

19

The Hunt

"THIS IS IT." STANDING across the street from NBB, I craned my neck up to the cracked twentieth story of the building that once housed a robust force of people working on creating life-changing antibiotics. But Nick Barnes screwed up and now he was stuck in demon prison. *Sucks to be that guy.*

"Last time we were here, it wasn't fun," Edie said.

"Hope you brought your hiking shoes," I winked at her.

"Why?" Corvina asked, holding her arms across her chest.

"The elevators are out of service." I led the way across the street until we reached front the door. I teleported through the glass and waited for the others to follow.

The interior hadn't changed since our last visit, so I was confident I didn't need the purse to disguise myself. Thank hell. The crew followed behind, heads scanning the lobby for dangers or threats.

Edie shot a beam of light ahead of me, but I didn't need it. Teleporting through the heavy door, I waited until the others joined me in the darkened stairwell.

The hefty door pushed opened and in funneled the mismatched crew. The door closed behind them, leaving only squares of light from each floor's access doors.

"Now where?" Ford asked.

"Tenth floor. Meet you up there." I teleported and waited for the others.

The demon history texts marked the locations of all Hell portals. One was pegged at this building. Andras's office was on the tenth floor. It was also the location where he ran into us. Even though I'd cleaned this office space as a demon for years, I didn't know exactly where the portal was. Now that I thought of it, that was weird. Why wouldn't I have known about it? It's almost like pieces of my memory were stitched onto other pieces, blocking important information and leaving irrelevant information. Adding another task to my list of saving the world—finding the memory demon who scrambled my eggs.

Voices carried up the echoing stairwell. A flashlight beam shifted around like a disco ball. Ford teased Edie about her stamina. Corvina shuffled up alongside them. Lewis's quiet steps were almost impossible to hear, considering his size—silent as a mouse.

I shivered.

Mice weren't *that* silent. I hated that simile. For some reason, the filthy creatures haunted me, and entering an abandoned building and creeping in a darkened stairwell didn't help any.

Around the final bend, I watched my crew ascend. "I thought you were stealthy hunters?"

"The building's empty," Ford said. "You didn't tell us we'd be tracking and killing Supers here."

"Don't you own a security company? Isn't being on your toes kind of your modus operandi?"

"Don't get smart with me, cat," Ford said.

"Where's the portal?" Corvina asked.

"Somewhere on this floor."

"Somewhere?" Ford asked. "What we supposed to do—knock on every door?"

"Not quite. Let's go." I turned to face the steel fireproof stairwell door leading to the tenth floor.

Ford pushed on the door, but it didn't open. "It's locked."

"Let me try." Lewis shifted around the women in the tight space and gave a shove. Bupkis. "That's weird. Aren't these doors supposed to be unlocked in case of an emergency?"

"Seriously? Move aside, men. Let the women handle this." Edie faced the door and waited until the others gave her clearance. With a swift kick to the door, Edie said, "Ow."

"Looks like no one's getting through this door without a key," Corvina said. "Is there another stairwell?"

"Seems like whatever caused the explosive damage on the top floor sealed off the stairwell from the outside, preventing anyone from running into danger," I said, from what I knew of the building. "I'll pop over and see if I can unlock it. Hang tight." I teleported through the door.

Looking up, the lock mechanism was far too high for me to reach, and there was no furniture in sight to use. Unless I happened to find a pack of C-4 explosives, we were stuck. I teleported back to the stairwell side of the door. "I can't unlock it for you."

"Back away," Ford said, drawing his pistol.

"What are you going to shoot? It locks from the inside," I protested.

"It's better than standing here all day doing nothing. Got any better ideas?"

Lewis stepped forward, head hung low. "I can try something."

"Be my guest." Ford waved him through and holstered his pistol.

Everyone gave the lumbering man beast plenty of space to shift. Lewis meekly kept his head down, just like when he'd been telling his story of the contract from his family and the ghoul farm.

My patience ran dry. "Any day now, wolf."

Facing the door, as if hiding his face, Lewis said, "Promise me you won't shoot."

Ford chuckled. "No can do."

Corvina stepped forward and touched Ford's arm. "It's fine, Lewis. If you think shifting will get us through the door, do it. But I do have a question."

"Sure, kid," Lewis said, still facing the door.

"Can you control yourself in animal form?"

Lewis shook his head, and I caught a smile there. "I promise I won't hurt you."

"Great," Corvina said.

"Here it goes." With a shimmer in the air and a blur of the big man, he disappeared.

"Where did he go?" Edie asked. "Do you see him?"

"No." Corvina asked, astonishment in her voice. "How do you miss a wolf? Can shifters teleport now?"

"Maybe he wasn't a wolf shifter?" Ford said with uncertainty, turning in place, looking up, and then looking down. "Or a really tiny one."

I looked down just as the others did. There Lewis was. White fur, four tiny feet, long scaly tail, and those white wispy whiskers. The purest of evil. I screamed and leaped into the air, landing on Ford's back with claws extended—not on purpose—and Lewis waddled right under the door.

Ford gripped me with a grimace and tore me off. My complete terror caused my legs to start pedaling in the air, refusing to touch the floor. A few of my claws tore, but the pain didn't register. I panted, but oxygen wasn't reaching my brain. Before my eyes, an army of mice charged me, climbing up my arms and legs (for some reason, I pictured himself human-shaped during this nightmare), and chewing... All the chewing. Tiny nails like razors slashing at my skin as the gnarled toes climbed my flesh.

"Guess he really is afraid of mice," Corvina said.

My vision tunneled into darkness. The last image in my mind was of a sea of infected wounds festering, instantaneous gangrene climbing up my body like a sentient black ooze devouring me from the outside in.

BEHIND CLOSED EYELIDS, I smiled. Warmth coddled my body, and a heavenly gentle scratching behind my ears had Mittens purring. Having no clue what the hell happened, I blinked, willing my eyes to adjust to the dim interior. My paws weren't on the floor. A faint whiff of vanilla entered my delicate nose, and the scratching became long strokes.

I was in Corvina's arms, being pet like a cat. A little freaked out, I said, "Ah! Put me down this instant. What do I look like to you?"

"A cat." Corvina set me on the floor.

"I'm not. Got it?" The rest of the crew filled in around me, and I met their gazes. "What going on? What happened?"

"You fainted...dramatically," Corvina said. "But Lewis unlocked the door for us, and we've been scouting around for this Hell gate portal. Since you couldn't walk, I carried you. So far, we haven't found anything out of the ordinary."

Lewis shifted into a mouse, which was impossible if he were the brother of a wolf shifter. "We need to talk about this," I said to Lewis. "For now, follow me."

I didn't remember where the portal was either—if I ever knew, which was impossible. I worked here, and Andras brought me to Hell, so why couldn't I remember how? Starting at Andras's office was a logical first step. Down the hall and around a bend, I stopped at his office. I remembered that much.

"Through here." I nodded at the chief information officer's door, and Ford entered first, weapon drawn.

Flashlights lit up the tidy office, and I went inside. "Any doors in here?"

"No," Ford said.

"Hmmm. This way then." Instinct moved my feet back down the hall, tracing steps I didn't remember. Around a corner and further down, I stopped at a utility closet. Made sense. I'd come here all the time to restock. "Open this."

"The closet?" Edie asked. "Are you sure?"

No. But I didn't need to admit that. I worried they'd tire of waiting and return home. Worse—they'd think I was teasing them or distracting them from something important. I needed that trust, so very fragile, tethered only by a single frayed string.

Weapon lifted, Ford nodded to Lewis, who silently understood his instruction. The door opened with a soft creak, and Ford entered, flashlight shifting as he ensured the safety of the room. "It's clear, but I don't see any door in here."

Positive it was somewhere around here, I crossed the threshold. Blue light lit up an invisible doorframe on the far side of the broom closet. "It's there!"

The humans and shifters crammed into the closet and closed the door behind them. The phosphorescence and flickers of blue reminded me of something, but I just couldn't put my proverbial or metaphorical finger on it.

"You sounded way too excited to have found it. You didn't know where it was, did you?" Edie asked.

I mumbled something in my defense, and then said, as a distraction, "Watch out for that, it's sharp."

Heads turned, and I flicked my tail.

"I don't see anything sharp," Edie said. She reached out for the glowing rectangle on the wall. "And there's no knob on this door. How do we open it?"

Not a clue, but I didn't want to admit that either. Buried instinct guided me to the frame where I waited. "Well, here's where we figure out if your spell worked, Ford."

"If not, it's Edie's fault," Ford reminded us.

"You can't blame me for your incompetence," Edie said.

"You interrupted my spell. My skills have nothing to do with it."

"Technically, they do," Corvina mumbled.

"Stay close," I said. "Keep your eye out. If we're approached, don't say anything." I walked toward the light. The area where a door would be split down the middle, revealing a glowing blue portal to Hell.

Taking a deep breath, I crossed the threshold, where legions of demons awaited an unauthorized intrusion.

Let's hope no one tipped them off.

20

Warning

"I DON'T KNOW WHAT I expected from Hell, but this wasn't it. It's freezing in here," Edie rubbed her arms for warmth. "Where's the blistering heat? The tortured screams? The endless flames?"

Corvina hugged her bag tighter. Either out of fear or to conserve body heat, I wasn't sure. Flaming sconces lined the damp stone floor and walls. A moldy scent accompanied a soft trickle of water, like a medieval dungeon's passageways.

One perk of being a demon meant the cool air didn't bother me.

"Our Hell, the real Hell, isn't what the stories led you to believe," I said.

"Is this an old sewer line under the city?" Lewis asked.

Huh. Interesting thought. "The only way to reach this place is through the various portals around the globe. So, by that definition, I would say no, but I've been fooled before. This way." I cringed as dampness permeated my fluffy paws. I forced myself to focus on the task at hand and keep alert for incoming guards—and not on potential mice lurking around the corners.

None of them were as terrifying as the silent and large, hulking mouse shifter behind me. Soon, this nightmare would be over. Just a little farther.

"Where is the front desk guard we needed to sneak past?" Corvina asked.

"That was the other portal. This one is more...backdoor."

"Why didn't we use this one first? We could've avoided the wolf shifters," Corvina added.

I sighed. "This is—or was—a popular portal. I was trying to avoid running into demons unnecessarily. Okay now? Shush, before we get caught." A scuffing sound stilled my paws. "Wait."

The others behind me slowed to a stop, and I listened again.

"What is it?" Ford slipped a metal blade from a leather holster at his hip.

The scuffing stopped.

"Guess it was nothing," I said slowly. "Let's go."

Corners and long halls passed by. I'd expected to encounter someone by now. Glitter was down here somewhere in the north wing. Whichever way north was. "Ford, did you bring a compass?"

"Are you lost?" Ford's exasperation led me to believe asking for an assistive device, no matter how mundane, was a mistake.

"You didn't bring us down here for fun, did you?" Edie said. "If you leave us in this maze of hell, I'm going to hunt you down and kill you myself."

I believed every word. "Relax. I don't exactly have the schematics memorized, but torture is in the north wing. In the words of Ford, *ergo*, the prison cells are in the north wing—where my body is, and where we will find Nick Barnes. We need to go north."

"Take a left," Lewis said.

Skeptical, I asked, "How do you know?"

"Growing up as a mouse with wolf brothers, getting lost meant death."

"Fair enough." I swung left, and the others followed. Muffled screams echoed down the hallway. I smiled. "We're almost there. You were right. Try not to get distracted by what you see."

"What are we looking for? I mean, how do we know we found your body? Are there name tags above the cells?" Edie asked.

"Search for a human-looking body that's not moving but also isn't rotting."

"So, sleeping?" Corvina asked, clarifying my gruesome visual.

"That works, sure."

We quietly stepped from iron gate to iron gate, observing the prisoners one at a time. Most of them lounged in their cells, staring at the walls, or sleeping. Yellow ooze, purple scales, red flecks like dandruff—man, I was glad I'd started out human with...skin.

"Some of these demons are just gross. Hey, this one, iKat! He looks like a human who's sleeping," Corvina said, pointing into a cell.

I skittered over, and a body laid supine on a cot, but at this height, I could only see the dirty treads of the demon's boots pointing toward the ceiling. "Pick me up for a better look?" At this point, I was willing to suffer a little indignation if it meant the end of this cat punishment.

Corvina lifted me up, and I frowned at the gruesome face. "Not me."

She set me down. The prisoner lifted off the cot and gripped the bars. "What's going on down here?"

More prisoners approached their bars and rattled the iron with little effort. They snarled and shouted, but their scare tactics didn't work on my crew. However, the commotion started to concern me. Time was a limited resource.

Lewis said, "What about this guy?"

Knowing the north wing held hundreds of prisoners, my enthusiasm for escaping my fur prison waned. I jogged over and Lewis picked me up for a better look, without me having to ask.

The long layered brown hair, strong curves of the jaw, and stubby beard matched the face in the mirror. "That's me!"

The crew closed in around my body and gazed upon my magnificent face.

"How can you tell? His face is in darkness," Edie said.

"Demon vision mixed with cat vision. I can see better than you."

"Oh, right," Edie said with interest.

"I'm going in, and I need you to get me out." I calmed my excitement and centered my thoughts. With a focused visual, I shifted out of the cat's body and toward my own, but I hit something. An invisible field, preventing me from crossing the bars. "Damn it."

"What's wrong?" Corvina asked.

"There's a protective ward on this cell. I can't get through. The gate needs to be opened first."

"How?" Edie asked.

"A key ring should be hanging nearby," I said.

The crew moved fast, searching the walls between the cells for keys on a hoop. Passing dozens of prisoners only roused them more.

"We're running out of time," I yelled over the noise.

"They're here!" Ford yelled and darted toward the keys at the end of the hall, but the access door next to it opened, stopping Ford short.

Stopping me in my tracks, too.

"What's going on down here?" Heather strolled toward Ford, blocking his reach to the keys, heels making their telltale clicks against the stone floor. The smirk on her face had Ford walking backward, away from her approach. Smartly, he shut his mouth.

"Heather?" I asked, redirecting her.

"Hello, Malaikat. What brings you..." she trailed off, tilting her head and lifting a brow while sizing up my crew.

"It's good to see you again, and nice to see you healed well," I said, trying to distract her from looking too closely at the veiled crew. So far, Ford's spell was working, at least a little. "My friends and I are busy."

"Friends?" Her nose scrunched, and she glared at Lewis. "Something about them isn't right. You, big guy, have we met before?"

Lewis shook his head, but he also remained silent.

With narrowed eyes, Heather moved her gaze back to Ford. "What are you wearing?" She walked up to him and reached out to the amulet hanging around his neck. I needed to draw her attention before the little flying flags became blaring alarms.

"Heather, hey, I've been meaning to ask you something."

It worked. Heather gazed down at me. "Like what?"

"If you wanted to go out on a date. With me." Yep, I said it. Desperate times called for desperate measures.

Heather scoffed. "Maybe in your natural form I'd consider giving you a ride." A memory brought a smile to her face. "You know, if you were who you're supposed to be, I'd love to take you anywhere, after lots and lots of groveling, of course."

Edie's brows popped, and she shared a look with Corvina.

"Me?" What was she talking about? What did I do?

"As fun as that sounds, though, it can't happen," Heather finished.

Inspiration hit. I could use her sentiment against her. "Don't you think being cursed inside a cat is an unfair punishment for borrowing a sandwich? Help me get my body back. Then I'll take you up on the offer." I tried my best charming smile despite the leathery nose and puffy whisker pads.

Heather cringed. "You want *me* to help *you*? Oh, that's rich."

I'd underestimated the amount of groveling I needed to do. "Please?"

The urge to lick my paws overwhelmed me. *No, no, not right now.* The paw came up and Mittens demanded a foot washing. I cringed with each lick. "I'm not...choosing...to do...this."

"You're supposed to be doing your job on the surface. If the king finds out about your little side quest down here, he may just change his mind about keeping you alive."

"Look at me." I held back tears. So close to being a whole person again, and the one woman who'd helped me learn the ropes in Hell laughed at my uncontrollable licking. "Take pity on me."

That was some seriously pathetic pie, and I was munching through it.

Heather glanced at my veiled friends and back to me. "We've been doing just fine all these millennia without you. The zombies threatened to upend everything, destroy everything, but somehow, they're in control. We don't need you, but for some reason, the king wants you alive. But if you slip out of line, I will kill you."

"You just...said...the king...favors me."

"Forgiveness is easier to ask for than permission. But I'll admit, it's no fun when you're like this—for you—so I'm going to enjoy sitting back and watching the shameful punishment continue. Your unusual buddies are not welcome in here." With a dramatic and unnecessary snap of her fingers, Heather teleported my crew away. To where, I didn't know.

She didn't even need to touch them. Heather was much stronger than me.

The forced licking ended, and I stood on all fours. "Why are you doing this? What did I do to you?"

Heather folded her arms across her chest. "Of course, Andras erased that part. Don't want the little king's pet to carry guilt."

Her sarcasm was both confusing and irritating. Andras said it was an electricity-and-water accident. My friend erased my memory and lied to me about it?

"Enough!" Andras's booming voice stole both our attentions. My friend had teleported right next to us. He filled out his suit in a way that rivaled the mouse shifter's unusual size and strength. "Heather, you're interfering with the king's plan."

"Like I care."

"You should. During war, there is no room for disobedience. And you, iKat, don't belong down here. Both of you, get in line or the king will make changes and neither of you will like it."

"Oh," Heather said with mock terror. "You mean the king will leave that dreadful office of his and actually *do* something?"

"Same M.O. with you always," Andras said with a shake of his head in disapproval. "Hundreds of years and you've never changed. Please, this once, for your own good, leave iKat alone. And you—"

I smiled, waiting for my friend to help me out.

"Don't ever come back down here again, or you'll be behind these bars, too, and anyone else helping you"—he glared at Heather—"will find themselves without a pulse." Andras folded his massive arms across his thick chest. To anyone else, his commanding posture might be terrifying, but not to me. I'd seen the demon's natural giant, purple-scaled, shiny, iridescent lizard-demon look, and he wasn't intimidating at all—just pretty.

But now the stakes to my crew's lives were just raised. Assuming they weren't already dead.

Heather glared with hatred at Andras and said, "Here's what I think of your precious pet."

I had totally lied about wanting to take her out on a date. Before I threw that tidbit of truth in her face and defended myself, I was forcefully ejected from Hell. A teleport against my will. In a blink, I was dropped into a darkened field...ripe with mice, and my crew was nowhere to be found.

21

Search

Tall, dry grasses crackled under my paws. Trees surrounded the nighttime field, and the only light shined from the quarter moon. The cool air was completely still. Not a single fur on my body fluttered. The flapping of wings overhead belonged to bats swooping at insects. To me, that was Mother Nature at her finest. (If she could've skipped mosquitoes and mice entirely, the world would've been a better place.)

Not a footstep came from anywhere—both a relief (because mice) and a worry (because where were they?) And not a groan reached my ears—also a relief—because I didn't need a zombie ambush now either.

"Edie? Corvina? Lewis?" I called, my voice swallowed by the shrouded landscape. "Ford?"

Where did Heather send me? And where was my misfit crew? Were they even still alive?

A soft rustling nearby, so soft it could only mean one thing, sent my stomach lurching. Of all the places Heather could've dropped me off, the middle of a grassy field squarely in the middle of nowhere was the worst.

I was curious about what I'd done to make her so angry and demand groveling, but that was a problem for another day.

Desperate to escape the tiny hellbeasts, I darted through the field, keeping my eyes peeled for signs of my crew, but not holding onto much hope. Heather wasn't known for being nice.

Paws pattered against the ground, but still I saw no one, nor did I see the end of the vast field. Mittens ran out of energy too soon. Slowing to a walk, I called, "Edie? Corvina?"

Still nothing.

I couldn't get anything done staying out here. With a moment's concentration, I teleported to the cabin.

The lights were out, the door closed, and the driveway empty. That wasn't a good sign, but just in case Heather somehow managed to drop them off at home, I strolled up the porch and teleported inside.

"Edie? Hello? Anyone here?"

There weren't many places to hide in the small cabin. I checked the bathroom and under the bed. Both places were void of humans and mouse shifters.

Where else could they be?

With a worried and tired sigh, I teleported straight outside the utility closet at NBB Pharmaceuticals. With no electricity and darkness having descended upon the city, only the orange glow of streetlights penetrated the exterior glass walls. No one, in either direction, was around. I listened closely and not a single sound reached my sensitive ears. Normally, a light bulb would hum, or the heating system would kick in, fans would turn, the whisking of equipment. A creak of the foundation.

Nothing.

I teleported through the stairwell door—the one Lewis crawled under in his mouse form—the only memory I'd love to forget. Popping my ears up like little satellites homed in for delicate sounds, not a noise echoed through the stairwell. Not a footstep. Not a shuffle. No throaty moaning, either, but at least that was good news.

Since Heather didn't react violently to my crew, it would make no sense for her to have teleported them into a prison cell. And if she did, I wouldn't have a clue how I was going to rescue them. I had one more place to check before venturing down the possibility she'd locked them away, and I'd have to ponder the effort involved in a rescue or replacement situation.

I teleported to the sidewalk outside the NBB building. Staying in the shadows, only a few people walked along the sidewalk. Across the street, the Prius, Silverado, and Ford's SUV were lined up at the curb, but no one was inside. I craned my neck to see if they were loitering nearby or just returning from a nearby business when sprinkles of rain fell.

Hadn't I been pissed on enough lately?

Across the street from NBB was a twenty-four-hour coffee shop, and without a thought to customers' reactions, I teleported inside. Something was oddly familiar about this place, but I didn't know why. Janitor pay wasn't conducive to barista-brewed coffee.

"Cat?" A whisper.

I spun at Edie's voice, excitement taking over. Around a small circular table, my crew sipped on steaming coffees. Edie set hers down and scooped me up into her arms. "Hide. We don't need to be kicked out now."

And for that moment, I was totally cool with being cuddled.

"For a while, I thought Heather sent you to join my body in a Hell dungeon."

Corvina chuckled nervously. "She can do that?"

"Sure. I'm more surprised you're alive, honestly."

Corvina's wide eyes focused on her drink.

"It was touch and go back there." Lewis sipped from his cup. "That demon sensed something off about me."

"She almost recognized you from the Menominee massacre," Ford said. "But the good news is, my spell worked."

"Almost doesn't count except in horseshoes and hand grenades," Lewis said and sipped again.

"I can think of a few other things," Edie said with a sly grin. "So, how does a shifter with a wolf brother end up as a mouse?"

Lewis set down his mug and tugged at the neckline of his shirt, and I curled up for story time. I didn't know everything about every faction myself.

"When a shifter reaches the age of maturity, his chosen spirit animal at that moment becomes his. For generations, the Gard household was one of wolves. Our coat of arms features the wolf. It was expected I'd become one as well."

Lewis sipped from his coffee, as if the story was painful to tell, but I wasn't interrupting him. "Before my change, I was scrawny, believe it or not. Skip and his friends picked on me. They refused to include me in anything they did, and living out in the woods, there wasn't much for me to do without a driver's license. Both my moms were gone on council business all the time."

Edie and Corvina exchanged glances. Ford lifted his brows, but no one said anything about Lewis's revelation.

"I had a pet. His name was Cheese. Every day, I'd bring him food in the field near a pile of old lumber, and he'd come hang out with me. Many days I wished to be like him, so I'd have a real friend."

I couldn't stay silent any longer. "You had a pet *mouse*? Voluntarily? What is wrong with you?"

"iKat!" Edie and Corvina hissed.

The coffee shop manager shot them the stink eye. Ford hid his grin behind his mug.

Ignoring my outburst, Lewis finished, "When my first shift began, I wished to be like Cheese."

Lewis sipped and swallowed, staring at the table's imperfections. "My first shift was earlier than usual, so I was able to hide it for a few years, but when my moms found out, the demons mediated a contract between my moms and the vampires. I've been working for the vamps ever since."

What did his moms get in return? "Well, that explains why the Wolfsbane didn't sicken you. Not a wolf."

Everyone else stared at the table, silence thickening like an unpleasant, lumpy gravy.

"Tomorrow night we try again?" Corvina asked.

I lifted my own furry brows. After that kerfuffle in the dungeon, I thought I was going to need to pull out some serious, manipulative begging. "You're willing to?"

"I mean, we were so close," Corvina said. "Your body was right there, and the keys were within our grasp. Hardly any demons were there. Just a little more luck, and we'd get your body and find Nick. I think we can do it."

"We need a stronger spell," Ford said. "Something that will stop us from being sent away by a snap of the fingers."

"Heather almost recognized me." Lewis shifted his weight in his seat, uncomfortable with the atmosphere. "I don't want to be the cause of your failure. And if we're caught, I can't exactly shift."

"I can't wait to get my hands around Nick Barnes's throat," Edie said. "With Heather lurking around, we need arms like yours. We need you, Lewis."

Lewis looked up, and his lips curved into a small smile. "You want me to go with you?"

"This is iKat's party. What do you say?" Edie asked me.

On what planet would I turn down free muscle? "As far as I'm concerned, all willing are welcome."

"Then I'm in." Lewis smiled broadly, but it quickly turned to a yawn. "But first, sleep. I have a shift in the morning, and I'm gassed out."

"I'm off tomorrow," Edie said.

"I have a shift at the library in the morning, too, but I'm available the next couple of days."

"I'm available at night, as long as someone doesn't call off," Ford said.

"When humans are sleeping, demons don't have surface work to do, so there's more of them in Hell doing administrative work.

We'll have better luck going as early as we can in the daytime," I said.

"I'll text a day and time that works. Plan for after shift, but before dark," Edie said.

"I'm going home," Ford said.

"Same here," Lewis said, standing.

"I'm going to the dorms. I don't want my roommate getting me kicked out for not being there. I have to assert my dominance over my half of the room."

"I'm heading back to the cabin. You coming with me, iKat?" Edie asked, still cradling me in her arms.

"I like that plan. The fridge is a nice nap space."

"Then it's just you and me tonight, cat," Edie said. "Let's go before the manager sees you."

Slumber party with the slayer. Too bad I didn't have my body back tonight. I could've used it, and I was certain Edie would've liked it. At least the crew was willing to try again. I was so close to having a normal life I could almost smell those clouds.

22

Extra Help

Steam roiled off the pot on cabin's small stove. Ford promised us a delicious feast if everyone helped scour the books for a stronger veil. Corvina's nose was buried in the stacks of books on the wobbly card table. Edie paced the small space, open book cradled in her arms, lips moving with the words. My neck hurt from watching her. She stopped and said, "What about this one?"

Ford rested the ladle on the spoon rest. "Let me have it."

"Cow's Tail, Dew of the Sea, Hare's Foot, and Catgut."

"I must object at the last two ingredients, I said, scrunching my nose in disgust. "No wonder witches were burned at the stake."

Ignoring me, Ford said, "I have the rosemary and clover, but I don't have the others." He snapped a fistful of dried noodles in half and dropped them into the pot. "Any unusual directions?"

"Oh, this one requires a Blood Moon," Edie said, finger pressed against the page.

"That's too far away. Keep searching." Ford stirred the shallow pot of sauce and licked the ladle. He tipped his head side to side, deciding if the flavor was worthy of his name. I couldn't eat noodles, so I couldn't care less.

Corvina slammed shut the top book. "This is useless. There's nothing here about a stronger veil. Is there a stronger witch—man or otherwise—we could call?"

The dirty look Ford sent her made her recoil. "I mean more experienced. Someone who knows what we're looking for and where to find it."

I sighed. "Wildabeast."

Everyone turned to me.

"Who?" Edie asked. "Sounds like something that needs slaying on principle."

"Wilda Rivers, I presume?" Ford answered. "She's a very powerful witch."

"That's the one, and best buds with the king, so I'm not sure how much she'll help." I stretched my long spine, itching to get back into Hell.

"How do we contact her?" Corvina asked.

"Summoning spell," Ford said. "Or if you have her cell number. That works, too."

"I think I can get her cell," I said. "Be right back."

"Wait, where are you going?" Edie asked.

With a quick smile, I teleported to the alley Hell gate—the one the shifter pack had stopped us from using in the first place—and I passed through the portal before my brain focused on the filth. Hiding behind a potted plant from the distracted desk demon, I teleported to the hall of management offices. (Screw office policy.)

Andras was an information demon, so he usually lurked at the surface, extracting whatever data Hell needed. When he was between assignments, Andras drowned in paperwork.

The true hell.

Unable to knock, I yelled through the door, "Andras? Are you in there?"

"iKat?" The surprise in his friendly voice was clear. "Come in."

His office down here wasn't much different from his NBB office—sparse, tidy, and windowless. But Andras wasn't his usual stacked bouncer-type in a sharp suit. The overly large demon didn't bother glamouring himself from me. He was covered in purple scales that glinted in the overhead lighting, like an oversize iridescent lizard.

Glancing down at me, he shifted into his human shape.

"I already saw you. No reason to stress yourself to hide your lizard form."

Andras frowned. "Lizard? I'm dragon-like. I'm not a lizard."

I shrugged. Whatever made him feel better.

"Are you alone?" he asked.

"Just me. Are you going to throw me in prison, or was all that puffy threatening an act?"

"Welcome to my office. How've you been? What's the weather like?" Andras said, patting his desktop for me to meet him face to face. I leaped onto the desk, careful to avoid messing his papers. No need to extend the torture for my friend.

"Your office is comfortably organized," I said, appreciating the neatness. "I like it."

Andras smiled and leaned back, lost in thought. "We always did get along."

"We did, which is why I need your help to get out of this cat, and you didn't answer the question about throwing me in prison."

With a casual motion, Andras scratched my back. Mittens didn't hate it, so I let the demon do it. "I told you it's not safe for you to be down here, and I meant that."

"I figured as much. Was your threat to kill my friends real?"

"I wanted to scare Heather into backing off, but you have to stay out of the dungeons. Otherwise, she'll know it was a fake warning, and she'll use that against me with the king. I don't want the king upset. You've met Glitter. You understand."

I shivered. I had. "I don't intend to come back again." I would've crossed my furry toes if I could've. I didn't like lying to my friend, but did Andras really expect me to let my body go after I was so close?

"Good. But I can't help you. No matter what I believe about the king's punishments, I can't go against his orders." Andras rubbed my head, and Mittens purred. "This is awkward, isn't it?"

"Eh, I'm not complaining. Look, I'm not asking you to disobey him." My tail reached up with the euphoric feelings pulsing beneath my fur.

"What do you need from me?"

"I need to contact Wilda Rivers. Aside from asking the king directly, I don't know who else knows how."

Andras smiled. "But you assume I can."

"You're the king's number one. If you can't, then no one can."

Andras brushed the loose fur from his hands. "You're right." The demon released his human glamour, showing his lizard shine again. He glanced at the office door. "I want to help you."

"Can you write down the instructions for my crew to understand? I don't have pockets or thumbs, though."

"Crew?" Andras lifted his brows as if he had no idea.

"A mouse shifter, a man-witch, a hunter, and a...uh..." I wasn't sure what Corvina was, so I left out that detail. "Young human woman. They're kind of helping me while helping themselves. It's a tenuous truce."

"Interesting." The thoughtful look on Andras's face made me uneasy. Did I say too much?

I frowned. "My instructions, please?"

"I want to level with you, iKat. After all that's happened, you deserve my cooperation and apologies."

"Is this about my memories? It wasn't an electricity-and-water accident, was it?"

Andras raked a hand through his natural hair and stood up. He paced the small office. "It's not safe for me to tell you."

"Then write it down. I can still read."

"You were my assignment," Andras continued, ignoring my request. "But I screwed up. If the king knew..."

"Screwed up what?"

Andras paced, speaking to himself, "No, no, no. It's not right. This whole thing is such a mess. Could I? No. The more he knows, the worse it is. Just like last time."

"Last time?" I spun around on the desk, facing the stressed demon. "Are you taking about the demon trapped in a ferret?"

"If only Gremory were here, I'd ask him whether or not I should..." Andras trailed off.

"Andras!" I leaped down to the floor and faced my panicking friend. "I just need you to write down how to contact Wildabeast. That's it. No one's getting in trouble."

Andras stopped pacing just before stepping on me, face drawn with worry. "You must leave at once. Hell's guards are on high alert after your last unauthorized visit. You coming here now is just..."

"My only option?" I finished.

"Unwise."

"Then help me and I'll go," I pleaded.

The worry knitting Andras's brow never faltered. After a stretch of silence, the big demon nodded. Turning to his desk, he scribbled on a piece of paper. "Here's how you summon her. But I must warn you, her price is steep."

After being trapped in a cat's body, nothing was worse. "Got it."

Andras wrote the instructions for far longer than I expected.

"What kind of phone number is it?"

He folded the paper. "You know what magic does to electronics. This will work." He held out the paper and shifted it around as if searching for a place to tuck it. "Um."

"Put it in my mouth. You'd think I could find a pouch to tie around my neck, but then again, I don't have thumbs to use it... The longer I'm stuck like this, the more depressing it is." I held my jaws apart, and Andras placed the paper near, and I clamped onto it.

"Good luck. This isn't how things were supposed to go."

I nodded and teleported to the gate. Without the desk clerk noticing, I slipped behind the potted plant and darted through the portal. In an instant, I teleported back to the cabin. I didn't know what upset my friend so much, but after my run-in with Heather, I didn't want to stick around, risking mine and Andras's lives.

Not until I was ready.

But now I knew someone messed with my head, and they were on my list next.

INSIDE THE CABIN, CORVINA, Edie, and Ford were eating spaghetti dinner at the cleared off card table. My stomach grumbled. I should've detoured for my own meal.

"Hey, did you get it?" Edie asked, setting down her fork.

I dropped the paper to the floor and tried to unfold it with my paws. No luck. "Right here."

"What does it say?" Ford asked.

"I don't know."

"I thought you could read," Ford said, teasing.

"I thought you could do a basic veil, man-witch, but here we are."

"Don't call me that." Ford squinted at him, aiming his fork in a potentially threatening way. After a beat, he added, "There's food for Mittens over here."

I followed his fork, and on a small plate was a can of cat food.

"It's salmon and chicken. Hope you like it," Corvina said.

I blinked back tears of gratitude and dove in face first. After licking alley-grime-coated fur and areas of a cat that should never be tasted, anything would be delicious. But this stuff had just the right lumpy soft texture with slurpy gravy. It sounded gross, but it wasn't half bad. "It's better than it looks. Thanks, Ford."

After licking my plate clean, Edie scooped it up and started the dishes.

Ford unfolded the paper and stared. Frowning, he turned it upside down. "I don't know this language."

"Let me see," I said and jumped up onto the table. It shook under my weight. "You guys really need a new table."

"Gonna buy us one?" Edie asked.

"Sure. I'll pull my credit card out of my ass."

"You don't need to remind us that you're a freeloader," Ford said.

Ignoring that dig, I said, "Let me see the paper."

Ford continued squinting and turning the paper, and finally the man-witch slid the square across the surface. I studied the markings. "Demon language. He really wanted to be sure only the right people understood the information."

"Translate and I'll write," Corvina said, pen to paper.

I studied each word and the syntax and translated the demon language into English. "Come forth, wise one. In brackets, write her name, Wilda Rivers. We command thee to answer the call. No harm shall come to thee."

"That's it?" Corvina asked.

"There's a potion to be mixed and a ceremony to be performed. That was the chant."

"Oh. List it out and let's get started."

I read the remaining instructions and the list of ingredients until I reached the last one. "Hmmm. Not sure if I've got this one right. Ever heard of Witch's purple? I don't think that's quite it."

From the floor near the bookcase, Ford dragged out his tackle box of supplies and set it on the table. He opened the lid. "You mean Sorcerer's Violet?"

I studied Andras's paper and played with the words in my head. "That sounds better."

"It's periwinkle. I have some."

"All right. I got it." Corvina tore off her transcribed translation and handed it to Ford.

"Are you missing anything?" I asked the witch.

Ford read the list. "I have all this. Let's do it."

Finally, a break. This whole human body retrieval thing was taking far too long.

23

A Price

I WISHED FOR POPCORN while standing on the folding table. On the eastern edge of the chalk circle, outlined in symbols and lit with candles, Ford stood with a wand, chanting. A swirling cloud of gray formed in the middle, a small, temperamental tornado about to rip apart whoever disturbed it. Corvina and Edie stood off in the corner, free of weapons but uncertain what would happen, looking nervous as the mystical gray cloud condensed and fell.

Wilda Rivers appeared in the middle with a scowl that could wilt plants.

"Is she a demon?" Corvina whispered to Edie.

Edie shrugged her shoulders.

"Who summoned me here?" Wilda Rivers folded her arms across her chest. The woman favored tight athletic wear and wore a short blond pixie cut. It was her stature and broad arms that made her intimidating. Add in the respect of The King of Hell, and Wilda was one scary woman.

Now I could ask a real witch how to make us invincible to the demons in Hell. "The King of Hell requested your assistance on spell 247,014, but you declined."

Wilda traced my voice to me and smirked. "Oh, hey, fluffy. Of course I remember that. It was stupid to try it, but I see Corson did it, anyway. Figures. And I'm guessing he didn't read the fine print."

Well, that couldn't be good news. "Fine print?"

"If you don't reverse the spell, it's permanent."

"Yeah, I figured I got about nine lives or about eleven years to get myself out of here, whichever comes first."

Wilda shook her head solemnly. "Far less than that, tough guy."

"Er, how much less?"

"Look, I'm on a tight schedule, and I'm not in the business of *giving* help."

With a grumble, I asked, "How much?"

"Depends on the request but make it quick. I'm busy."

"We need a spell to veil their true form from demon detection." I nodded toward the crew, as if Wilda couldn't figure out who I meant.

"Is that it? Shrouded in Safety," Wilda said.

"I tried that. Wasn't strong enough," Ford said.

Wilda flipped her hands in the air, annoyed. "There's one other option, but you'll owe me a very expensive favor if I disclose it. *Very* expensive."

"Anything." As long as she didn't need cash, I would do whatever she wanted. Hindsight would probably tell me that was a stupid thing to say, but at the moment, I didn't care.

"It's called *Demoniška eksperimentų knyga.*"

"English, please?" Corvina asked.

Wilda darted her a look of annoyance. "The Demon Book of Experiments. There are only two known copies in the world. The king keeps his personal copy locked away where only he can access it. Believe me, I've tried." A sly smile lifted her lips. "The other was lost centuries ago. In the witch circles, rumors are the demons move it around regularly, but even those in charge of its location don't know what it is. It's highly coveted and incredibly dangerous. Anyone who possesses it instantly becomes a target of all factions of the supernatural world on, under, and above the earth. It has the capability of destroying the planet as we know it."

"Sounds impossible to get," Edie said.

"Thus, the crux. I upheld my end of the bargain. iKat, you owe me, and you better never forget."

"What if I do?" I hated to think of the consequences of slighting the most powerful witch in known existence.

"I'll remind you."

"Oh. Uh, thanks."

With waves of her hands, the gray cloud reappeared, swallowing the witch whole, and when the clouds drifted to the floor and dissipated, Wilda vanished.

"That was dramatic," Edie said.

"I'd like to learn that trick," Ford said.

The front door to the cabin opened. Lewis took in everyone's faces and the markings on the floor. "What did I miss?"

Edie and Corvina took seats at the table next to me. Lewis closed the door behind him and lowered himself onto the last open seat. Ford packed up his candles and supplies.

"There's only one way for us to get into Hell without the demons tossing us out or locking us up for an eternity of torture. But the answer is in a super dangerous, incredibly rare book. One copy is in the hands of The King of Hell, and the other has been lost for centuries, circulating with a secret demon guard group who don't know what they have," Edie said.

"So, we either wing it down there and hope to live or iKat goes alone?" Lewis clarified.

"There's another option, I think," Corvina said slowly. All eyes fastened on her. "At the university, there's an antique books area of the library. It's locked down hard. I'm not even supposed to know it exists."

"You snuck in," Edie assumed.

"Duh. And I'm pretty sure I read a book cover with a Lithuanian title on it resembling what the witch said."

"Are you sure?" Ford asked.

"Sure enough to go look. What's the worst to happen—I get fired? Kicked out of school?"

"Arrested for breaking and entering, possibly burglary, unauthorized use of government ID—" Ford started.

"It's a college, not the CIA," Edie said.

"State school," Ford said, closing the tackle box on the table.

"Okay, fine. Mr. Security Company and Miss Unlawful Employee, what do we do?" Edie said.

"We go in disguise. No weapons, no leather. Just us and a couple of backpacks. Wear torn jeans and hoodies," Ford said.

Lewis lifted a lip in disgust. "You can't be serious."

"Have you been on campus lately?" Corvina asked. "Late at night, classes are over. Average students are gone. Slackers never showed up in the first place. So only the overachievers are pounding the coffee for late night cramming. It's our best chance."

"Do students bring pets in purses?" I asked with a note of hope in my voice.

"No. Animals aren't allowed, except service dogs. You can't even fake that," Corvina said.

I didn't have the ability to glamour myself, but I couldn't let my crew go without me, and there was no way I was waiting in the car like a dog. "You can't leave me behind, so bring me in the purse. I'll be quiet, and no one will find out I'm a cat."

"My pink purse?" Edie asked.

"It fits the college culture." Corvina shrugged.

I sighed. "Can you put a different scent in it?"

"We don't have time for that," Ford said. "Get dressed and meet at the college. Which parking lot?"

"B, north side of the school," Corvina said. "It's right outside the library, but park on the far side, away from the lights, and don't group up. It'll look suspicious."

Ford smiled, hands on the tackle box. "You would make a great security guard."

"Really?" Corvina beamed at the compliment.

"If you can handle a gun." Ford winked and carried the box back to the bookcase.

Corvina burned bright red. Her mind was definitely in the gutter.

Why would The King of Hell keep his most valuable possession in a local university library—the most powerful book, sought by factions across the globe? I had been a little lucky lately, but finding this ultra-rare, super-duper book sounded too good to be true.

All we could do was prepare...for the worst.

24

Rare Antiques

I SQUINTED THROUGH A hole in the purse seam while trying to hold my breath against the eye-watering vanilla, but I couldn't. Instead, I focused on not coughing while Edie strolled down the university hallway in her squeaky sneakers and pulled the library door handle.

It was locked. A badge reader blinked at the side of the door. The lights were on, and a few students sat at tables or picked through the stacks.

"Now what?" Edie whispered.

The sign on the door said badge access only after six o'clock. Corvina had left that detail out. "Wave your hands to get their attention. One of the students can let us in."

"Yeah, and security will be the first to notice."

"Text Ford."

Edie pulled her phone out of her back pocket, sending me jerking around in the bag. She tapped out her message and a moment later, her phone chimed with the response.

"What did he say?" Too much longer in this purse and I was going to start sneezing.

"Just shut up, okay?" Edie's tone was angry and sharp.

Interesting. I tipped my face up to the magnetic top and tried to catch a glimpse of her face. I couldn't. "I don't want to stay in here all night. What did he say?"

With a grumble, she said, "Wave my hands until a student notices and lets us in."

I chuckled. "What's wrong with that idea?"

"It's stupid. I'm not a student. I don't look like a student. And he wants me to bring attention to myself while carrying a cat in a pink purse? This whole idea was a waste of time. We should've suited up and stormed Hell like..." Edie trailed off.

"Kamikazes?"

"Shut up." The sharp tone was back.

Footsteps approached from the other side. A student pushed the metal crash bar, and the door swung open, sending a blast of air. I inhaled through the seam in the stitching. Sweet relief.

Edie's hand caught the edge of the door before it closed. "Silly me, forgot my ID."

"Sure, whatever," the student said, completely disinterested.

The student walked away, and Edie slipped inside. She headed straight for the back corner where we'd planned to meet, bypassing a few students at tables, and many rows of books sitting undisturbed.

At the end of the stacks, Lewis sat on the floor, legs crossed, squinting through his glasses at a book.

"What are you doing?" Edie asked.

"I'm incognito. Guess it worked." Lewis shut the book and stood, slipping it back on the shelf. He pointed to a door next to him with another badge reader and a sliver of a window. "Through here is a hallway of unmarked doors. I'm guessing we're going that way."

I used my demon vision to search the area for wards, but I didn't see any. There weren't any demons around, either. "I expected more security if the book is that important."

"The witch said they might not know what they have," Edie said.

"Let's hope so," I said.

Ford and Corvina appeared around the corner, both carrying backpacks. Corvina was all smiles.

"Right this way." Corvina pressed her student ID against the door's gray security pad, and nothing happened. She tried again.

"Is it supposed to work?" Edie asked.

"I haven't tried it before, but it should. I work here."

She swiped it near the pad a third time.

"Don't do it again. You might get flagged, and because of that, I'm not using my handy tool belt buckle." Ford set down his backpack and unzipped the front compartment. He lifted out a small spice container and grinned. "We do this my way."

"Isn't that going to trigger something, too?" Edie asked.

"I'm hoping for a jumbled signal that makes the security guards, if there are any, smack their console. If it lasts longer than that...well, just move fast." Ford zipped the bag and tossed it over his shoulder. With a few words mumbled, he waved his two primary fingers and tucked the spice container into his pocket.

Magic fingers. I stifled a chuckle.

"What spell was that?" Corvina asked.

"Doesn't matter. Any spell disrupts electronics. Oh, check your phones, guys. They might be glitchy."

Everyone glared at the man-witch. Ford kept waving his fingers, but no sounds came from the lock.

"Try it," I said, desperation for a second helping of fresh air threatening my patience.

Ford pulled on the door handle, and it opened. With a self-satisfied smile, he said, "Imagine that."

"You sound surprised," Edie said.

"I only half expected it to work. Good news, no one came running."

"Yet," Lewis mumbled.

The crew entered the plain hall, and I teleported out of the purse. Dramatically, I inhaled a few deep breaths and jogged to keep up.

"Up here on the left," Corvina said.

Rounding the corner was another hallway with only one door. This one had a biometric fingerprint scanner and a number pad.

"Can you get through this door?" Ford asked.

"I did once," Corvina said.

"How?" Ford asked.

"A power outage."

"If the circuit breaker is nearby, Ford could fry it," Edie said.

"Or I could just turn it off. Why do you always jump to the most destructive solution first?" Ford said. "That's assuming I can find the breaker, and we can get back here through all those locked doors before someone figures it out and flips the switch. Not likely."

"How about conjuring a lightning storm?" Edie asked.

"Can you do that?" Ford asked with mock astonishment.

"No, dummy. I meant you."

"Why would you think I could do that?" Ford shifted the heavy backpack on his shoulder.

Edie shrugged and mumbled, "Powerful man-witch there."

I cackled.

"Excuse me?" Ford spun on her.

"You're excused," Edie said. I remembered why I liked her...for a hunter. "Corvy, what do you think?"

"I think the best way in is another of Ford's magic fingers."

Ford growled. "Can we not?"

"Why not try your 'tool' this time, or does it only announce your personality defect?" I asked.

Ford glanced down at his belt buckle. "It's a custom multi-tool, and no, nothing will work on a lock like this."

"Hey guys," Lewis said, interrupting the entertaining banter. "The longer we're in here, the higher the chance of us getting caught. I'm not too worried for myself, since I can squeeze..." the shifter drifted off and his eyes widened with the answer.

I figured it out at the same time. "Go under."

"On it."

"You know, you're kind of useful after all," I said.

Edie sent me a glare, but I only shrugged. Humans didn't like liars, but apparently, they didn't like honesty either. So confusing.

Lewis shifted into a mouse. Despite myself and the warning, the visual of a human-shaped being morphing into a tiny critter of Hell made me scream. Ford, Edie, and Corvina shushed me while Edie clapped a hand over my mouth.

Corvina checked over her shoulder. "C'mon cat. You knew what he was going to do."

My frantic panting wasn't lessened by her ill attempt at comfort. "Easy for you to say. Have you ever been afraid of anything? I can't control it. It's like a thing following me around, ready to spring a jump scare on me with no notice. It's horrible. And pardon me if it's inconvenient."

"You had notice," Corvina said, calmly. I wanted to tell her where to shove her infallible logic, but the door popped open.

A proud Lewis held it for us. "All clear."

I trailed behind the others. Just like the rest of the library, rows of books filled the tight space, but unlike the public facing side, these were ancient texts and scrolls, and the dim lighting was enough to give anyone a headache. The floor was covered in crushed burgundy carpet, and the ceiling's recessed light pucks were surrounded by dark fabric. Moody and soundproof.

This was the kind of place prideful snobs wearing expensive suits sat reading books for 'enlightenment.' I wished for so much leisure I could ponder about the meaning of life. Instead, I spent an inordinate amount of time running from death. And with that, an ick feeling settled over me. Hesitantly, I followed after the others, crossing the threshold. A cold blast of air pummeled me from above. Dread numbed my toes. Might have been the air, but dread was more likely.

I shouted, "We tripped demon wards. We have to get out now!"

"What?" Edie said, turning toward me. "We just got here. What are you talking about?"

"You don't feel that frigid air blasting you?"

Edie held up her palms as if catching drops of rain. "Nothing. The mouse scare probably has you on edge. Just wait here."

Not a chance. I jogged up to the student. "Corvy! Is there an emergency exit in this room?"

"I never looked, but I would guess so."

The door we entered slammed shut, but no one else seemed to care.

"We have to get out of here," I said. My pulse quickened. That ick feeling was part of the warding to keep wandering demons away. I'd failed to listen to my instincts.

"It was just the wind, cat," Edie said, walking back to the closed door to reopen it.

"From what? There aren't any windows."

"The air conditioning?" Edie turned the handle and pushed. With a frown, she shoved harder and jiggled the handle. "Well, this sucks."

"Lewis, Ford, find us an exit! Corvy, get that book now! Edie, stay with me. We're going to have company."

Edie bent at the waist and slipped a knife from her ankle holster.

"You were packing anyway?" I asked.

"Always."

"Good." I extended my claws in preparation.

Boots thundered down the hall outside the biometric door.

"Maybe they won't be able to get inside?" Edie asked hopefully and then groaned at the beeps from the electronic door lock. "This reminds me of that time I was trapped in a mansion, fighting vampires."

"Yeah? How'd you escape?"

"I was ten years old. It was also the day I learned bullets don't kill vamps. After the mangy monsters cackled at my lame attempt to shoot them, my parents cut their heads off."

"How does this story help us now?"

Edie shrugged. "Cut their heads off."

"I'll keep that in mind." With my tiny, useless claws.

The door swung open, and demons in human glamours and wearing suits poured into the room. The first one shouted, "No guns. Don't harm the artifacts or you will answer to the king directly."

That was convenient.

All of them rushed right by me as if I were invisible. Edie took on two of them, swinging and striking with her knife. The remaining demons split up, hunting the rest of the invaders. I trailed the one headed in Corvina's direction. Around a set of stacks and behind a box, Corvina sat on the floor, prying open a duffel-bag-sized wooden crate.

"It wasn't locked before," she said and did a double take at the incoming demon. Her mouth gaped open in surprise, and she said nothing more.

I had to do something, or the young woman would be slaughtered. "The King of Hell commands you to freeze!"

The demon turned around in confusion, and I leaped at his face and clung to his flesh with sharp little claws. I scratched while the demon pulled, making the gouges worse. The demon tumbled into the stacks, knocking books free. I gripped his face like an octopus, wishing he had more limbs, too.

"Corvy, get the book and get out!" I yelled.

The lanky woman lifted the whole crate on shaky legs and rushed for the exit.

I positioned myself around the neck of my attacker while the meaty hands struggled desperately to remove my furry body. Secured in position, I rabbit kicked the demon's throat with razor-sharp claws. Blood gushed, and the demon yelled in frustration. He lifted a book from the shelf and swatted me with it, but I ducked one of the blows, and the demon hit his own head.

Sensing the demon's balance wavering, I leaped free, and the demon crashed to the floor, palm pressed to his opened throat, mouth gaped in panic.

Satisfied I neutralized the attacking demon for now, I chased after Corvina. Around the corner, Edie pulled her knife out of a second demon. He dropped to the floor, next to the first.

"Where's Corvy?" Edie asked, covered in gashes and sliced clothing.

"Didn't she come this way?"

"No."

We bolted down the aisle of shelves. At the far corner, hidden behind a bookcase, now tipped on an angle, another pair of demon bodies slumped unconscious. A low secret doorway behind them led to an unlocked iron gate with bloody handprints on the bars.

"This doesn't look good," Edie said and pushed the gate further open. Through that narrow passage, a grated square that looked like a heat vent opened to a normal hallway.

Edie ducked through, and I easily followed. Down that short hall was a heavy door with a crash bar and an emergency exit sign. Edie shoved it open hard enough to stress the hinges. The door shut behind us, with no way to go back inside.

On the library's back lawn, Corvina huddled, torn and bleeding, over the locked wooden crate. Just beyond the landscaping, cleverly disguising the emergency exit to the library's secret room, the remaining demon fought *with* Lewis and Ford—as a team.

The enemy of my enemy is my...I thought, watching in horror as a horde of zombies attacked.

Where the hell did they come from?

25

Zombies

IF A PERSON INFECTED with The Annihilator returned to life, which could happen in as little as minutes after death (and as long as days later, but that was a separate case altogether with embalming and rotting tissue), the newly reanimated person was incredibly dangerous, because they generally didn't know they died, and the infected retained the personalities of their former selves. So the family would be in denial and would ignore advice to flee. Once the bacteria took over the rest of the body's functions, the infected person became the mindless, mouth-breathing idiot who fed on the living to spread the bacteria, and a simple bite resulted in the newest victim becoming the next perpetrator, if they came back to life.

So there was a chance of being munched on and simply dying, and that was the best-case scenario.

We knew Nick Barnes was responsible for releasing it, but the mystery was why did the zombies randomly appear in pockets? And how did they seem to disappear without a trace? Regardless of the news warning people, life went on as usual on the surface for the most part, less some population and add in some crime. A sighting was nothing more than a police call. The brave ones carried knives to fight back, but they could easily be overrun, depending on the size of the group.

With our hands on the most valuable book in the world, a swarm (the term for a grouping of zombies hadn't yet been established, but since 'swarm' was used for parasitic insects, it seemed fitting) of zombies sprang up to destroy everything.

Demons showing up made sense—their wards protected their assets. The zombies didn't. I didn't have any more time to ponder. A variety of mismatched people, wearing jeans, T-shirts, high heels, trucker caps, and yoga pants snarled and grabbed, trying to bite or outright kill Ford, Lewis, and the remaining demon, leaving Corvina unprotected.

Edie rushed over to assist Ford, creating a shield between the zombies and Corvina. Without weapons for school security, Ford punched. Lewis lifted and threw zombies against the brick wall of the library. Many of them squished flat on impact. Edie used the knife she'd snuck in.

The remaining demon was getting two-timed. I didn't know him, but I didn't want to see him die. I spit a fireball at one of his attackers, and the demon tossed the second zombie to the ground. The demon conjured a fireball and launched it at the second zombie. The first zombie, currently with an eye socket on fire, was dressed like a football fan who'd staggered out of a bar. As the flames burrowed deeper, it flailed its limbs with a screeching cry.

The demon frantically craned his neck, overwhelmed by the incoming threat. He stared hard at Corvina and the prize in her hands. "Forget this. I didn't agree to die. I'm out." The demon teleported away.

A zombie with a business suit—a nice one at that—got past the shifter and hunter pair, and it headed straight for Corvina, who frantically tried to open the book-containing crate. I opened my tiny cat jaws and drew forth another tiny fireball. Being smaller, I had to work smarter to be effective. The businessman targeted Corvina. While it shuffled over to the lanky woman, I spit a fireball into its eye socket. The injury only disrupted its focus for a moment, and Corvina lifted her head. Seeing the opportunity, she kicked its knees, sending it falling. I leaped onto its chest, avoiding swinging arms, and sliced its throat with my front claw.

I'd just killed someone's brother, uncle, or father. All because Nick Barnes unleashed a devastating bacterium on the city. Good thing Nick resided in demon prison, or I would personally visit the bastard with my flaming cat jaws.

Maybe I would anyway just for spite.

The zombies blocked the path between Corvina and our parked vehicles. Lewis, Ford, and Edie fought, but they were wounded and outnumbered. If a zombie bit any of the crew, they were done for. "We need to get Corvina out of here!" I yelled.

"Go!" Edie yelled while slashing open a zombie's belly. The woman's face was impassive as her intestines spilled on the asphalt like a bowl of spaghetti. She tripped on her own innards and crashed to her knees. The zombie kept coming, but her hand-knitted sweater was toast. "Get Corvy out of here!"

I might not have thumbs, might not wield a gun or blade, but leaving reduced the chance my crew would survive, and I needed them, but I needed the book more.

I could always find a new crew. Still, I hesitated to leave, but another half a dozen zombies shuffled over, and I padded over to Corvina. "Put me in your lap and hug that crate like your life depends on it."

With a puzzled look, she nodded. I stood in her lap on all fours while Corvina squeezed her eyes closed and hugged the crate. I centered and cleared my thoughts, concentrating on moving her and myself to the cabin. With a mental shudder, I opened my eyes to find us sitting on the front lawn—if you could call it that—of the hunter's cabin.

Corvina fell over and placed a hand on her head.

"The first trip is a rush," I said.

"I'd say." She rubbed her forehead and lifted the box with a grunt. "The crate is so heavy. Let's get it inside." Corvina carried the crate to the cabin door, and with a turn of the knob, she walked in.

I followed. "You guys don't lock the door when you leave?"

"There's always someone coming or going, so it's a waste of time."

I searched under the bed and in the bathroom, just in case. "Besides the mangy wolf shifters, who else knows about this place?"

"Wilda Rivers, but no one else that I know of." Corvina set the crate on the floor and blew out a breath of air.

"Then the crate should be safe here for now. It needs a secure hiding place, like under the floor or behind a wall."

Corvina pulled out a stack of books from the bookcase. "There's a false wall in the back of this bookcase." She felt around and pressed, popping open a small cubby. "But it won't fit unless we get it out of the crate."

Clever hiding place. "What do you have for tools?"

Corvina sighed. "Edie has the tools in her car."

I distinctly remembered Edie's disastrous Prius. "Where?"

"In the trunk…under the garbage." She scrunched her nose.

"Ah, okay then. Is there anything around here we can use to pry it open?"

"I'm sure Ford left some utensils." Corvina opened and closed drawers, rattling their contents. She held up a metal spatula. "How about this?"

"Give it a try."

Corvina kneeled on the floor and pushed and pulled with the spatula.

It bent—the spatula, not the crate.

Corvina chuckled and bent it back. "Guess not this one. Maybe he won't notice." She put it back in the drawer and picked something else.

"How did you open it last time?" I asked.

"The box wasn't locked."

Hmmm. "They doubled down on security since you were there last. Lock the front door, just in case, and keep trying. I'm going to get Ford."

"If you think I should, then okay." Corvina rose and locked the front door. "Good luck."

"You, too."

I teleported back to the library. Calling it a war zone was an understatement.

BRANCHES OF DECORATIVE TREES were snapped. Bushes were bent over. Bodies scattered all over the lawn and areas of the parking lot. Blood. So much blood. I found my battered and bruised crew sitting at the open trunk of Edie's car. I rushed over, and Ford diligently tended a gash on Edie's thigh, while Lewis worked on her arm.

"I'm getting tag teamed." Edie chuckled.

"What happened?" I asked, ignoring her levity.

"Zombies just kept coming. Did that demon bounce out of here?" Edie asked and flinched when Lewis tightened the wrap around her arm.

"He did. Were any of you bit?" Once dead, the coughing was no longer an issue, only the bites. Since they were alive, that was the next biggest concern—that they wouldn't be soon.

"I don't think so," Edie said.

"No one touched me," Ford said. "The zombies felt organized. I thought they were too stupid for something that coordinated."

Ford applied butterfly bandages to her thigh and wrapped an elastic bandage over it, securing it with a hook. Lewis finished his wrap and helped Edie to her feet. She wiped her upper lip with her forearm, smearing blood across her face like a macabre mustache.

"Where's Corvy?" Edie asked.

"At the cabin, trying to open the crate."

"She's safe?" Edie relaxed her stance.

"I believe so."

"Good." Edie's face darkened once again with rage, only this time, she focused on me. After all the killing she'd just done and the injuries sustained, I didn't think she had the energy to fight. I backed up anyway. Edie spat blood. "We walked into that small room and demons tried to kill us, but not you. We escaped and zombies tried to kill us, but not you." She inched closer, and I retreated a few more steps. "And then you left. Poof. A magical exit to safety. Imagine that. Only after they were all dead, you returned."

"What are you getting at?" I backed away from her and the other two, who were now giving me apprehensive glares.

"You set us up."

Lewis and Ford closed the distance, shoulder to shoulder with Edie. A line of soldiers ready to attack on command.

"Is it true, cat?" Ford's snarl sent shivers down my spine. "Did you do all this to destroy a cabin full of hunters? Do you get a trophy in Hell for it? Is there a cake and ice cream party celebrating each death?"

"Even as a demon, I didn't think you had it in you," Lewis said, joining them. "I mean, you're a cat. Your lot is just as bad as ours, and I thought that made you one of us."

Now I was irritated. "We're colleagues at best. We had a deal, a mutual agreement. I plan to uphold that deal until it's complete." I wanted to tell Edie the truth, what I'd told myself since seeking Edie in the first place. "I did—" *plan to use you and leave...*I was going to finish.

Edie cut me off and snarled, "Just as I guessed! I trusted you, and you betrayed me. Us. Get out of my sight before I lop your head off, you despicable *demon.*" She emphasized the last word as if it were an insult. "You're just like the rest of them. Why didn't you just call your demon friends to the cabin and end us there? Why all this ruse?" While ranting at me, she stalked closer with her grisly, germy blade, and I swallowed a lump. All that work since the farmhouse, up in smoke. I was back at square one.

What else could I do? With the condition Edie was in, there was no reasoning with her, and she had backup—one of which was a horrifying, disgusting *mouse.* "But I—"

"Don't even give me excuses. If I ever see you again, consider your grave officially marked. Actually, I think I'll decapitate you and leave you for the crows. You don't deserve a grave."

That stung. With two angry faces—the hunters—and one seriously conflicted—the mouse shifter, I turned and scampered away.

"Go! Get out of here!" Edie shouted after me.

26

Caught

My furry legs carried me wherever they pleased, not knowing where to go. Avoiding alleys and their filth, I strolled the sidewalk under a depressing blanket of darkness. What was I supposed to do now? My crew, mangled and shredded, hated me. Their exhaustion and frustration at the zombies had to be the reason for it, but if they couldn't give me the decency of explaining, why should I bother?

Bullheaded, short-tempered idiots.

I didn't realize getting my body back would be so much work, and now I was even further from returning to a normal life. Wilda Rivers had said I had less than nine lives or eleven years. I didn't want to know how much less.

A car motored by, a soft hum through downtown at this hour. Two people laughed across the street. Probably drunk. Most definitely stupid.

I preferred physical fitness and maintaining my body's strength and stamina, but a bottle of rum sounded like the vacation I needed. How was I going to buy a drink with no money and no...human form? For that matter, I couldn't talk to anyone without risking getting shot or kicked. Although neither of those would kill me, I was concerned for my innocent ride along, Mittens, who was not supernaturally strong.

My stomach growled.

I came upon a darkened alley that, even with my demon vision, was still creepy and disgusting. Could I subject myself to the torture of dumpster diving? The alternative was to dig in the hunter's cabin for another can of cat food that I couldn't open.

This was so humiliating.

A small commercial van pulled to the curb alongside my lazy path. Two people came out, talking to each other. I paid them no mind. They weren't aiming guns after all. What could two humans do?

Their footsteps approached, and I glanced over my shoulder as a net fell over my head. Cage doors clattered and shut in my face. The latch dropped, locking me in. Engine started. Van lurched forward, knocking me off my feet. Even if I felt like trying to reason with these two humans, they'd probably shoot me for talking.

The humans in the front seats faced each other, lips moving. Just my luck Animal Control would find me. If only they focused their efforts on cleaning the streets of mice and other vermin...

To them, I was the vermin. After everything I'd done to the people who'd given me a chance, I deserved to sit and rot in a cage. So I didn't bother teleporting out. Maybe these humans would take pity on an orange tabby and feed me.

Hell, even I pitied Mittens.

Every turn shoved me into the steel wires of the cage, and I frowned. Eventually, the van lurched to a stop, flinging me again. The back doors swung open, and the woman who'd netted me collected the cage, not gently, and carried me to the side door of an animal shelter.

The man opened the doors for her, and a swath of fluorescent light stung my eyes. She dropped the cage onto a stainless-steel island in the middle of the sterile room and slid it further to the center with an ear-piercing screech. A weight scale sat next to my cage. Baskets of medical supplies lined the countertops. The walls were covered in glass-front stainless-steel cabinets, and diplomas hung in a blank space. Dr. Winifred Paxton, both MD and DVM. One smart woman.

"Got a fresh one for you, Dr. Paxton," the man said.

A woman in scrubs and smart round glasses waved dismissively at the pair of animal control officers. "Dr. Fred, please. I'll take it from here."

"Okay, fine, Dr. Fred," the man said with a hint of an edge to his voice. "I just think a woman like you deserves..."

"To have a feminine name?" she finished with raised brows.

"I was going to say more respect. Good night, doctor, and don't get bit. That one seems...off." The male animal control officer sent me the stink eye. I so wanted to stick my tongue out at him.

The doctor chuckled. "No kidding. Who knows if animals are carrying that dreaded bacterium? Last thing we need is a new variant."

"If I had it my way," the man said, "all these strays would be euthanized, just to be safe."

"Can't blame you for that," the doctor said and sighed.

"We're out of here. Hopefully, we won't see you for the rest of the night," the woman said.

The pair left, shutting the heavy steel door behind them.

"All right, what do we have here?" Dr. Fred leaned in close. A scent of hand sanitizer pinched my nose. She was an attractive woman, and yep, I gazed down her shirt. "Orange tabby. Filthy. Unusual eye color. I bet, after a bath, you'd be a very pretty kitty. Let's get you out of there." She opened the cage and pulled me out, hugging me gently and scratching behind my ears. For Mittens's sake, I didn't fight her. She inspected my ear canals and set me on the cold steel. She squeezed around my belly and lifted my tail. "There's a handsome boy. Not fixed."

I attempted a look of frustration, but I didn't think it was effective with all my fur. I flinched under her continued prodding.

"All we're going to do tonight is get you some preventative vaccines. Draw some blood to check a few things, and I'll get you added to the list for neutering."

I coughed. "Neutering?"

The doctor jumped back. "You talked. You just talked, right?"

Oops. When someone threatened the family jewels, I needed to say *something*, but now I kept quiet. No reason to have someone else try to kill me, a someone perfectly capable of rendering death in a way that looked innocent.

"It's late. I need more coffee." She shook her head and stepped out of the cramped room.

I sat on the cold steel, waiting for a chance at a meal. Then what? Leave and go where? At what point in my life did I become a drifter? A bum? Was there some official scale of bum-ness?

I'd had a job cleaning human toilets and picking up after them at the NBB building where Andras took me under his wing. I remembered running on a treadmill with my friend at my side and occasionally boxing with the demon, but the hazy details stung when I tried to conjure them. I had other friends, didn't I? And who were Chris, Stella, and Dennis?

So many questions, and I didn't know where to start. Or if I should bother. I suspected a memory demon tampered with my head. In which case, they didn't want me to know something. Because knowing meant I was a danger to them—Chris, Stella and Dennis?—or a danger to myself.

Considering the circumstances, I chose door number two.

Dr. Fred returned with a steaming cup of coffee in her hand and a fistful of syringes. She sipped and set the cup on the counter. "Now where were we?"

I was smart enough to stay quiet this time.

She brought the syringes over to me and carried over a form from a stack on the counter. She filled out the lots and expiration dates. "This is only going to be a quick pinch."

I braced myself for impact.

She signed the document and set down the pen. Dr. Fred frowned. "Usually cats are trembling in fear, hiding in the corner or searching for a way out by the door, and shedding all over the place. What kind of cat sits here like he understands what I'm doing?"

I just stared.

"Well, maybe in your wild days, you hit your head too many times. It's okay to be missing brain cells."

"I'm not stupid," I blurted.

The doctor jumped back and pressed a hand to her chest.

I meowed as a cover, but I didn't think it worked.

Dr. Fred sniffed her cup of coffee and pressed a hand to her forehead. "I'm losing my damned mind working nights. Good thing my shift is almost over."

She gripped the first syringe, uncapped it, and grasped a fistful at the nape of my neck. A rapid succession of pokes later, the doctor capped the needles and dropped them in the sharps container.

Eh, didn't hurt.

"Now that's all done. You can quarantine back here for a few days until your surgery on Monday." She picked me up and carried me without giving any scratches or pets. The doc was cautious of me now. Oh, well. I was getting used to people being afraid and hating me. What difference did one more person make?

Dr. Fred pushed me into a head-height cage stacked among many others—some occupied and some not. She latched the door shut and gave me a wary glance. The doc opened her mouth to ask me something, thought better of it, and left.

In my suffocating cubby, I had a clean litter box, bowls of dry food and water, and a blanket to sleep on. After Mittens inhaled the crunchy offering, I curled up on the blanket, and Mittens crashed hard to sleep. My need to function was exhausting the poor cat. But at least being in this cage, I was safe from anyone trying to kill me—zombies, hunters, et cetera, and so forth.

Mittens dozed while I watched the clock ticking away the time, unable and unwilling to do anything. I sighed (only in my head). The lights darkened on their timers, and other cats rattled their cage doors. One meowed its fear.

The restlessness of the other occupants had me focusing on what their problem was. They had a semi-okay meal, fresh water, a place to sleep, and a toilet—that for once humans were cleaning for them. I smiled at my contentedness to sit here, at least for a few days. I sure as hell wasn't sticking around by Monday.

It wasn't like anyone missed me.

The door to the quarantine room opened, and a light flicked on. I couldn't move, but the doctor lead Andras inside and point out my cubby.

"Thank you, doctor." Andras smiled at the woman, who sized up his bouncer-sized biceps. If only she knew he was a lizard in disguise.

"When you're sure you're taking him, just sign this form here. Please don't let him loose again. We have a population problem in our city and allowing an intact male to roam is…irresponsible."

"Understood, loud and clear. It won't happen again." Andras flashed her a charming smile, and the doctor blushed before closing the door.

Andras approached my cage. "iKat, what are you doing in here?"

With Mittens asleep, I couldn't answer.

"Hey, what's wrong?"

Yep, still nothing.

"iKat? Doc says you're alive and healthy. And...currently up to date on your shots." Andras chuckled. "She also said you're getting the big snip on Monday."

After a few beats, Andras rolled his eyes. He opened the cage and shook Mittens awake.

I stood. "What are you doing here?"

"Why did you stay?" Andras asked.

"Where else am I supposed to go? The humans helping me turned their backs on me. I'm not allowed in Hell. In case you haven't noticed, feeding myself is impossible."

"Cats eat mice," Andras said deadpan.

"Don't even say that word." I shivered. "I'll take this dried kibble instead. Thank you very much."

"It wasn't supposed to be like this," Andras said solemnly.

With a smattering of sarcasm, I said, "You mean the king didn't intentionally toss me into a cat's body, throw me helplessly onto the surface, and cut my lifespan from immortal to a maximum of eleven years, all because I borrowed a damned sandwich?"

Andras sighed. "That wasn't the reason for the punishment. It was an excuse."

That made sense. "Since someone messed with my head, please enlighten me. What was my real crime?"

"I cannot explain. If you know too much, the demons fear what will happen. I've already said too much." Andras paused and studied me. "How did you figure that out? Have you been experiencing headaches or migraines?"

"A few. If you tell me what's going on, I can choose not to do whatever they're afraid of."

Andras ran his hand down his face. "Every fiction dystopian book written has become a playbook for leadership. It's almost a joke now."

"Are you saying if I know I'm doomed to repeat my actions? I'm well aware of demon history, if I believe it's all true, and I'm fully capable of not being stupid."

Andras sighed, warring with the choice in his head. "You're my friend, and it hurts me to see you like this, so I'll help you."

Complete surprise had me sitting open-mouthed. "Uh, sure. Yeah, I'll take whatever you can give me."

"Humans historically don't do well with others of their own species. So asking your team to trust a demon, a different breed entirely, known for higher levels of intelligence but also short tempers and a lack of empathy, was a difficult feat. They might never trust you, but there's a way to get them to finish your deal."

"I'm listening." Andras was actually going to tell me how to get my crew back so we could get my body back. Why he wouldn't whisk me to Hell himself and hand it over wasn't a leap. Andras was under the king's thumb, and he couldn't get caught with a vengeful Heather lurking about. I still had no idea what I'd done to her, either.

Andras simply said, "Care."

That wasn't useful. "Huh?"

"Actually care. Treat them like friends, equals, not as humans, and a means to an end."

"But they are humans and a means to an end. You want me to lie to them?"

"If you respect them and treat them well, they will return the favor. Sure, there's a few bad eggs no matter where you go. But in general, if you treat people well, they will treat you the same."

Irritation ground at my jaw. I appreciated all Andras had done for me, but this came from nowhere. "Why do you assume I treat humans like dirt?"

"I know you, iKat." With sadness pulling Andras's features, he teleported away.

Huh. I never thought I treated anyone that terribly. I was rather good at my desk job and no matter how disgusting the toilets were at NBB, I'd never complained. What was Andras talking about?

27

Bribe

I DIDN'T BELIEVE ANDRAS at all. I treated humans well, until I realized in the cold small hours of the night, he'd meant my crew.

Little girls can catch a cat better than you, I'd said to Ford to shame him.

The dude is built like a tank. No need to make Ford feel less than, I'd said to Edie to embarrass Ford.

Shifters. Didn't you know that, miss hunter? I said to Edie, rubbing her error in her face. *Don't be a condescending ass. You lied to me.*

You had a pet mouse? Voluntarily? What is wrong with you? I'd insulted Lewis.

Insult Ford, check. Insult Ford again, double check. Lie directly to Edie, check. Embarrass the crap out of Lewis, check-ity check. What about Corvina?

Frustrated with Corvina's slow-to-process questions and apparent uselessness, I asked Edie, *What is she doing here?* That was rude, and Corvina had been afraid of me for a while.

Could I have been nicer? Sure. Did my current condition excuse such treatment? Lewis was a mouse shifter shamed and sold by his family to vampires. Edie's parents were hunters, and presumably dead now. I hadn't nailed down what happened between security guy Ford and whoever Pia was, but it likely wasn't good. And I still hadn't figured out why a college student and unknown Super had any interest in helping these people. Where were Corvina's parents? Siblings? Friends? Then there was Vale, a nocturnal Super I suspected could be a vampire, except his day job was literally during the day.

My previous life was empty, honestly. I exercised alone at home. I studied and started planning a fish tank, but I couldn't afford it, nor could I reasonably get one into Hell. What made my life so horrible to justify treating those people like they were lesser?

If Andras said treating them like friends instead of idiotic colleagues was the answer to getting my body back, then I'd do it. The effort required, in hindsight, seemed so...miniscule.

Just as I said, "I can do this," Dr. Fred pushed through the quarantine room door.

A broad smile pulled her lips. "I knew I heard you talk! I've treated all kinds of Supers, but never an actual cat. What are you?"

I stared. I had too much to do and wasting time chatting with someone who either knew too much (she wasn't afraid of me) or too little (she had to ask), meant more of my precious time dwindled. I teleported away before that whole disaster unfolded.

I needed something strong, something the humans would trust, something that would prove not all demons were evil, because I couldn't forget Edie's last words, *If I ever see you again, consider your grave officially marked. Actually, I think I'll decapitate you and leave you for the crows. You don't deserve a grave.* That sounded serious. Instead of begging forgiveness while teleporting around the cabin, dodging their blades, what could I offer them that would prove I was equally serious and seriously sorry?

Ford had already told me what fit the bill for him—beer and pizza. I was thankful for the conveniently low standards, but I had no money or opposable thumbs. I didn't have the ability to compel humans like vampires could. How was I going to accomplish such a simple task?

I teleported to the nearest carry-out pizza place and activated my demon vision. While waiting around the corner, one demon appeared on the sidewalk heading toward the liquor store next door, wearing jeans, a white T-shirt, and a black sport coat. A cigarette was tucked behind his ear. Gremory, the demon who had a unique and valuable ability, which likely explained the heavy cigarette and beer consumption.

I whistled for his attention, which came out more like the heaving of a hairball. Gremory turned his head anyway, and his irises flashed red. Releasing the door, he approached and looked down with his lips pressed thin. "What do you want, iKat?"

"I need three large pizzas"—figuring Lewis and Ford to each need their own—"and a six-pack of beer."

Gremory broke out in laughter. "I have not checked the updated future of our species but, seeing as how you are still in a cat's body, and I hear Heather is still breathing, I don't need to."

"Can you spring for the refreshments? It's my last request, I swear."

"You already owe me."

"I know. I promise I won't need you again. But I don't know anyone else who has a human face, money, and doesn't hate me."

Gremory blew out a breath. "That bad, huh?"

I nodded.

"Stay here. I'll bring it out to you."

"Thank you," I said, humbled by his generous assistance.

Gremory pushed his way into the restaurant and returned with a stack of pizzas that he set down on the sidewalk. In a blink, he teleported to and from the liquor store and set down the six-pack on top of the boxes. "You owe me two favors now."

I grumbled. "No problem."

"The hunter didn't tell you about her father, did she?"

"No details."

"Heather was responsible for Ray Randall's death."

That was likely just what I needed to sway Edie. "Is that three?"

Gremory nodded.

I teleported with the pizzas and beer to the cabin's front porch in the bright morning light, but I didn't see anyone around. Lewis's and Edie's vehicles sitting on the gravel driveway didn't matter. They could've carpooled somewhere.

On the bright side, maybe fewer bodies would be easier to convince. I stood behind the food, using it as a shield, and teleported it and myself inside. The cabin was dusty and dirty. Stacked books on the table, unopened canned food on the counter, and opened duffel bags on the floor. Almost like they'd just vanished.

I trotted over to the messy bed and leaped up. Using my better-than-average demon hearing, I listened for breathing.

One loud snore. Two sets of breathing.

An alarm clock's blaring stabbed at my ears, and I jumped away from it.

Lewis lifted from the bed with exhausted, baggy eyes and flung the sheets away.

Corvina walked in the front door, and after catching a glimpse of the big guy in his boxers, she turned around, bright red. "Oh, I'm sorry. I didn't know you'd still be in bed."

"Huh?" Edie sat up, also bleary eyed, and the snoring stopped. "What's that smell?"

That was good news. Talking to them while half asleep gave me better odds than when they were fully weaponized and alert.

"I'm late for work. Gotta go," Lewis said while collecting clothes off the floor and stuffing legs into pants. When his head tipped toward me, he paused. "Uh, Edie? You got a visitor."

"Huh?" she repeated, clearly not a morning person. Edie rubbed her eyes and waved to Corvina. "Hey, Corvy! Did you bring pizza?"

"Not her," Lewis said slowly.

Sensing the warning tone, Edie rolled off the bed and gripped a knife tucked under the frame. She glared at me with death daggers.

Remembering the decapitation party at the farmhouse, I said, "Last time I caught you in a kinky situation, it didn't go well for me."

Getting to her feet, in a tank top and shorts, she stalked closer to me with a grim line to her mouth. "I predict this won't go much better. I told you. I warned you. But I'm not surprised you refused to listen. Well, I won't be making that mistake again."

She launched at me, and I teleported to the other side of the room. Neither Lewis nor Corvina moved. They only tried to track her and my movements around the cabin, like a ping-pong match. After several attempts to chase and kill me, I landed on top of the fridge. Edie held the knife at a threatening angle with a nasty frown. "Get down here and fight with dignity."

"That's what I'm trying to do. I want to help you fight your demons—literally—but I need my body and my dignity to do it."

"We can't trust you," she said.

"How about I start with this—I'm sorry? I should've been more transparent with you. I should've trusted you to do the right thing. I shouldn't have taken advantage. I'm sorry, and I mean it."

Edie glared, still not trusting me.

"I brought pizza and beer, just what Ford said he needed to believe that not all demons were evil. Will you give me another chance?" I stood, stepping forward to the edge of the refrigerator.

Edie refused to relax her stance. The beer and pizza weren't what she needed.

"I have something you might want."

"What's that?" She still didn't move.

"The truth."

"Does it matter?"

I shrugged. "Maybe, maybe not."

"I'm listening." Edie relaxed her arm.

Lewis stuffed his pockets with his phone, keys, and wallet. "I gotta go. Garbage doesn't take itself out."

"Don't I know it?" Edie shot me a glare.

Lewis waved and left. The engine of his pickup roared to life, and the sound faded into the trees.

"I can't believe I'm saying this, but keep talking, cat."

"I lied to you by omission."

"I know."

I deserved that. "Heather is responsible for the death of Ray Randall."

Edie's glare burned, but her eyes misted. "My dad was fighting off a swarm of zombies when demons ambushed us. Demons killed him, and zombies killed her. I lost everything. I've been focused on nothing but killing all demons since, and you're telling me that snooty, evil twit I almost killed is responsible for everything I lost?" Edie's glare burned.

"If not by her hand, then her orders."

"Knowing this, you asked her out on a date right in front of me?" Edie's blade moved closer to my fur.

I backed up. "I didn't know at the time. I swear. Heather and I were colleagues in Hell for a short while. She helped me learn the ropes. I didn't know her *that* well. And she did threaten to kill me."

"Isn't that a kiss in demon-speak?"

I wanted to chuckle, but it wouldn't come out. "I'm sorry for not telling you everything I knew up front. I'm sorry for the way I treated you all. But for me, the non-deal is still on. Help me get my body, and we can take Nick Barnes down. Justice and vengeance for you and your family."

Edie sighed in frustration and exchanged a glance at the quiet Corvina. "You promise to be entirely open and honest with us?"

"Cross my heart and hope to…Never mind. Yes. I swear I won't lie to you anymore. I can't promise I won't insult Ford."

"What about Heather?" Edie asked.

"She's of one few in the king's trusted circle. Although the king is elected"—Edie scowled—"he won that election through strength. Taking Heather down will require more effort than the handful of us can manage right now. To charge after her is suicide."

Edie asked, voice sharp, "So, before, when you dangled her as a carrot, you were lying to us or wiling to kill us all?"

"I'm sorry?" I added sheepishly. "I wanted my body back, and I was willing to do whatever was necessary to get it. But I'm not like that anymore."

Edie sighed and mulled that over for a while. She looked at Corvina, and the unknown Super gave the slightest nod. Edie faced me. "Ford thinks he found a veil in that foreign book from the university."

"Wait, you were going to go without me?"

"Hadn't decided yet." Edie picked up the stack of pizzas and the beer from the floor. She placed the drinks in the fridge and spread the pizza boxes on the table. Edie opened the lids and Corvina came over to inspect the food. Edie served herself a plate, and Corvina had a slice, too.

"Save some of that for Ford." I nodded at the pizza. "It was his bribe."

"I'll convince him," Edie said, biting into a slice. "When he swings by around nightfall. Then we make a plan to kill Nick Barnes."

I still had my head, so that was a bonus, and all it costed was three favors for Gremory. I had no idea what that demon wanted from me, but as long as I got my body back, I didn't care.

28

Vale for the Veil

FORD STROLLED INTO THE cabin, dropped a duffel by the door, and his brows popped. "Who needs coffee when this shocks you wide awake?"

"What's wrong?" Edie asked with a sly smile, sitting at the table, feet resting on top.

"Did you...? Did you *clean*?" Ford's mouth gaped open in mock horror.

Edie swatted the air and made a dismissive noise. "iKat did."

Ford's face darkened as he spun on me, posturing for a kill. "You're allowing that furball back in here? Did he burn everything and hold the cabin hostage?"

Edie crossed the room, arms open to restrain the hothead. "No. He apologized, and he brought beer and pizza. There's leftovers in the fridge."

With a scowl, Ford marched to the refrigerator and opened the door. He bent inside with a grumble and pulled out a can and a chilled pizza box. He set the box on the table and popped the top on the beer. Ford inspected my offering.

"I can spot a bribe when I see one. Cat, you want to join us again? Heat my pizza," Ford said.

I tilted my head. "You said the pizza would let you trust me."

"I said beer and pizza with no strings attached would prove not all demons are evil. Do it or get out."

Did the man-witch want me to teleport his pizza to the next nearest neighbor's house and borrow their microwave? "With what?"

"Conjure your flames."

The things I had to subject myself to for humans. "For the record, I've never done anything like this before, so if the pizza goes poof, it's not my fault, and we're still even." I jumped onto the table and pooled fire in my mouth. I blew on the pizza like an oversized birthday candle. The air rippled with heat and the cheese bubbled from the flame.

I stopped when the box started curling.

Ford smiled. "See, Corvy? Don't need a microwave."

"Eat quick," Edie said. "We're going to Hell tonight after you whip up that spell you found."

"Whip up? Do I look like a chef?" A smug smile crossed his face, and he bit into the hot slice.

"You're the best at making something." Edie winked at him.

Corvina dropped her eyes, lips pressed thin. If I knew any better, I'd say the girl fancied the hothead. Shame she didn't appear to be his type.

"Well, I strive to please...anytime, anywhere."

Corvina smacked a book against the table with clear irritation, stealing their attention. We're going to Hell tonight, if you were listening. How about we get that spell going?"

Ford straightened and cleaned his fingers on a napkin. Back to business. "Let me see that recipe again."

Corvina dragged the *Demoniška eksperimentų knyga* out of its hiding place behind the false wall in the bookcase. She opened the book at a marked page and held it out to him, catching glimpses of his lips and blue eyes. "Right here. This is the one?"

Ford only looked at the page. "That's it."

Lewis strolled in, hair still damp from a shower. Good to know he didn't carry the garbage scent with him. "Are we sure messing with that book isn't a bad idea?"

"Hey, Lewis," Edie said. "Pizza and beer in the fridge. iKat stopped being an ass."

"I'm surprised you left any for me," Lewis quipped and headed for the food.

Ford skimmed the text with his finger and set the book on the rickety table. Corvina leaned by his shoulder. Lewis joined them, digging into the box of leftovers. "Oh, it's still hot and fresh."

"iKat breathed on it," Edie said.

Lewis held the slice in front of his open mouth.

"With fire," I added.

Lewis shrugged and ate.

I leaped up on a folding chair next to the studious pair. "Do you have everything you need?"

"It's not that simple," Ford said. "And no, I don't. This is heavy stuff. There are things in here I never thought possible, and I think that witch—"

"Wildabeast," I supplied. "Or, if you don't want to become a toad, Wilda Rivers."

"Uh, Wilda, yeah, if you don't fully trust her, she should *never* get her eyes on this. Honestly, she shouldn't know we have it. Ever."

"Agreed," I said. "Guard it with your life."

Ford frowned at me. "I'm only going to guard it with my life because it's the right thing to do, not because you said so."

"If that makes you feel better," I said.

"Seriously?" Edie said, taking another slice of pizza. "I thought we took care of this."

"I was being honest. If doing the right thing makes someone feel better, then by all means. But time's ticking away guys, and you're not getting any younger."

"Neither are you, cat," Corvina said with a grim set to her mouth.

I hated when she was right.

"Ford, what do we need for this spell? It isn't another Tuesday one, is it?" I asked, the urgency biting me in the ass.

Ford dragged his finger down the fragile paper, and he wrote down the layman's version of each ingredient. At least, I assumed the pages were paper. Best to keep that to myself.

"I don't have Mouse Tail." Ford paused from transcribing the recipe and glanced up at Lewis.

The big guy swallowed a huge mouthful and gestured in the negative. "I'm willing to help, but I'm not an axolotl. Sorry."

Enjoying the shifter's discomfort, Ford smiled. "That's the witch name for arisarum, not a literal tail, but I wouldn't say no if you offered."

"Where can we get some?" Edie asked.

"The grocery store?" Corvina said, with a questioning lilt.

"There's a spice shop downtown." Ford closed the book. "Corvy put this back."

Corvina dutifully retrieved the heavy book and returned it to the secure location inside the bookcase.

"We have a spice store. There's enough demand for that?" Edie asked, brow raised.

"They sell other occult wares, but I think the spices are the public facing products. Where do you think I get all the good stuff?" Fold folded his recipe and tucked it into his dark jeans. "Didn't your parents ever cook?"

"Uh, no," Edie said. "I lived off fast food and TV dinners. Spent years in motels until I was old enough to tag along on the hunts. Now if you're okay with eating boxed macaroni and cheese, I'm your girl. If you need various powders measured and mixed, don't ask me."

Ford chuckled. "I expected nothing less. I'm heading over. Are you guys staying behind to pack?"

"Me in an occult spice shop? They don't have enough insurance for me to walk in the door." Edie retrieved black duffel bags out of the closet. "I'll pack extra for this trip and catch a nap."

"I'll be back." Ford turned on his heel.

"Mind if I join you?" I asked. The more I knew about the human side of the hidden world, the more leverage I'd have, and finding this place might be useful in the future. Besides, I could use more bonding time with the hothead hunter.

Ford stopped.

I teleported in front of him. "I just want to come along. No funny business."

The man-witch sighed. "Let's go, but I'm watching you."

Unlike Edie's Prius, Ford kept his SUV pristine. Everything was in its place, no dust, no crumbs, no litter. "Your carpet looks clean."

"It is." Ford turned the wheel at the light, bringing us into downtown proper. "If I see one cat hair on my leather, you better brush it off. If I see one cat hair on my carpeting, you better scrub it off. Understood?"

I grumbled. "I got it. I mean, I'm still a cat. There's only so much I can do without thumbs."

"Use your tongue; that'll be a good use for it." Ford navigated the SUV down an alley and turned into a gravel parking space. His headlights beamed on a dumpster. Gross.

A single crooked light fixture poorly illuminated a sign reading Northern Organic Spices. Ford shifted into park and unbuckled. "The identification of who you're going to see in there cannot leave this store. No one at the cabin can find out. Understood?"

"Rules, and more rules with you. I get it. Is she some secret mistress and you need to keep it hidden from Edie and Corvina?" I teased.

"What? What about Corvy?" Ford opened his door, frowning as he walked around the vehicle.

I checked the darkened corners and teleported out. "Tell me you haven't figured out both of them are into you."

Ford stopped with his hand on the back door to the spice shop. "What Edie and I have is playful teasing. It would never go anywhere beyond that, and it's mutual. Corvina? I've never looked at her like that." Ford paused, as if considering her for the first time. "She's young."

"She's old enough to notice you."

Ford lifted one side of his lips with sly presumption. "It's normal for women to notice me."

I scoffed. "You remind me of someone. I just can't put my finger on whom."

"Whom? No one talks like that." Ford opened the door to an antique bell, and I followed on his heels.

An overpowering aroma slammed me in the face, and tears formed a protective layer against the assault. Glass jars with handwritten labels huddled shoulder to shoulder on thick wooden shelves. From my vantage point, I couldn't tell how far the shop stretched. Bins lined the narrow aisles to scoop one's own amounts by the pound.

By the *pound*.

Who needed a pound of cumin? And I thought I had issues.

"Hey," I whispered. "I'm not going to get kicked out, am I?"

Ford called over his shoulder. "Stay out of customers' sight."

With the overstuffed shop, that shouldn't be a problem. I scanned the shelves for an empty, non-stenchy bin I could climb inside to hide in case of emergency.

At the counter, a customer rounded on her heels carrying a paper bag. I ducked behind a barrel of coffee grounds and waited for her to pass. The woman's eyes fixed on Ford, saving me from a painful kick to the rib. At least something good came from Ford's magnetic appearance.

She checked out and left, and I rushed up to Ford's feet. "Can I jump up? Don't want to sit down here like...uh..."

"An animal?" Ford finished. "It's fine to come up."

I leaped onto the counter and pulled up short at the memorable Super with gray eyes, gray pallor, and black shaggy hair. I still hadn't figured out what animal remained buried beneath the man's skin. Vampire was still on the table. "Vale? You work *here*?"

"The way you say that gives me a negative vibe. You didn't mean that, did you?" Vale asked.

"Perhaps. A spice shop, huh? That's why you're never available to help during the day."

"My employees cover the day shifts."

Strange. Why would a Super and store manager never help during the day, if he was available, but kept himself unavailable each night? Most Supers fight. It was their nature, but Vale here avoided it. Even vampires liked a good fist swinging and staking here and there. "Shouldn't you be doing what Ford does?"

"I'm not fond of guns, and I own this store." Vale flashed a look at Ford, and the resident security chief nodded. Vale added, "And you've been warned to keep this information private."

"I have and I will," I said carefully. "Can I ask you something personal?"

"Maybe," Vale said.

"Are you a vampire?"

Ford's shocked gaze moved from me to Vale and back.

"No," Vale said simply.

"No, I can't ask that, or no, you're not?" The context mattered.

Vale only stared at me. He shifted his gaze to Ford and blinked. The dude was still as a statue, and I had a feeling he wasn't going to come clean on that suspicion.

"Do we have a problem?" Vale asked us both.

Ford cleared his throat and pulled the list out of his pocket. "Uh, no. We need an ingredient for a spell."

"I'll do my best."

"Got any mouse tail?"

"I do. Right this way." Vale zigzagged through the store, and I followed on Ford's thumping heels.

For the pale Super to not admit to being a vampire meant he probably wasn't one. With their victims pawing over them, they tended to have egos. That meant the only thing the pale Super could be was a shifter. Unfortunately, there were endless kinds with their own strengths and weaknesses.

Shifter, it was.

Vale climbed a rolling ladder mounted to the wall and reached for a small glass jar. Creaking the wood on his descent, Vale held out the powder. "Is this enough?"

Ford shook the container and read his recipe again. "I think so. If not, I know where you are."

"Fair enough." Vale led us back to the register where Ford quickly paid. The shifter wrapped the glass jar in paper and set it inside a stiff bag. "So, what spell is this for?"

"A veil."

"Shrouded in Safety?" Vale asked.

"Tried that one, but it wasn't strong enough."

"Then you haven't tried Smothered in Secrecy?"

"That one's not as strong."

"Cloaked in Concealment? Shaded in Stealth?" Vale's voice rose with each option and subsequent answer in the negative. Vale's blanched face somehow paled further. "You're not trying...? No, it's impossible. Did you find" —he whispered— "the *book*? *The* book?"

Ford glanced both ways to check if he was within earshot of anyone. "*Demoniška eksperimentų knyga* or however it's pronounced."

Vale shushed Ford and glanced around the store again. He placed a hand on his forehead. "How? How could you possibly...? That doesn't matter. You must destroy it. It's too dangerous to be loose. If that book falls into the wrong hands..."

"The witch told us the book was highly sought and incredibly rare." I validated his worry, which didn't help any, I supposed.

"Which witch?" Vale asked.

I snickered.

"Wilda Rivers," Ford said.

Vale gasped. "You must never let her hands touch that book. It's far too powerful, and with her wielding it..."

"Egads, Vale, I've never seen you so worked up. Before today, I wouldn't have said it was possible."

"There are two copies in known existence. The rumor is demons move it around every decade or two."

"Relax, my friend. We have it taken care of. Nothing bad will happen," Ford said, stuffing his wallet back into his jeans.

Famous last words.

"Then you must be doing the Mantle of Obscure Asylum," Vale said.

"How do you know about this spell?" I said, suspicious of his in-depth knowledge for a shifter.

Vale leaned against the countertop. "I've seen what it can do."

That was handy. "Can it make a veil strong enough to stop demons from teleporting humans away?"

"It can and much more. Be careful. Guard it with your lives, for in the wrong hands, it will mean your lives," Vale said ominously.

"Little morbid, don't you think?" I asked.

Vale darted me a look. Eh, I was used to it.

"Don't worry, Vale," Ford said. "Hey, you coming with us tonight?"

"Where?"

"We're going"—bells chimed on the front door—"to Hell to get my body back."

A woman's gasp behind us interrupted our chat. "Did that cat just..."

"Nope, just some chatter on the radio," Vale said with a friendly smile. "Can you give us a moment?"

"Sure," the customer said, hesitantly.

Vale ushered us to the end of the counter, and he spoke in hushed tones. "I told you, I protect; I do not attack."

"All right, all right. I'll remember," Ford said.

"Don't tell the other hunters where I am. Remember *that*," Vale said, and I suspected he also meant *'what I am'*.

"Why?" I asked.

"I have work to do." Vale turned and grinned for his new customer, returning to the register. "How can I help you?"

"Let's go," Ford whispered and used his body to block the woman's view of me. Out of the customer's sight, Ford said, "No need to incite mass hysteria by looking at you."

I laughed. "I knew you thought I was a handsome beast. You should see my human form. I'll have to pry your mitts off me."

"Keep it up and you won't be able to pry my mitts off...your throat."

"Oh, tough guy."

"Let's do this spell," Ford said. "Just a warning, if any demons lay a hand on me, I'll take their heads clean off. I don't care who they are."

"Sounds good," I agreed.

"Yours included."

I frowned as Ford climbed into the SUV, and I teleported inside. With the looks of this spice shop's exterior, I'd expected to get ambushed.

It wasn't every day I was pleasantly surprised.

29

They're Back

As Ford pulled into the cabin's gravel driveway, headlights illuminated the ajar front door. His brows pulled low in alarm. The best soldier the crew had, according to Edie, unbuckled and drew the gun at his hip.

"What is it?" I asked.

"Something's wrong." Ford exited the SUV and closed the door with a gentle click. He dashed to the cabin, keeping his head low. Without an announcement, he slipped through the door, swallowed by darkness.

I teleported into the cabin, and a pungent metallic stench hit my nose like the flick of a fingertip. I flinched. Blood. And lots of it. Well, the hothead was right: something was definitely wrong.

Turning on my demon vision, I scanned the small space. A group of Supers, several of which looked familiar, including Skip, had infiltrated the cabin and were now trying to kill everyone.

Edie, taking swipes and giving stabs at a shifter, still wore her pajamas. A trio ganged up on Lewis—one was Skip, using a knife, another was Wallace with a club, and the last one had the razors imbedded in his baton. These were the same shifters from before. Lewis's family.

The mouse shifter swung and punched and took a beating himself. After watching him heave a stone the size of my whole body so far it was no longer visible. Why was the big guy holding back?

Corvina huddled in the corner, watching the fight in paralyzing terror. Just as puzzling as Vale, what kind of Super was she? Two who didn't want to fight.

Strange.

I couldn't fire on Edie's shifter without risking the fireball going through the shifter and killing her. Same for Lewis, but I was less concerned about the fall-out since he could heal quickly. I extended my claws. Before I could pounce, a fifth shifter, the short one, entered the back door, and this one went straight for Corvina.

Using the element of surprise on his side, Ford cleared the shadows and sidestepped all the action, intercepting the short shifter. Stalking up behind him, Ford sliced the head off the one who'd decided to kill an unarmed young woman. The head bounced off the hardwood and rolled, sending blood decorating the floor and walls in a way only Glitter could appreciate.

I groaned. I'd just cleaned this place.

With a sigh, I leaped onto the shoulders of one of Lewis's attackers, who suddenly decided getting a pesky feline off him was more important than obeying attack orders. Holding on with all four sharp claws, I wrapped my razors around the meaty throat. "Hold still and no one else gets hurt."

The Neanderthal of a shifter didn't waver, so I pierced the flesh beneath my paws and formed a golf-ball-sized fireball in my mouth. I leaned my head closer to the shifter's neck until the skin sizzled. With a yelp, the shifter's hands opened, reaching out for mercy. "Stop! Brant is gone. Brant's dead."

About time.

Skip glanced at his fallen soldier and then followed the light to my flaming fireball. He lifted his hands palms-out in surrender. "Stop, everyone! Lord Fluffybutt, I presume? Let Aaron go."

The second-in-command shifter, Wallace, didn't listen quick enough and shoved Ford backward into the wall with a head-splitting crunch. My brows rose (sort of). They had real power hidden beneath layers of human form.

Ford groaned and cracked his neck, stalking closer. With a glare at Skip, the man-witch said, "Try that again, one more time." The shifters sent confused glances at each other.

Aaron craned his neck beneath my claws and only managed to further slice his own skin. Bright ones, the lot of them.

"You're stronger than we expected, and your loyalty is baffling," Skip Gard said, sheathing his knife. "But we have a problem."

"We certainly do," I said, but Skip ignored me.

"We do," Ford repeated. "You broke into our cabin again and threatened one of ours." The hothead considered Lewis to be one of the crew only days after insisting he'd cut the guy's head off on principle. I wondered if this wasn't just a power play.

Skip folded his arms over his chest—not as large and defined as Lewis's but close enough. "Perception is everything, isn't it?

We came to this cabin to complete our contract terms, but now we have a fallen brother someone needs to answer for."

Edie and Corvina cringed at Brant's head on the floor.

"I took his life before he killed one of us. That's understood when one attacks another," Ford said in a mocking tone. "Lewis, this is your dysfunctional family. Anything to say here?"

Lewis, with swollen eyes, a split lip, and gashes all over, stood in the corner. Two shifters pointed their dented clubs at his skull. "Don't...risk your lives...for me," Lewis said with a slur.

Skip grimaced, a sadness of one brother regretting what he'd done to another.

My fury rose. "Explain to us why you need to kill Lewis."

Skip turned to me. "Lord Fluffybutt, release him." His tone darkened when his eyes met the bleeding marks on his friend's throat.

"Answer me or walk home with one less buddy," I said.

Skip met the haunted eyes of Aaron under my claws. After a deep exhale, the leader said, "Our family was shamed by a mouse shifter and further shamed when he failed to serve the vampires to satisfaction. Our family received warning of his failure, so when the C&D was placed on his head, my family urged me to fulfill it, rather than the filthy demons, to preserve what little dignity the Gard family still had."

"C&D?" Corvina asked, confused.

"A cease-and-desist order issued by the mediating demon for a breach of contract. Also known as a hit with no chance of resurrection. Expiry papers. Order of curtain fall. Annihilation of the target. Clear enough for you?" Skip said, with an edge that made Corvina flinch.

"Who ordered the C&D?" I asked, hopeful to give the hunters a demon target less impossible than Heather.

"Heather," Skip said.

Well, damn.

"How am I not surprised?" Edie said rhetorically.

Skip added, "Heather told me there was a possibility you survived our first attack, so she put a tracking device on your pickup, Lewis. That's how we found you here the first time and knew you were still here."

Heather had been at the Menominee massacre to make sure Skip and his brothers made good on the cease-and-desist order she'd sent out. I didn't know I could think any less of her. She gave demons everywhere a bad rep.

"Someone could've stolen my truck. How did you know I survived?" Lewis asked.

"Called your work and your boss said you showed up for a shift. When you're supposed to be dead, don't do that, just a tip. How you survived the beating and burning in Menominee and our prior meeting here still baffles me. But this won't be an issue much longer."

Ford stepped up closer, radiating rage. "Why's that?"

Skip stepped forward, meeting his challenge. "There's four of us left, and I can hardly count two and some fractions of you."

"Hey!" I said after the shifter slighted me, Corvina, and probably Lewis's weakened condition. "I'm small, but not insignificant."

"Lord Fluffybutt, release my brother. I'm not going to tell you again."

I hated that guy. They were about to see who the real boss was. Plus, my claws were getting sore, and the blood on my paws was sticking my fur together, the ick making my focus sketchy. Hidden behind the shifter's mop of hair, I opened my small jaws and formed a fireball. Before the idiot between my claws realized what was happening, I launched the flaming orb through the shifter's skull. It passed through him and embedded in the refrigerator across the room, sending steam billowing out through the hole.

Oops.

The shifter dropped to the floor like a sack of potatoes, and I retracted my claws, hopping off his neck and landing safely on my paws. My claws cramped from holding on for so long. "I think that evens things a bit."

After a glance at the body, a wide-eyed Corvina backed up. Edie engaged the shifter holding Lewis hostage. Ford struck at Skip, and I scurried after the last shifter, Wallace. I shouted (because they frequently pretended not to hear me), "No settling the score, pal. Stop right there or you're next."

With a club in his hands, Wallace stopped and turned, genuine fear taking over. "You mean that? You won't kill me? I didn't want to do this, but Skip said we had to, and he'd pay me when it's done. I don't want to be here, please."

I paused. As the moment dragged on, a flash of a smirk danced at the corner of Wallace's lips. Not bad acting, but not good enough. I opened jaws and launched a ball. The shifter's reflexes sent his palm to block the shot, like an idiot, and the fireball passed right through his hand and lodged in his chest. Steam rose from his mouth, and he dropped to the floor.

Behind me, Edie stabbed a club-carrying shifter in the neck with her knife, and he dropped, cradling his neck. Skip's buddy gurgled as blood seeped between his fingers. Even with his super shifter healing, it was fatal, and within moments, he softened with the release of his life.

Skip wore a proud variety of wounds, and Ford had a few badges of honor himself. They were exhausted, panting and standing knees bent, just out of swinging reach.

"Come on, dog. All out of juice, and I didn't even see the fur," Ford taunted.

"We're not dogs. We're wolves. Only idiots don't know the difference." Skip growled.

"There's only you left. Think you can take us all on by yourself?" Ford asked.

I conjured another ball and aimed at Skip.

Lewis yelled, "Don't!"

Unable to say anything with fire in my mouth, I choked down the flaming ball and said, "Why?"

Limping and cradling an arm, Lewis shuffled over. "He's my brother. Don't."

The shifters had attacked twice now, three times, including before we'd met Lewis. And the mouse shifter wanted to defend this sack of fur? "Are you sure? It would only take a sec—"

"Of course, I'm sure. How could you? Don't you have a brother?" Lewis's drawn eyes made me glance away.

I didn't remember a brother, but Dennis, Stella, and Chris's faces popped into my head again. Considering one of them was dead, why did they insist on haunting me?

"I don't know," I mumbled.

"You don't know if you have a brother?" Lewis asked, astonished.

"I really don't." But I wanted to.

"Oh, well, generally, despite one's differences, one still loves their brother, their family." Lewis spoke as if teaching a child a basic human concept.

I shrugged. "They don't act like family—selling you, shaming you, trying to kill you. I guess I don't see the value in the word."

"You wouldn't, would you?" Lewis said, but it wasn't really a question.

"What does that supposed to mean?"

"A demon wouldn't understand." Well, he wasn't wrong. I said nothing, and Lewis addressed everyone else. "I call a truce in this cabin. No more killing."

"Tell that to your friends," Skip said.

Lewis pointed a puffy finger at his brother's chest. "You broke in here, so you pipe down."

Skip's brows lifted.

"Skip will be spared," Lewis ordered, nodding at the last shifter. "In exchange, he will no longer attempt to kill me." At Lewis's pause, Skip nodded once in agreement. "And...he won't harm anyone else in this cabin."

Skip flinched. "If I don't fulfill the C&D, someone else will."

"I'll handle it. You disappear, and I better never see you again."

"What should I tell our Moms?" Skip asked.

"It doesn't matter."

With a reluctant step, Skip shuffled to the door. With a hand on the knob, Skip glanced at the bodies of his brothers—at this point, I believed they were all figurative brothers, except for Lewis. "What about them?"

"We'll handle it," Ford said.

Skip turned, paused, and left.

Ford glanced out the window. "He's gone."

A collective sigh of relief washed over everyone.

"Now we spend the evening cleaning instead of infiltrating Hell. Just great. What a waste. Corvina, you okay?"

Corvina stood and cringed at the leaking head on the floor. "Yeah. It's over now."

"Where are the shovels?" Edie asked.

"Shovels aren't the first thing I think of when someone wants to clean," I said.

"You haven't been around long enough," Edie said.

Ford cringed. "I hate to say it, but shouldn't we bring the bodies to wherever Lewis brought vampire leftovers? The ghoul farm?"

Lewis shook his head and flinched at the pain, but the swelling in his eye reduced by the minute. "I'm never going there again. Let's bury them with dignity like people."

"They aren't people," Ford said.

"Every one of us has a darkness lurking." Lewis pointedly stared at me. "Some are just easier to see."

I never pretended to be anything but a demon. I shrugged at the silent accusation.

Corvina stepped out the back door and returned a second later with a garden shovel. "I used it to bury a dead snake out back. It didn't belong in the garbage or rotting in the sun."

Sympathy for a snake. I didn't see that coming.

"Ford and I will carry and bury. Corvy, can you patch up Lewis's bleeders?" Edie asked.

Corvina went to the bathroom and returned with a first aid kit. She sat at the shifter's side. Edie and Ford carried ankles and wrists as they hauled the bodies out the back door.

"I guess going to Hell is off the table tonight," I said with disappointment.

Corvina shot him a look. "Be happy you're alive."

I prowled closer, ready to ask the question I'd been eager for an answer to. "What are you?"

Corvina wiped blood with antiseptic, revealing the real damage beneath the ugly exterior. She glanced at Lewis and whispered to me, "What do you mean?"

"You're not human."

Lewis was in and out of consciousness while his large body worked on rapid healing, so he didn't react.

Corvina cleared her throat and avoided my eye contact. "What do you mean? Of course I'm human."

I flipped on my aura vision to double check. "No human cloud means no human soul."

"You're a cat. You don't know what you see." Corvina worked on Lewis's face. Her hand movements quickened.

"It's fine," I said. "When you're ready to talk about it, I'm here. In the meantime, Lewis and I won't say anything. Lewis? I think he's out."

Corvina looked at me for a long moment.

"Ow," Lewis said after she wasn't paying attention.

"Sorry."

"He's right. I won't say anything," Lewis said.

Corvina scowled.

"I mean, if he's right about you...you know, I won't say anything either way, just in case. No worries," Lewis corrected.

"Won't say anything about what?" Edie asked, as she and Ford stood at the ends of the last body.

"Don't try being a hero now, cat. It's not a good look on you." Ford scowled at me with a death wish, as if I'd spilled the beans about Vale's spice shop. That whole secret seemed pointless, but whatever.

"I'm no one's hero."

Ford nodded, a silent message received. "We have a rotting corpse by the bed. Lift on three." He and Edie bent at the waist. "One, two, three, lift."

They shuffled out the door. Lewis slept while healing. Corvina cleaned up her supplies and began cleaning the floor.

I wasn't anyone's hero. I think I wanted to be, but I couldn't do anything like this but fling fireballs into perfectly functioning refrigerators.

30

North Wing

AFTER A DEEP SCRUBBING, the cabin looked habitable.
Smelled better, too. As much as it annoyed me that all my prior
cleaning was wasted, the wash of relief at the organized and
neat space put me at ease. But now, my veins were electric for
a chance to return to Hell. This time, we were going prepared.

"Put these on," Ford said, handing out an amulet wrapped
in silver wire on a leather cord to Corvina and Edie. He already
wore his own. Ford dug in his pocket for one wrapped in gold
wire. "This might not work as well, since you aren't human,
and I had to improvise on the materials. So, keep our fingers
crossed?"

"I'm not allergic to silver," Lewis said. "I'm a mouse."

"Eesh, don't say that word," I said, but they all ignored my
plea for understanding. And they called me the insensitive one.

"Why didn't you say that before? Now the whole plan is
going to be at risk," Ford said.

"What are these?" Edie asked, lifting the amulet around her
neck.

"Mantle of Obscure Asylum. As long as you wear it, Supers will not be able to see your true self, and humans won't notice any difference. The best part is demons can't snap you away unless they touch you, but they'll think you're one of them, so they won't. These should buy us much more time than before."

"You know what the most dangerous word is?" I asked. Corvina, Edie, Ford, and Lewis gave me a bored look. I finished anyway. "*Should*. A non-quantifiable probability stacked against you."

Edie frowned. "If someone is risking their life for another, a pep talk is more valuable than a defeatist attitude, especially considering what we're about to do for a *demon*."

"Just making an observation." I shrugged.

"We ready to go then?" Ford asked.

"Guns, knives, battle gear, amulets of obscure something... Am I missing anything?" Edie said, pointing each item out on her fingers.

"First aid," Corvina said. "But I have that covered."

"Suits," I said, and everyone turned to me with astonishment. "If you want to blend in, demons all wear suits."

"I don't do suits," Edie said.

"Tonight you do."

Edie grumbled. "I'm driving, but we can't all fit in one vehicle, and I'm not about to rent a short bus."

"We'll take Ford's SUV and your Prius. They have the most space," I said, thrilled they were listening to me.

"And which portal are we entering?" Ford said.

"The NBB portal is long and windy. We might get lost again," I said.

"So the alley?" Edie asked.

"The alley portal has a secretary. I think it's the better choice, so we can test Ford's magic rocks before getting too far to get out alive."

Ford mumbled something about magic rocks.

"That works for me. You guys?" Edie asked.

Corvina and Lewis nodded.

Ford said, "Let's go."

While Edie, Lewis, and Ford packed up and complained about finding suits at this hour, I stayed behind a moment. I sent Corvina a hard stare.

Corvina's worry wrinkled her brow.

I whispered, "If the amulet doesn't work on you, the whole plan fails, and you'll have some explaining to do."

"I don't know what you're talking about," Corvina said and shouldered her backpack stuffed with first aid. Without a backward glance, she rushed out the door after the others.

"I think you do."

EDIE GLANCED DOWN AT me, and I put on my best poor-me cat eyes. "I'm not carrying you in my purse. You can handle some alley grime."

"What kind of human has no sympathy for a cute cat?"

"You're not a cat, as you keep reminding us," Edie said.

I gritted my furry jaw. Just because we rode together didn't mean we had to walk together. "Fine. Let's get this over with." I teleported to the alley door and held my breath against the dirt, raw meat juice, maggots, flies, rotting food scraps, and every other disgusting thing all around me like a suffocating tomb of a blackened dumpster.

My crew sauntered forward on wary feet, covered in practical steel-toed shoes and boots, but their upper half was all business. They'd struggled to find a suit to fit Lewis's massive arms and chest. As long as Lewis didn't need to button the coat, he'd be okay. Probably.

Corvina and Edie opted for pant suits, just because they were easier to run in, a wise choice. Corvina's eyes kept drifting toward Ford. I admitted the man filled out a sharp suit. He'd fit in just fine down in Hell. Might draw too much attention.

"Can you hurry?" I asked the misfits as they approached.

"I thought running would set off alarms?" Edie asked with a playful tone.

"If you don't hurry, I'm running in there screaming, so there's going to be even more alarms."

Edie laughed and searched the alley door. "Well, we're here now. How does this work?"

"Stand by." I craned my neck for witnesses and leaned closer to the dented metal door. Blue luminescence traced around its perimeter.

"It's like it reacts to you," Corvina said in awe.

"I have a magic tattoo," I said. At least, I thought I still had it on my cat chest, buried in fur. I said to the door, "Open sesame."

Nothing happened.

"Was that supposed to work?" Edie asked.

"Still lacking thumbs here. Also, vertically challenged. Someone turn the knob, please?"

Edie opened the door and backed up. Blue glowed from within.

"Don't freak out and don't act weird," I warned.

"What's your definition of weird?" Lewis asked.

Fair question.

But I ignored it and stepped into the light. In this Hell entrance, a waiting room greeted visitors, complete with fake palm plants and a table full of magazines. Wi-Fi wasn't great through all the layers of topsoil, subsoil, groundwater, and bedrock, so print still had a decent run in Hell.

"It's like 1990 down here," Ford said.

Corvina hushed him. "We're supposed to belong here, not act like tourists."

At the visitor's desk, a man in a suit typed on a computer. I strolled to the desk and leaped up. "Hi, Reamus."

Reamus was a simple demon. He did his job and went home. He couldn't be bought or swayed, and he never smiled. Hell didn't receive any visitors that didn't belong, so human pleasantries were unnecessary. With the personality of a log, I would bet the demon had no friends. Not an envious life.

"iKat," Reamus said by way of greeting and inspected the newcomers with a suspicious eye. "Last I heard, you got promoted."

"Field Agent, yep. I'm looking for a friend. Have you seen Heather around?"

"What?" Edie whisper-yelled and the others exchanged nervous glances.

Reamus sent her a critical eye. "I have not. Would you like her paged?"

"No, that's not necessary. I'll find her."

"Your funeral," Reamus mumbled and watched us move through the lobby. "iKat?" Reamus called after us.

I turned and swallowed a lump. The amulets didn't fail already, did they? I glanced at Corvina accusingly and followed the secretary's gaze, but he wasn't scrutinizing the unknown Super. "Yes?"

"Who are your friends? I don't recognize these demons."

Time to make up crap. With mock surprise, I said, "Oh, you haven't met Edina, Corvina, Fordus, or Lew-G?"

Reamus shook his head and squinted at their faces.

"They're from the northern quadrant—Canada—visiting some friends."

Reamus's suspicion hung on like a pesky cat hair with static cling. "You don't have any friends down here."

Ouch.

Little did he know. "I do now."

"Then what is the nature of this visit?"

With a groan, I said, "To meet Heather, of course."

"She can meet you at the surface, and you're not supposed to be down here." Reamus stood and lifted the handset. "I can't allow this."

Ford pulled out a handgun from behind his suit coat. With Reamus's eyes fastened to the keypad, Ford aimed and squeezed, adding a new hole to Reamus's lapel.

The secretary's mouth opened. After a beat, he dropped the handset and touched the tear through his suit. Pulling back blood on his fingertip, he fell back onto his chair and rolled toward the wall.

Ford approached, removed a blade from a hidden holster, and sliced off the demon's head. It fell, plopped to the floor, and rolled, making a squishy noise. "We can't leave it here."

"Agreed," I added.

Corvina rushed to the phone and returned the handset to the cradle, while Ford holstered his gun. Lewis approached and the hunter and shifter lifted the body off the chair. "Is there a bathroom around here?" Ford grunted. "Demons are heavier than they look."

Lewis wasn't struggling, but out of respect to the hunter, I didn't remark.

"Just over there." I nodded to an ordinary office door with demon markings on it.

Ford and Lewis shuffled the body across the lobby and deposited him on the toilet. With a press of the lock on their way out, they brushed off their hands.

"That'll buy us time," Ford said.

"Let's go," I said.

"Why did you give us weird names?" Edie asked. "Well, not Corvy. That was her real name."

"I just demonized them a little."

"My name is demonic?" Corvina asked in horror.

"Hey, don't worry. Mine sounds like loogie," Lewis said, and Corvina smiled.

"Why did you ask for Heather?"

"You'll see," I said, walking ahead of the group, trying to remember the correct turns to find the dungeons. North wing, north wing. Which way was north around here? At junctions in the hallways, placards with arrows pointed out directions.

"Dungeons and torture, left. This way," I followed the sign, and the tile floors, white walls, and bright lighting abruptly stopped at a set of double doors. I teleported through, while the others pushed their way across the threshold. A blast of chilled air ruffled my fur. Cold leaky stones underfoot gave me a shiver, and dim flaming sconces took a minute to adjust to. I wished the helpful signs continued. Didn't want prisoners who managed to escape to find their way out.

Partially on instinct, partially on a guess, my twisting and turning through the dungeon hallways finally led to a rattling sound in the distance.

"Are we there yet?" Edie asked. "It's freezing down here."

I shushed her and listened. A tiny clink of a chain followed a whimper. I smiled. "Hear that? We're almost there."

"I'm afraid to ask what you hear," Corvina said.

Following my sharp ears, I rounded the corner and broke into a jog. "We're almost there!"

The others rushed after me, and around the next corner, at the farthest end of the gloomy hallway, hung the dungeon keys. My heart pounded in my tiny chest. This was it! Finally, my punishment was almost over.

"Ford and Edie, grab those keys. Corvina and Lewis, watch for incoming. Time to get my body back." I jogged down to the cell holding my body. Excitement coursed through my fur, and I flexed my paws in anticipation.

Ford and Edie's footsteps moved down the damp corridor. A jingling of keys in the metal ring had me beaming with the prospect of freedom.

"Hurry up!" Edie said as they ran back to me.

Ford shifted through the keys and inserted them one at a time, tugging at the tumbler. Key after key didn't work.

"Come on! Come on!" I chanted to myself.

Corvina wiped her hands on her thighs. Lewis stood, arms folding over his chest as if his first plan of attack was intimidation.

Metal clunked.

"Got it!" With the key still in the lock, Ford shoved the iron bars open, sending a squeak dancing down the passageway.

I ran inside and stopped at the cot where my human-shaped body laid in a silent slumber. Edie and Ford followed me in. "No, don't," I protested.

Edie leaned over the cot. "I can't see your face in this light, but you have fabulous hair."

Ford sent her an annoyed look.

"Jealous?" I chuckled. "Fordie has competition."

"Don't call me that. iKat, you haven't been on your feet for a while. You won't be able to walk."

I hadn't thought of that. "But you could get trapped in here."

With an exchange of glances and a shrug on Edie's end, the hunters returned to the hall to stand watch.

I centered my thoughts, and like teleporting, I focused only on my inner self. Gathering up what I needed to move, I mentally launched my essence from the cat. I floated toward my dormant body, trembling with excitement, and my essence flattened over the body like a blanket. I drifted down onto the firm surface. And I stopped. Something blocked me from moving to the interior.

"We have incoming!" Ford yelled.

I pressed down harder. So close. I was so close! I floated up high, near the ceiling of the cell, and dropped down as fast as possible.

I bounced.

Again and again, I tried, desperation refusing to see the truth. My body was warded, too.

No, no, no. I pushed and pushed. I slithered under my own clothes, but all with no effect. I tried sliding in through my nostrils, but that only led to a coating of dust and a tickle of hairs. My body shifted with the invisible effort.

"What's taking so long?" Edie asked.

Unable to speak as a floating cloud of essence, I drifted back to the sleeping cat's body, so frustrated I could launch a fireball through the king's head. For a flash, I worried the cat would wake up and run off. Then I'd really be in trouble.

"It's not working," I said, returning to the orange tabby.

"What? How could it not? You're right there." Edie gestured to my dormant human form as if I hadn't seen it.

"My body is warded, too."

Edie grumbled. "You need to get out there now. Demons are coming, and judging by their faces, they don't want to talk."

31

Not So Sneaky

A HALF DOZEN DEMONS rushed down the dingy corridor, weapons in hand. A mature and calm chat about the crew breaking into a warded dungeon cell was off the table. Figures. Edie and Ford drew their pistols.

"No guns!" I growled as the demons approached. "We don't want to set off the alarms. No weapons yet."

The hunters exchanged glances and reluctantly secured their pistols. They unsheathed knives instead, but kept them discreet. I braced myself next to Lewis, Ford, Edie, and Corvina, ready to prevent this conflict and collect my body.

The first demon came in hot, but stopped short and cocked his head. "Demons? No one's supposed to be down here." The guard squinted at my group. "What kind of demons are you?"

At least the magic rocks were working.

I cleared my throat. "They're Canadian demons. You know, visitors from the north."

Suspiciously glaring at each of my cohorts, the guard said, "There are no demons in Canada."

Edie sent me an annoyed look.

"Chinese demons?" I answered with a question in my tone.

The guard squinted. "None of you resemble a Chinese demon."

"Our glamours need tweaking," iKat said.

"No one leaves Hell without being able to fully glamour," the suspicious demon countered.

"We're Russian, then," Edie said with a forced smile and a plausible accent. "We thought you'd hate us."

The guard turned to her. "Russians are our friends, but you, I don't recognize. What was your name?"

"Oh, forget this," Edie said. She lifted her knife, and the guard reacted defensively, swinging a shocked fist like an offended drunk at a bar.

Lewis approached the suspicious demon and dodged a swing. Using the demon's momentum against him, Lewis pounded his thick fists on the demon's spine, dropping him.

I watched the demon for movement. A hand flopped over. "Most of these guys know nothing but their loyalty to their jobs. They exist in their own little box, so don't hold back."

Hmmm. Actually, a box sounded comfy right now.... Stupid cat thoughts.

Lewis bent over, splitting his suit coat down the back, and picked up the injured demon and tossed him like a limp rag doll against the cell bars. Iron rang under the force. Prisoners pushed their heads against their cells, trying to see the evening's entertainment. They cheered the fight, rallying further prisoners until the whole cell block rocked with noise.

This time, the demon remained still. Lewis brushed his hands clean, as if demons were filthy. I didn't know what to think of that.

The next two dungeon guards held knives of their own and engaged Edie and Ford. While they were busy, another pair tag-teamed Lewis. Flaps of his torn suit fluttered with his movements.

One demon in the rear of the group, a meaty male in a suit wearing a perfectly devious smirk, sauntered up to Corvina as if prepared to play with her. The trembling woman slipped a knife out of her waistband. Corvina wasn't a fighter, but I admired her gumption.

"Hey, down here," I said.

The demon, willing to take advantage of a lesser opponent, glanced down and his brows lifted. "iKat? You can't be down here!"

I didn't recognize the demon, but with all the attention I'd gathered with the coffeepot riots and the star chart, my name was likely well-known. "I didn't expect a red carpet, but a 'Good evening' would've been nice."

The demon shifted the knife in his hand, as if considering how to fight a cat. With a shrug, he swiped low, and like a sloth striking a cobra, I easily leaped away. Seriously.

Nearby, metal clanged as knives clashed. Boots squeaked against the wet floors—which I tried very hard not to think about. Grunts and groans filled the space as people and demons took hits and slammed against the walls, all to the chorus of a sporting event.

More demons flooded the corridor.

I dodged another swipe and jumped up onto my opponent's back. I cradled the demon's throat, ready to rip. "Call off your guards and live."

The demon stiffened. "A real demon doesn't take orders from a half-demon."

"Shows you never really know someone until shit hits the proverbial fan."

The demon twisted his head, helping me carry through with my threat. I sliced the demon's throat and leaped away when he fell.

"I've got three notches in my belt today," Edie said with pride.

"Three for me and more to come!" Ford said, beaming.

Ford and Edie finished off their attackers and rushed to Lewis's aid. The mouse shifter had three on him, which looked more like theatrical juggling than a fight to the death. Two flew back while one flew in the air.

Another demon approached Corvina, but he paused when he spotted the fresh claw marks on his dead friend's throat. The demon skimmed the area and settled on a new target. Fury twisted his features. He pointed at the fatal wounds and said to me, "iKat, did you do that?"

"Yep, and you're next if you don't call off the guards."

"What part of 'not allowed in Hell' don't you understand?"

"All I want is my body back. Why is that too much to ask?"

The conflicted demon said, "By orders of the king, your life is to be spared, but since I'm assigned to protect these cells at all costs, I'm burdened with choosing which order to disobey. You placed yourself in this situation. You placed this burden upon me." The demon shifted position. "I've made my choice. Understand it's nothing personal." He stabbed at the air but missed. He stabbed again, and I dodged, waiting for an opportunity to unleash my favorite move—not that I had many to choose from as a cat.

A squeak of a mouse tensed me. "Lewis, is that you?"

The massive fighter grunted with a punch. "I didn't say anything." He picked up a demon and flipped him over his shoulder. With his massive hands on the demon's thighs, he threw the demon to the stone floor with a wet thump. Only a demon could survive the magnitude of punishment Lewis was capable of. His strength was impressive.

Using my superior vision, I craned my neck and spotted a mouse not two feet away. I sucked in a breath.

A hot pinch registered from somewhere in Mitten's abdominal region, but all I focused on was the tittering whiskers, gangly claws, and scaly tail. A searing, breath-stealing pain roared through my tiny, borrowed body, and all strength flushed away. I fell to the cold stone floor and cringed at the millions of invisible bacteria rushing toward me for their snacking, defecating, and multiplying pleasure.

My body was paralyzed, and a tugging sensation stole my attention. I tracked the demon pulling a knife from my body with a smirk on his face. "Thank you for the choice. You made me a hero, the demon who killed the abomination."

I pulled in a heavy breath, and a crushing pain locked my lungs. Desperation for oxygen forced me to try again, but my lungs wouldn't budge. A pounding in my head added to the growing panic.

There was nothing I could do.

Edie, Ford, and Lewis fought off attacker after attacker. Bloodied, panting, shredded, but smiling.

Corvina rushed up to me and dropped to her knees. "iKat! Oh, this looks bad." She touched my fur, brushing it over to see the damage. Tears flooded her eyes, and she sniffed. Corvina pressed against the wound. "I didn't bring anything that would help with this. There's nothing I can do."

Incapable of saying anything more in the tiny broken body, I released myself into my essence, now a living consciousness, without any way to communicate or affect anything around me. Never to have my opinions shared or rejected. I was less than a ghost. I just existed, doomed to watch and never participate for all eternity. A fate truly worse than death. I should've treated Mittens like a god, because Mittens was all I had, and I threw that away, because of a stupid fear, and a stupid need to have what I didn't deserve.

Corvina sobbed. Edie and Ford, sliced and bleeding, finished the last of their attackers. Lewis punched one in the face so hard, the demon flew back into the stone wall.

The demon got up.

"To hell with this," Ford said and pulled a pistol out of a holster hidden behind his shredded suit coat.

Edie struck out a hand. "iKat said no guns. We can't fight off more of them. Look at Corvy."

They both turned to the young woman.

"Corvy?" Edie asked. "What's wrong?"

Lewis punched the indestructible demon twice more and finally he stopped getting up. The cell block of prisoners cheered, and many begged for release with promises of helping.

The hunters and shifter approached Mittens's bleeding body. Edie gasped. Lewis looked away. Ford rested a hand on Corvina's shoulder. The young woman stood and launched herself in Ford's arms. He cradled her, patting her back.

"He's dead." She squeezed the man-witch.

Ford didn't say anything.

Sadness in Edie's eyes turned hard. "We can't stay here. Let's get his natural body and bury him like one of us. Lewis?"

Lewis returned to the cell and flung my human-shaped body over his shoulder. "Ready to go."

Edie rested a hand on Convina's back. "We need to go now."

"We can't leave Mittens. He can't just stay here like roadkill. They'll feed him to the hellhounds!"

I hadn't thought of that either, but she was right.

"Okay. We'll take him, too. They can be buried next to each other. I'm sure Mittens is sick of iKat after all this time, but at least they won't be in the same grave."

Corvina pulled away from Ford's embrace and scooped Mittens into her arms, immediately staining her blouse.

"Ready?" Edie asked her.

Corvina nodded.

They rushed down the pungent hallway, and I kept my essence close. If I couldn't do anything, I could at least watch. Rounding the corner, they stopped, and I caught up.

"Which way was it?" Corvina said.

"I thought we came this way," Edie said. "Ford? Lewis? Any opinions here?"

"I thought this was the right way, too." Ford wrinkled his brow and scratched his head.

"It was. Let's go," Lewis said, taking the lead.

They followed in a rush, and I glided along with them, watching my handsome face bob against Lewis's firm ass. At the next intersection, they stopped again.

"This isn't familiar at all," Edie said.

"We should've left breadcrumbs," Corvina said.

Ford swore and kicked the wall.

Corvina sat down on the cold floor, cradling Mittens like a limp baby, her long, blond hair draping across her face. She stroked his fur—my fur?—and smiled through tears.

"More demons will be coming once they discover what happened. I can't tell if they have security cameras," Edie said.

"I'm guessing not, otherwise they'd be here already," Ford said.

"Or they do and they're having fun placing bets. They are demons," Lewis said.

I resented that.

"We shouldn't have come," Corvina said and sniffled. "How did we really expect to break into Hell, find the right key, and escape all the demon guards? Saying it now seemed—"

"Suicidal," Edie finished.

"Homicidal," Ford corrected.

Lewis sat next to Corvina, and tilted my limp human feet so they rested on the floor, reducing his burden. My face rested on the cold, damp stone floor.

All I could do was sigh.

"But we did get to kill a bunch of demons, so there's that." Edie smiled.

"Pizza, beer, dead demons. That's my definition of a good day," Ford added.

"Even cold pizza was still good. The pizza iKat brought," Lewis said slowly. "How many miles of tunnels are down here, do you think?"

"Far too many to take guesses," Edie said.

Silence stretched, and no one made eye contact. Were they contemplating their decision? Were their lives flashing before their eyes? *I'm sorry, too,* I tried to say. Sorry I'd led them to their deaths in a fruitless attempt to break into Hell and steal from a locked and warded cell surrounded by armed demons. Sorry I hadn't treated them better from the get-go. Sorry I couldn't help them with their personal problems. Their impending deaths were my fault, and poor Mittens had to suffer the most, without having a voice for his own autonomy.

Corvina laughed, and everyone looked at her. "Remember when Ford first learned he was a demon? That was funny."

"It was a perfectly normal response to meeting a talking demon cat," Ford said, hiding a small lift of his lips.

"And it makes fire, too!" Corvina repeated his phrase, using a deep mocking tone. "I wanted to punch him and laugh with him."

Edie laughed. "I wanted to cut his head off." Corvina stopped laughing. "But after all this, he wasn't such a bad guy...for a demon."

Always with the disclaimer.

"Oh, and when he fainted seeing Lewis? How many cats are actually terrified of mice?" Corvina asked.

"None," Lewis said with a straight face. "With my size, you'd think people cower in fear when I walk into a room, but that's not the case. I have to thank iKat for his genuine fear."

"The first time I met him, he walked in on me hunting zombies. He thought I was having kinky sex. Sounds like something a virgin would say."

I resented that.

Ford chuckled. "I wouldn't be surprised if 'ol cat here was a virgin." Ford gripped my human hair and turned to see his face. Ford's brows popped. "Egads, he's a good-looking dude. Edie, you are banished from gazing upon his face."

"What?" Edie laughed. "Let me see."

"Not a chance."

Edie scooted forward, but Ford held his arm out to block her. She play-fought back. "You can't tease me like that."

"Seriously, you're not looking at him. I will be relegated to the used sock bin after you lay your eyes upon his perfect skin and angular jaw."

"Oh! You have to let me see now."

"No can do. He's just too magnificent," Ford said. "If I swung the other way, I'd pay to have him pose for me. Hell, I'd pay for a lot more..." Ford sent her a devious smile.

Edie stopped fighting him. "You're just saying all that, so I'll be let down when I see him, and I'll still only have eyes for you."

"You got me." Ford grinned.

Jerk. I almost liked Ford for a minute there.

Lewis noticed Corvina hung her head low. The shifter rose with a grunt, bearing my limp weight, and said, "For iKat's sake, we should try to get out of here. All things considered, I'd rather die trying than waiting here like sitting ducks. Not that you guys aren't great or anything, but I've got the urge to punch something."

Ford stood. "You and me both."

Corvina joined them. "Which way. Anyone got a coin to flip?"

From down the hall, a clicking against stone echoed, turning their heads toward the flame-lit pathway. I knew that sound. The demon I wanted to see, but now I couldn't do anything about it.

32

Helpless

If I could've told the demon off, I would've. More importantly, if I could've teleported all my friends out of Hell, I definitely would've tried. But since my consciousness was trapped as an incorporeal cloud floating through space, I had to deal with watching the disaster unfold, helpless.

Heather rounded a corner and blocked their exit. The cranky demon wore her usual curve-hugging skirt suit with her black hair pulled into a tight bun. Maybe she had no plans to fight in those clothes, but I knew better. Even though I didn't remember seeing it happen, I just knew Heather could take a wallop without a hair falling out of place. She scowled at my cat body in Corvina's arms.

"Well, well, well. After all your warnings, you still had the gumption to come down here." She glared at my body. "And you brought your pathetic friends."

"Hey!" Edie yelled, but Heather ignored her, like the insignificant bug demons believed humans were.

"Not going to snark at me tonight?" Heather asked my cat body, and after a beat, the realization sunk in. The scowl fell. "He's dead?"

Corvina sobbed.

Heather's eyes widened in shock. "He's really dead?"

"No pulse means dead, at least for earth cats," Corvina said.

"It wasn't supposed to end like this. He's too..." she trailed off with a huff, shock turning to anger. Heather gritted her teeth. "Who did it?"

"One of your minions stabbed him with a knife," Edie said.

"Which one? I want to know the demon responsible."

"You want us to walk you down there and point out the correct dead guy?" Corvina asked, unusually brave in the face of certain death.

Heather groaned and briefly covered her forehead with her palm. "What happened back there? A demon disagreement?"

A light glowed around Mittens, and since no one reacted, I figured I was the only one capable of seeing it. The light grew until I would've closed my eyelids if I had any, and a gentle breeze floated me toward it. Wasn't that the rule—go toward the light?

I didn't want to die for real.

Once I reached the bright Mittens, cradled in Corvina's arms, I felt a tug, an invisible leash forcing me closer to the light. I fought it. Without arms or legs, or any real capacity to do anything, I fought against the pulling of the light in the only way I knew how as a floating essence. But the force continued, unimpeded, dragging me toward whatever awaited me next.

I was honestly afraid.

The light burned bright as the sun, prickling my cloudy form, like being shoved through a net and turned into jelly. Hard to imagine, since not many people experienced jellinizing, but it was incredibly uncomfortable. I'd rather visit the proctologist, but since I literally couldn't do anything about this blinding, painful force, I continued to complain incessantly about life not being fair.

The light faded away, but the pain in my eyeballs and the pain of the squeezing net sensation took longer to fade.

"Wow, that sucked," I said and dragged in a breath. Sweet air filled Mittens's lungs. I...I wasn't dead. I had control of Mittens again. I shifted a paw, appreciation surging through my body like a smooth rum and Coke. Except with every movement, my borrowed body ached like I'd been flattened through a wringer.

Everyone stared at me.

"iKat?" Corvina asked with a wet smile, looking down at me bundled in her bloody arms.

"I'm here. Hey, I'm here! Ow. I hurt. Everything hurts."

The young woman brushed around my fur, searching for the wound. "It's healed! The wound's gone, but you're still full of drying blood. Do you want me to put you down now?"

I chuckled and groaned. Wound or not, my pride was injured. "Yes, please."

With gentle hands lowering me to the floor, I lightly planted my sticky paws on the filthy stone. I was all out of cringes at this point.

Heather stared, wide-eyed with wonder. "How did you do that?"

I exhaled deeply as if my body was a few liters low on oxygen. Guess dying did that to a cat. "Mittens has nine lives, right? I think I just spent one."

Edie laughed.

Heather did not. "All this just to steal your body?"

"Not exactly. I was hoping you'd make an appearance," I said, thrusting my tail upright.

Heather's devious smile made my sticky fur crawl. "Oh, really?"

"Lewis Gard has a contract and a C&D. I want to buy the contract and cancel the hit."

Lewis nervously shifted his weight, adjusting my human-shaped body on his shoulder.

Heather focused on him and slyly smiled. "I thought you looked familiar." Her eyes shifted to the amulet around his neck. "Someone's been dabbling in magic, but yours is wearing off."

Lewis stiffened, and Heather's smile broadened. "I don't get my hands dirty, big guy. You're safe...for the moment."

The big guy did not relax.

"Are you interested in my deal?" I pressed.

"Hmmm. What do you offer in exchange?"

"Since I'm broke, I can offer a favor."

"A favor?" Heather laughed. "What could you possibly do for me?"

"That's what I'm offering—one task, whatever you need."

Heather considered for longer than I thought necessary. "No."

"Why?" I asked.

"I'm not in the business of making wishes come true."

"It's a deal. We both get something."

Heather folded her arms across her chest. "There's only one thing you could do that would make me happy."

Desperate, I said, "Anything."

"Die."

I snorted. The range of evil among demons varied significantly from one to the next, not unlike humans themselves, but that was a bit much. "What did I ever do to you?" I asked, and maybe she'd answer it.

"Fortunately, I think, or perhaps not, you just don't remember. Andras messed with your head as a condition of allowing you to live." She scoffed. "An information demon trying to do a memory demon's job. Well, he failed. I insisted on just killing you to save the risk, but the king has his favorites."

"You're right about one thing. I don't remember." But at least I knew for sure Andras played hide and seek in my skull. I wasn't crazy, but I was unsettled.

"I'm right about so much more than that." Heather conjured a flame in her hand and formed it into a ball the size of my head.

Well, crap.

"Run!" I shouted. My crew fidgeted as if deciding to follow the order or fight the demon. "Move now!"

War raged on Edie's face. She knew listening was the right answer, but the call of revenge was strong. I understood her dilemma, but the longer they hesitated, the worse their odds were.

"You were responsible for my father's death. Remember Ray Randall?" Edie said, features twisted in pain and rage.

"Who?" Heather asked with a smirk.

The fireball flickered light across Edie's angry features. "The cat knows you best, but I promise you, this isn't over, Heather."

Corvina ran, and Lewis followed behind her, hauling the extra weight without effort.

Ford and Edie exchanged glances. Ford gestured to follow and took off after the other two. Lips pressing thin, Edie rushed after, hugging his toes and shouting her promise. "I'm going to kill you, demon!"

This time, I was sure she meant Heather.

I stood between them and the high-ranking contract demon. She watched their panicked retreat with glee.

After several yards, Edie stopped. "iKat, let's go!"

"No. You get out of here. This is for me to handle."

"iKat!" Edie pleaded. "We already lost you once. Don't make us do it again."

"You won't."

Edie's face fell, but she ran. Good. I didn't have to carry the burden of her death on my narrow shoulders. The hunter was smart and cunning, and she could see when the odds meant fleeing was the best course of action. I appreciated her cooperation. On the rare occasion it appeared. The footsteps of my retreating crew quieted in the distance.

Heather looked down at me, strumming her fingers along her arms. "I love a demon with confidence. I always thought there was a chance for us to be a thing, after I slapped you around for all the humiliation I suffered at your hands. We would've been an indestructible Bonnie and Clyde, tearing up the surface like a pair of crazy kids with no limits. But it wouldn't be right if you're a cat."

There was so much to unpack there and no time to do it. A glimmer of hope had me asking, "Can you get me back into my body?"

"The king said you were too dangerous to have that kind of freedom, so he coddled you. Kept things from you. And when you still wouldn't cooperate, he had Andras turn you into an empty-headed monkey, all in the name of preserving your memories of him. So instead of letting nature take its course, reverting you back to the evil you were destined to be, or instead of letting me kill you for all the humiliation you put me through, he turned you into this disgusting furry thing."

"It's not over for us," I insisted.

Heather screwed up her lips in disbelief. The fireball in her hand grew. "We're beyond that. Such a shame that still I hesitate, but you are his pet, and the king's warnings are not to be trifled with."

It was her or me, and with my friends lost in the cavernous corridors of Hell, I also couldn't hesitate any longer. I gathered Hellfire into a ball in my mouth, not as large or as impressive as Heather's, but I had something she didn't: perspective.

At this height, throwing her off balance was the best strategy. I fired through her high-heeled foot, from toe to heel, which cauterized immediately. I gathered a second ball and hit her other foot.

Heather unleashed her larger ball with a scream of fury and pain, but I teleported to the side. Heather fell to her knees, sweat beading up on her skin, and she propped herself up on her trembling hands.

Anger twisted her face. "You...damned cat. I should've killed you when you were a useless sack sitting at a desk." She ignited flames all over her body, loose hairs and the edges of her sport coat fluttered in the heat wave.

"Probably." I gathered another ball. I'd put up with a lot from her, and a sudden déjà vu told me we'd fought before. If only I could remember! The growing frustration at her knowing more than I did grew the fatal ball larger.

My crew, this motley group of strangers, helped me when no one else would. They listened to me when my own demonkind mocked me. They welcomed me without torturing me. And they didn't rummage around my memories. Heather was behind everything Lewis and Edie had suffered, but this time, I was ending her threat for good. I launched a fireball between her wide-open eyes.

She ducked.

Damn it.

With shaking limbs, Heather scooted back, resting her spine against the stone wall. She held her palm out, pooling another fireball.

As fire coated my soft fur, I raced to conjure my own, and right when I was ready to launch again, Andras appeared, blocking my line of fire. I swallowed the toasty fireball with a hiss. "Andras? We're busy here."

The information demon ignored me and faced my adversary. "Heather, you're under arrest. Come with me." Andras held out his hand, ignoring her flame, but she refused to take it. Of course.

My brows lifted at the sudden turn of events.

"On what grounds?" She still trembled from the pain, and nothing made me happier at this moment.

"Failure to heed the king's orders." Andras leaned over and grabbed her by the upper arm.

Heather flinched as she was dragged to her burned and steaming feet. The flames around her snuffed out. "And which were those?"

"Murdering iKat."

Heather scoffed. "He's clearly alive."

"He wasn't. Now I'm here to collect you for Glitter."

I made a noise of disgust and fear. Sounded close to that throaty grumble after a long vomit into an unclean toilet. Not that I had direct experience with that. I just knew.

"That wasn't me! You can ask…" Heather turned her head in the direction my crew ran. Too bad for her, she chased away her alibis, and I wasn't sticking my neck out in her defense. With a tone of defeat, she asked, "What happens after?"

"If you survive Glitter's punishment, the king has ordered your imprisonment. All your contracts will be redistributed."

"Uh, can I have one?" I asked Andras.

Andras craned his neck down, finally acknowledging my presence. "They've already been assigned."

"Who has Lewis Gard's?"

"I'll have to check the spreadsheet. Heather, let's go. You don't want to keep Glitter waiting. iKat, get out of here." Andras dragged a limping, grunting, scowling demon to a nasty fate she brought upon herself.

I was left alone in Hell. All things considered, that went well, but I had a crew lost in the maze down here. Shouts turned my head toward the aftermath of the guard slaughter. The bodies had been discovered and more demons were coming.

I ran after my crew and stopped at an intersection. I listened. Soft but rapid footsteps came from the south. I tore off after them and turned another corner in the corridor. Hunter and shifter feet pummeled the floor just ahead, casting eerie shadows along the seeping walls. I closed the distance.

"You guys look lost," I said, slowing.

They all stopped and turned. Edie picked me up with a smile and a glisten in her eye. "I thought that was suicide. How did you do it?"

"A little of this, a little of that, but we have bigger problems."

More shouts echoed our way, but this time they were from the direction we were heading. In moments, my crew was going to be sandwiched between an army of angry demon guards.

"She is dead, right?" Edie asked.

Ignoring her, I said, "We have incoming on both sides. We're trapped."

"You sure? We can keep going," Edie said.

"I can hear them."

"Is there another way out?" Ford asked.

"Or somewhere to hide?" Corvina asked.

There was one option, but I had never tried it. "Everyone, hug."

They stared blankly.

"How does this help?" Lewis asked, skeptical.

"I'm going to try teleporting us all out of here. Get close. Hug like your life depends on it, because it does."

Everyone glanced at each other with awkward hesitation.

"Hurry up," I ordered. "They're coming fast. And Lewis, watch my ass."

"I've been watching it. It ain't going anywhere."

"Edie, come on, you guys, get in close. Just don't smash me."

Edie opened her free arm and wrapped it around Ford. Corvina took his other side, and Lewis bear-hugged them all. My human ass was firmly in Ford's face, but now wasn't the time for jokes.

I focused. I pictured each person. Their hair, their faces, their clothes, their shoes, Lewis's precious cargo. I pictured my ass in Ford's face, and I snickered. I cleared my throat and focused again, picturing them all linked into one being. Securing everyone and everything necessary with my mind, I shifted my thoughts to the location we needed.

"Stop right there!" a demon's voice interrupted my precarious process.

Ford shifted, relaxing his grip on the women.

"No!" I yelled. "Hold tight."

The male demon in a suit with a buzz cut pointed a pistol at the group. "I said stop. All you demons are being charged with criminal trespass. Don't resist or you'll have more charges. Hands where I can see them."

"He forgot homicide," Lewis added.

"Thanks, Lewis," I said dryly. "Hold tight."

"Hands up now. Last warning." The trigger squeezed.

I focused harder. I recollected my thoughts of each person, one at a time, but much quicker, and then focused on a location far from here. A tugging sensation pulled at my fur.

I was going to get us away.

I rode along with the force, keeping my focus on each person. The bang of the gun reached my ears. I hoped my first attempt at teleporting more than one person was successful.

If not, all my friends were dead.

33

Underlings of Lord Fluffybutt

It was like running through the desert, chased by a starving vulture, with no water in sight. Feet burned on the baked sand. Lungs screamed for cool air. Head swam with impending exhaustion. I squinted into the blinding sunlight.

Up ahead, a boulder on a rocky hill promised shade, safety. Rushing through the torment of sun and squawks, I scrambled up the steep embankment. Gravel broke free, sending my feet sliding back, back toward the hungry beak. Deep breaths loaded with dust stung, but still I climbed up and up to the shade.

Panting from the hot air, I leaned against the boulder, relieved by the shade and dainty breeze. Lips cracked. Head floated. It wasn't enough.

A vulture landed on the rock overhead and squawked. I flinched under the ear-piercing noise. Gravel rained down from its claws, contracting and opening in anticipation of a hot meal. Spots danced in my eyes, and I fell over, too spent to fight any longer.

Dinner was served.

Instead, the bird's impatient shifting broke the boulder loose. It knocked me over and rolled until it crushed my chest. Death by suffocation sounded like a better way to go anyhow. I laid still, gasping shallow, insufficient breaths, ready for the darkness to free me of the chains of mortality.

A blunt object poked me in the ribs. A beak? A claw? "Just eat me already." The words were a slur, but I was sure the bird understood.

"Wake up, iKat. Wake up." That was Edie's voice. How did she get to the desert?

I blinked. A bright haze burned my retinas. I blinked again and squinted. Corvina kneeled in front of me. A burning deep in my lungs caused a reflexive gasp. Sweet relief.

I sprung to my feet on wobbly legs, and my vision cleared. Corvina steadied me while Ford, Lewis, and Edie watched with concerned faces.

"He's alive!" Corvina said, sliding her hand away.

"Barely." Ford stood and stretched. "About time, cat. You had us actually worrying."

"Where are we?" I asked, feet burning from the sand. I looked around. Wooden boards, wobbly folding table, kitchenette. Why was I burning up?

"The cabin. Don't you recognize it?" Edie asked and held up fingers on her hand. "How many fingers?"

"I'm fine, I think."

"You don't look fine," Lewis said.

"What happened?" I shook my head to clear it, but that just made the floaty sensation worse.

"We were blockaded on both sides by demons, and you teleported us to safety. Can't say I have any desire for a roller coaster ride anytime soon, but I'm grateful to be in one piece. Thanks, cat," Ford said.

"You did good, and I appreciate your help with my contract. You have no idea what that means to me," Lewis added. The big guy was still in his shredded suit, but his shoulder was empty.

I gasped. That better not have all been for nothing. "Where's my body? Do we have it? Why am I not in it?"

"We set you over there." Edie pointed to the corner of the cabin. Sitting on a folding metal chair, leaning against the corner, my body was slumped over in a catatonic slumber.

I approached myself and tried to teleport inside, but I bumped against an invisible barrier. I sighed. I needed rest before trying again.

Edie kneeled beside my human body and craned her neck to see my human face, obscured by amazing hair. "You look kind of familiar. And definitely as hot as Ford said. Me-ow."

I blushed, but no one saw—one perk of being covered in fur. With my hot goods—pun intended—I'd expected fall out, an attack, revenge, something. "Did anyone ambush us for the stolen body?"

"Negative," Ford said, scrolling on his phone.

One positive slice of news didn't balance out all the negative. "Well, I didn't find Nick Barnes. I didn't kill Heather. I didn't get your contract, Lewis, and now another C&D team will be on the way. And I still don't have my memories. I'm sorry I failed all of you."

"We," Edie said with a gentle smile.

"Excuse me?" I asked, completely confused. I thought my slurring had passed.

"*We* will find Nick Barnes, make him fix the zombie mess, and then I'll kill him. *We* will kill Heather if there's any chance she can get out of her cell, and *we* need to deal with Lewis's contract. *We* will help you get your memories back. You aren't alone in this," Edie said. "You're one of us now…unless you plan to ditch us."

I had spent all my known memory being kicked, insulted, trapped, and thrown to the wolves (figuratively, and debatable if literally). I'd never would've guessed a messy group like this would've been the first to care. I met the gazes of a mouse shifter, a pair of demon hunters, one of which on his way to becoming a real man-witch, and a Super in denial. I'd considered them my friends, but I didn't know the feeling was mutual. *If you respect them and treat them well, they will return the favor.* Thanks, Andras, you memory-messing bastard. I blinked away the misty tears.

Corvina lifted her eyes from her phone and smiled. Lewis smiled, too. Ford stuffed his hands in his pockets and said, "What's it going to be, cat? *We* or *I*?"

I cleared the emotion from my throat and affected a lighthearted air of authority. "If it be true, thou peasants shall become the Underlings of Lord Fluffybutt, and I welcome thee to thy lordship."

"Don't ever call us that," Ford warned.

"My brother was always great with insults. You should've heard some of the things he picked for me," Lewis said. When all eyes met his, Lewis's face flushed. "Well, I didn't mean I would actually tell you. I was being facetious."

"What do we do with your body in the meantime?" Edie asked.

"Oh! We can decorate him." Setting down her phone, Corvina hopped onto her tiptoes and clapped her hands. "Like a Christmas tree."

Edie snorted.

Ford shook his head, hiding a smile.

Lewis covered his eyes with his wide palm, and his shoulders bounced with silent laughter.

I sighed. "Fine, but I get veto power."

"Yes! First, I was thinking Hawaiian luau. I'll find a grass skirt and a lei. Oh, and sunglasses."

"If you say coconuts next, that's vetoed," I said.

"I'm making dinner," Ford said. "This time I have a can of cat food ready for you and all the seasonings I need. Who's hungry?"

I smiled and sat with my crew, my friends. Tomorrow was another day to sort this mess, but I wasn't doing it alone. "Can we have cake?"

Heather

"I don't belong down here, and you know it," I said, arms restrained in heavy iron chains, while a barrel of water waited overhead. Fiery sconces dotted the wet walls, and a crackling fire illuminated the small room, casting an eerie light over a tray of dirty implements. This was no place for a lady, but I couldn't teleport out of the torturemaster's main cell even if I wanted to. It was demon-proof. Besides, I'd already tried the last time I'd visited Glitter. Fortunately, I always had tricks up my fine-pressed vicuña sleeves. With a pouty lip, I said, "I brought you many fine specimens over the centuries. Cut me some slack this time, Glitter?"

Glitter, wearing an outfit an 8-year-old human girl would envy—complete with tutu—wore his hair in a unicorn-colored braid. Despite his outward appearance, he was a fearsome demon. Calm, structured, and immune to screams of agony. And completely oblivious to my pleas. He crossed the room with a music CD and placed it into a boombox. (Hell had terrible Wi-Fi, and the dampness wasn't good for electronics, anyway.)

The disc reflected off the firelight, where Glitter had been preheating The Torture Device of Screams.

My mouth stretched in horror, and my heart raced. "You're not putting on... No, no, you can't subject me to them again!" I begged. The music was the worst part—even worse than the water coming next. Always the water.

Glitter closed the lid and pressed play. Without a glance, he approached and reached over my head. A squeak of metal made me cringe. Anything but the water! Drips from the spigot fell onto my head in a slow endless succession and rolled down my face. The music grated my ears like a whiny child scratching metal along a chalkboard for the fun of it.

Drip.

"Please stop. Anything but the music." I whined. It wasn't the stage of torture on the verge of breaking me, it was the anticipation. I knew Glitter's favorite toys, and I didn't want to play again.

Drip.

While The Torture Device of Screams was preheating, Glitter retrieved a pair of scissors and a rusty spoon from a collection of cringeworthy tools. He cut the slit in my skirt higher, exposing my toned thigh. "No, no, please, Glitter. Anything. Please!"

Drip.

I flinched. With the edge of the spoon, Glitter silently sawed at my flesh just above the knee. Small even strokes with a little pressure. My skin burned from the friction. But it was a dull tool. This was going to take...days.

Drip.

"Please no. Anything but the music, the rusty spoon, and the water. Glitter, come on. I've been good to you."

Drip.

The torturemaster ignored my pleas, like usual. Dirty water rolled into my eyes, but my secured hands prevented me from dashing it away. It burned. I'd get out of this again, one of these days.

My feet were still healing from Nick Barnes's fireballs, and he was going to pay.

And so was Corson, the pathetic "king".

Drip.

Dear Reader,

THE NEXT CHAPTER, **STAKES** Up, is coming soon. In the meantime, get **Demon Experiment (A Demon Cat Chronicles Special Report) for FREE!**

Think Hell is above filing incident reports? Think again!

The exclusive behind-the-scenes report from The King of Hell, detailing what happened during the spell that "successfully" turned Nick Barnes into a demon.

Claim your copy HERE or discover more titles by Marie Flynn at https://stephanieflynn.net/marie-flynn-books/

If you found any typos or errors, I fully blame my cats strolling on my keyboard and resting their rear-ends on my mouse cord. But please feel free to submit them to: stephanie@stephanieflynn.net, and I'll fix them!

Your reviews are very important to me, so if you enjoyed this book, please consider leaving one for the next chapter of Nick Barnes's story, **Twice Cursed.**

To my dearest pile of cats, thank you for your crazy inspiration.

Also By Marie Flynn

Demon Cat Chronicles series
Demon Experiment special report
Demon Curse
Twice Cursed

If you like steamy romance mixed in with your paranormal tales,
check out Marie Flynn's other name, Stephanie Flynn!

About Marie Flynn

Marie Flynn is a pen name for Stephanie Flynn, and she is the author of the Demon Cat Chronicles and a big fan of the gray area between good and evil. She loves stories with supernatural beings who go bump in the night and some that slay during the day. She lives in Michigan, USA with her family and a small horde of demonoid cats, from which she draws endless inspiration. Check out her website for more books: **StephanieFlynn.net/marie-flynn-books**